THE CONSUL'S DAUGHTER

Jane Jackson

Published by Accent Press Ltd 2016

ISBN 9781786150165

The story contained within this book is a work of fiction. Names and characters are the product of the author's imagination and any resemblance to actual persons, living or dead, is entirely coincidental.

Chapter One

'Drunk again?'

Rage flushed Teuder Bonython's pallid complexion. He tugged with shaking fingers at the neck of his white nightshirt. 'He needs a thrashing to knock some sense into him.' He closed his eyes, labouring to breathe, the grooves in his forehead deepening.

Seated on the side of the bed, Caseley leaned forward. 'Are you in pain, Father? Will you have your drops now?'

'Where is he?'

'Ben is putting him to bed.'

He looked up at her. The wretchedness and frustration in his gaze wrenched her heart. 'How many times is that this week? I want the truth.'

'Four, I think.' She looked at his blue-veined hand clenching the sheet. 'He's going through a difficult –'

'Damn it, Ralph is twenty-five years old.' Bitterness and despair twisted his mouth. 'My only son.' He looked at her. His pale eyes, usually so sharp beneath shaggy grey brows, now held bewilderment. 'Why, Caseley? Why is he doing this? To me, to the family?'

'He's unhappy,' she said softly.

A strangled laugh tore itself from her father's throat. 'Good God in Heaven, what's he got to be unhappy about? How much more does he want?'

Not more, less. Caseley said nothing. She reached forward to the bedside table and unscrewed the top from a fluted brown bottle resting on a silver tray. Pouring several drops of amber liquid into a glass she added water from a carafe.

'I don't need that,' Teuder growled. But as she held the glass to his lips he drank obediently. The burst of anger had drained him, and though the purple tinge had faded, beneath the flush on his cheeks his skin was grey.

'You're a good lass,' he muttered. 'You should be tending a husband and children, not burdened with me and the business and your wastrel brother.'

'You're no burden.' Caseley smiled. He had no idea how much the well-meant words hurt.

'If only your mother were here.'

'It wouldn't help Ralph, Father,' she said as gently as she could. 'Try to sleep now. Dr Vigurs is coming tomorrow, and if you don't look better than you do now, he'll keep you in bed for another week.'

'Doctors,' Teuder grunted, his papery eyelids drooping. 'What do they know?' But he didn't protest as she straightened the covers and blew out the candle. She leaned down and kissed his forehead.

'Goodnight.' He grunted again and she limped out. She closed the door quietly. Turning she saw a stocky man in his early thirties carrying an oil lamp coming along the passage.

'How is my brother?'

'Sleeping. He've parted with most of it, begging your pardon, miss. But I brung the bucket back up, just in case.'

She hid her distaste at the all too vivid image Ben's reply conjured. She should be used to it by now. Hadn't she done her share of holding Ralph's head? She understood the desperate battle raging within him, and admired his talent. But she was tired of his self-destructive behaviour.

'He'll have some thick head come morning.'

'Where was he found this time?'

'In the alley behind the Marine Hotel. Henry didn't know how long he'd been there. He wouldn't have seen him at all but for taking out a couple of barrels. He put him in a cab and sent him home.'

'I'll see Mr Voss is paid for his trouble.' Caseley mentally added this to the already long list of tasks for the morning. She opened the kitchen door. 'I expect you'd like something to eat before –' She broke off.

The large scrubbed table was set with a knife and fork, a mug of ale, and a plate of cold beef, pickled onions, and a lump of cheese. A spotless white apron tied over her grey calico dress, mousy hair gathered into a bun, Liza-Jane, thin as a willow and strong as an ox, emerged from the pantry carrying a crusty loaf.

'Evening, miss.' Her brown eyes slid past Caseley and a blush crept up her throat to stain her sharp features. 'I just done a bit of supper for Ben.' Picking up a long knife in a work-roughened hand that trembled slightly she began to slice the bread.

Despite her exhaustion, Caseley had to smile. 'He's earned it, Liza-Jane.'

The maid's colour deepened and in the soft light from the gas-mantle she looked eighteen instead of twenty-eight. What must it be like, to care so much for someone that his mere presence was transforming?

Caseley looked round. 'Where's Rosina?'

'She've gone up bed, miss,' Liza-Jane said. 'Got one of her headaches. I brewed up some mint and marjoram, and when I looked in a few minutes ago she was sleeping.'

Caseley had a strong suspicion that the housekeeper's headache was more diplomatic than real. Until her husband's untimely death, swept overboard from his fishing boat ten years ago, Rosina Renfree had been blessed with a very happy marriage, and she took every opportunity to encourage the growing attachment between Liza-Jane and Ben Tonkin, who had joined the household a year ago as valet, gardener, and handyman.

'Want a cup of something, do you, miss? It won't take a minute.'

Caseley shook her head. 'No, thank you.' She took a lamp from the shelf, lit it, and replaced the glass funnel. 'Ben, I'm grateful.'

'No trouble, miss.'

'Goodnight.' She paused at the door. 'Liza-Jane, make sure the copper is lit first thing, will you? Dr Vigurs is coming and Father's bed linen must be changed. Mrs Clemmow will be here by eight thirty.'

'Right, miss. 'Night.'

Caseley sensed their relief as she closed the kitchen door. As she climbed the stairs once more, the brass lamp cast distorted shadows on wall and ceiling.

In her room she set the lamp down on top of her writing cabinet. A tall clothes press filled an alcove. The brass bedstead gleamed above the lilac spread. Behind the door a flower-patterned ewer and basin stood on the marble top of the night table and several white towels were folded over a rail at the side.

She sank into her chair, gazing at the litter of invoices, orders, requests for quotations, and other paperwork generated by a busy and successful shipbuilding and repair yard. The long narrow drawer holding her pens and ink was pulled out, everything exactly as she left it when her father had called, woken by Ralph's drunken shouting.

Caseley rested her head against the chair's high back. What would Miss Hester say seeing her now?

Under the meticulous eye and strict discipline of the Misses Hester and Amelia Wills who ran the School for

Young Ladies on Florence Terrace, she had learned to compose and address correspondence for every occasion in beautiful flowing script. She had studied literature, mathematics sufficient to ensure she could balance a household budget, deportment, piano and watercolour painting. Miss Hester deemed her embroidery exquisite.

Though being able to dance was another important accomplishment, she had been excused due to the accident that had left her with a crushed foot and pronounced limp. Her classmates sympathised, but no one wanted to partner her. So while they mastered the complexities of the waltz and mazurka, she studied Spanish.

It would have shocked Miss Amelia deeply to know that instead of reading Castilian poetry, her star pupil was gazing at a letter penned in Mexican Spanish requesting information concerning the qualities of different steam pumping engines for use in the Guanajuato silver mines.

Propping her elbows on the paper-strewn writing slope, Caseley buried her face in her hands.

There was a quick tap on the door and Liza-Jane walked in carrying a cup and saucer. 'I know you said you didn't want nothing, but you're looking proper wisht. I've brung you some camomile tea.' Beneath the severe centre parting her forehead puckered in concern. 'All right, are you?'

Caseley looked up, her eyes hot with unshed tears. 'Actually, I was laughing.'

'Bleddy cry if you didn't, eh, miss?'

Caseley lifted one shoulder. 'It wouldn't help though, would it?' She sat up straight. 'Thank you for the tea.'

Liza-Jane placed the cup and saucer by the lamp. 'Drink it while it's hot.'

'Ben's a lucky man. I hope he realises it. And Liza?' The maid turned in the doorway. 'Thank him again for taking care of Ralph. I couldn't have faced it tonight.'

After Liza-Jane had closed the door Caseley picked up the cup and cradled in between her palms. Sipping the honey-sweetened liquid she stared into space, disjointed thoughts and images tumbling through her mind.

Ralph's ashen, sweaty face had lolled against Ben's shoulder, as the manservant carried him upstairs.

Her great bull of a father, weakened by illness, was unable to understand his son's rejection of the business that should have been his inheritance. She remembered finding her father hunched over the desk in his office, his face dusky grey and creased with pain.

'Tired, that's all,' he gasped. 'A few days' rest and I'll be fine. You can stand in for me.'

The responsibility terrified her. 'Father, I can't. I don't know enough. Surely Uncle Thomas or Uncle Richard would –?'

'This is *my* business, girl,' he croaked. 'Thomas can only think in figures. While there's no one to beat Richard at finding cargoes for our vessels and those we're agent for, neither of them knows a thing about shipbuilding or repair. You must stand in for me.'

He clutched her hand, his grip painful. 'If word gets out I'm sick, people will take their work elsewhere. Once we lose a vessel to another yard we won't get it back. You've been translating letters and replies long enough to know what's needed. You must act for me, Caseley. It won't be for long. In a week or two and I'll be fine.'

So under the disapproving eye of Dr Vigurs her father had – through her – continued to run his business. But he was not recovering as quickly as either of them had hoped.

Unable to remain in the office after official closing time, partly to avoid speculation about the true state of her father's health, but also because Bar Road linked the docks with the town and at night was crowded with sailors and prostitutes, she had started bringing work home.

A soft knock on the door brought her head up as Liza-Jane looked in.

'I'm going up bed, miss. Doors is all locked and the lights out. Finished your drink, have you?'

Caseley looked down at the still-full cup, now cool. 'Not quite,' she smiled. 'But I will. Goodnight, Liza-Jane.'

''Night, miss.'

Swallowing a mouthful of tea, Caseley set the cup on the saucer and studied the letter from Mexico. But the words would not register.

Obeying an impulse she slipped off her shoes, opened the door, and padded quietly along the passage and up the dark narrow staircase to the small tower that gave the house its name.

The captain who had built the house had added the windowed tower so he could point his telescope over the narrow spit of land at the back of his property to the bay beyond and know which ships were coming into port long before they arrived.

But it was not to the open sea that Caseley looked. Resting her forehead against the cold glass, she gazed out over the inner harbour. Below her, on the far side of the road, the Bar with its warehouses, boatyards, saw pits, and timber pools curved round to the left. They were quiet during the hours of darkness. But daybreak would bring renewed noise and activity.

Above the wharves and quays, the town rose from the river to sprawl over the hillside. A fat pale moon, veiled by scudding cloud, hung low over the village of Flushing on the far side of the harbour, its ghostly light silvering the dark, rolling water.

The rising wind keened and sighed in the rigging of

ships moored in the harbour and alongside the quays. It clapped ropes against masts and made the beech trees creak and rustle in the garden next door.

Along the road the door of the Dock and Railway Inn opened. A man staggered out, his arm around a laughing woman. As they stopped in the shadows she turned away and went back to her room.

Chapter Two

Jago Barata eased himself up, leaned against the wooden headboard, lit a thin brown cheroot, and blew a thin plume of fragrant smoke. Cropped short, black curls clung to his forehead and temples. Sweat glistened on his broad shoulders, chest, and flat belly. Against the damp sheets and pillows his caramel skin glowed with animal health and as he raised his arm to tap ash from his cheroot, muscle and sinew flexed, gleaming in the lamplight.

Why was there no news? Alfonso Gaudara, his father's agent in Spain, had promised the writ holding his schooner in the blockaded port of Bilbao would be rescinded. Word of this should have been waited for him yesterday when he arrived back from South America.

Twice today he had called to see George Fox, vice-consul for Spain at his office in Arwenack Street. Both times the man had been out and, though apologetic, the clerk had been adamant. There was no message for Captain Barata.

Tomorrow he would go to the telegraph office. Each day the *Cara* lay idle in Bilbao he lost money. He had only a part-share in *Cygnet*. Though she handled well, and he was glad to have use of her, he wanted the *Cara* out of Spain in time for the fruit trade from the Azores starting in December. In the meantime he would use *Cygnet* for whatever deep-water runs he could get.

Unloading at the docks had been completed this evening and the hides he had carried from the Rio Grande were in the warehouse ready for transport to leather factories. He would need to allow a couple more days to rid the ship of the stench and for repairs to the jib boom and two jib sails.

It had been a close call, a collision that should never have happened yet could have been so much worse. That master would not tangle with him again. In the wrong place at the wrong time he had lacked the seamanship to get himself out of the way. Jago had little sympathy for him.

They had made a fast passage, only fourteen days across the Atlantic from the Gulf of Mexico. But it was more than two months since they had touched Cornish shores. His men would welcome a day or two with their families.

He knew the value of a contented crew. At sea since the age of sixteen, he had neither time nor inclination for any but brief casual relationships. He was baffled by his mate's willingness to walk the eight miles from Falmouth to Feock to spend twelve hours with his wife and children then walk back to be on board in time to catch the tide. Yet when turnaround was expected to be even shorter, he supervised the unloading himself so the mate could still make his visit home.

He gained the mate's gratitude and unswerving loyalty, and used the time for paperwork. Knowing he was in his cabin ensured the crew worked hard and fast.

He knew he had a reputation as a hard but fair master with eyes in the back of his head. An ironic smile lifted one corner of his mouth. Despite the old tales about dual ancestry, his had produced no special powers or sorcery. His gifts were simply an instinctive understanding of human nature, and intelligence that required him to curb his impatience with those less mentally agile than himself.

The woman beside him stirred and sighed, drawing her legs together from their abandoned sprawl as she pulled the sheet over her full breasts in a gesture of studied coyness.

'You've forgotten I'm here,' she pouted.

Jago stubbed out the cheroot. 'My dear Louise, how could I forget you, even for a moment.'

The hotel's bedroom window faced out onto Market Street. Porters shouted names and information to the desk clerks. Parties who had enjoyed a good meal and fine wines in the dining room laughed and chatted beneath the portico while awaiting their cabs. In the passage outside the bedroom, guests came and went, pageboys carrying messages knocked on doors.

Then the blast of a horn and the thunder of hooves and iron-rimmed wheels announced the arrival of the late evening mail.

Jago reached for his watch on the night table beside the bed.

Louise stuck her lower lip out even further. 'I suppose you want me to go.'

'Will your husband not wonder where you are?' He asked mildly.

'Him?' She gave a derisive snort. 'He wouldn't notice if I lay naked on the slab between a side of beef and a leg of pork.'

Jago's mouth twitched. 'No man worthy of the name could fail to be moved by your beauty, Louise.'

She tossed her untidy mane and preened. 'You got some lovely way with words. 'Tis true though. He've got three shops, and when he isn't working in one he's visiting the others. Money, money, money, that's all he think of.'

Jago regarded her with faint amusement. 'But surely that was why you married him?'

‘’Course it was,’ Louise agreed readily. ‘I got three older sisters. I wanted a nice house, and nice clothes nobody else had worn first. He’d have got good value from me. But I aren’t no ornament, just for show, to be took down and dusted off once a month.’ Sighing, she lifted Jago’s hand to her breast. ‘I’m a woman and I do need a man.’

The blend of coyness and invitation in her soft purr stirred him not at all. He freed his hand without haste. ‘No, Louise.’ As her full mouth grew sulky he added, ‘I am concerned for your –’ He hesitated over the word *reputation*, aware that, offended by his rejection and her husband’s neglect, she could with truth accuse him of having little concern for it before. Guarding her good name was her responsibility, not his. But that would carry little weight with her in this mood. ‘For your well-being. What if your husband should return home and find you not there?’

‘He’s at a Chamber of Commerce meeting. They talk for hours in the Council Chamber, then go and talk some more in the King’s Head.’ She raised herself on one elbow, allowing the sheet to drop as she arched her magnificent breasts towards him. ‘C’mon, Jago. Just once more?’

He smothered a pang of irritation. He liked her earthy honesty. But she never seemed to realise when enough was enough. He pushed back the sheet and with one lithe movement rose from the bed. Taking one of the towels from the washstand he wrapped it without haste or shyness around his lean hips.

‘Go home, Louise.’ He spoke softly, but the steely edge to his voice had her scrambling quickly into her clothes.

‘See you again soon?’

‘I expect so.’ He took two notes from his wallet and

picking up the little blue velvet drawstring purse trimmed with ribbon that matched her dress, pushed them into the gathered neck.

'You don't have to do that.' Her tone was a blend of resentment and gratitude.

'I know. But a gift is always welcome, is it not?'

'Come again next week, shall I?' she asked, twisting her frizzy hennaed hair into an untidy coil, then pinning her hat on top and tilting it at a rakish angle.

'No. Tonight you bribed a porter to let you in here while I was out. You will not do that again.'

She gazed at him, clutching the little purse, hearing the paper money crackle beneath her fingers. 'But you said you'd see me soon.'

He hadn't said that. '*I* will make any future arrangements.'

'I might decide not to come.' She shook out her skirts.

Jago inclined his head. 'That would be your choice, and I shall accept your decision.'

Louise's shoulders drooped and suddenly she looked much older than her thirty-one years. 'You arrogant bastard.' There was no malice in her tone, just weary acceptance and a hint of admiration. Unlocking the door, she glanced up and down the passage then left without another word, closing it softly it behind her.

Rubbing one hand over his dark beard, Jago's aquiline nostrils flared at his own scent. After opening the sash window he tugged the bell-pull.

When the boy appeared, he ordered hot water. 'I want a bath.'

'*Now,* sir?' the boy asked, startled.

'Now,' Jago growled. The taste of wine was sour in his mouth. 'Bring a pot of coffee as well.' As the door closed he lit another cheroot and propped himself on pillows against the headboard. He had much to think about.

In the big double bed, his striped nightshirt buttoned up to the neck, Thomas Bonython looked up from a large leather-bound ledger and peered over his spectacles.

'What was that, dear?'

Seated at her dressing table his wife glared at him in the gilt-framed mirror as she rubbed cream into her fleshy face. A lace-frilled cap covered her hair and she wore a voluminous peignoir of peach satin with deep flounces of lace at the neck and cuffs.

'I said it's ridiculous, Caseley in Teuder's office trying to look as if she knows what she's doing. At least she hasn't the cheek to use his desk. When I called in yesterday she was working on that little walnut bureau of her mother's in one corner. I told her Teuder should have done the proper thing and appointed you to take over while he was –'

Thomas jerked upright. 'You did *what?*'

'She said *you* could discuss the matter with Teuder when he's better.' Her tone was venomous. 'Just who does she think she is?'

'She's young,' he placated automatically, his thoughts racing. 'She'll be finding the situation difficult.'

Margaret swung round on the tapestry-covered stool. 'That is exactly my point, Thomas. She should not even be there. You are next in age to Teuder. You should have been asked to take over.' She turned back to the crowded dressing table, opened another jar, and began to rub almond-scented cream into the backs of her plump white hands.

'Teuder would have had to raise your salary, or at least increase your share of the profits. We need the money, Thomas. Look at this place.' She gazed with obvious discontent around the over-furnished room. 'Heaven knows what Bess did to those curtains when she had them down in the spring. They have never looked right since. And Charlotte needs at least three new dresses for Christmas.'

'Three?' Thomas bleated.

'In case you hadn't noticed, our daughter is now fourteen years old. She's a young lady and will be a laughing stock among her friends if she has to wear last season's clothes to the parties and dances.'

'Yes, but do they all have to be new?' He hesitated. 'Surely some different trimmings, an alteration here and there.' He waved a vague hand.

His wife's thin mouth tightened in disapproval. 'Regardless of our grievances against certain members of the family, we Bonythons have a position to uphold. If Charlotte appears in last season's dresses she will be snubbed.'

'Come now.' Thomas felt his smile wilt as he tried once more to defuse his wife's wrath. 'I am certain Charlotte's friends would not be so unkind.'

Margaret raised her eyes to the ceiling and sighed. 'How can you be so naive? I'm not talking about her friends. Though I don't doubt some young hussy would delight in sharpening her tongue and her wits at our daughter's expense. People in our position excite jealousy, Thomas. It is the mothers we have to guard our little girl against. And I cannot possibly invite the Trembaths here again until we have the Chesterfield re-covered. I saw Maria Trembath eyeing the worn patch on the seat. Apricot velvet would look nice.'

She stood up and blew out the candles in their gilt holder, then took off her wrapper to reveal a long white flannel nightdress with a pie-frill collar and full sleeves.

Climbing between the starched sheets, she settled herself on the two feather pillows and pursed her lips. 'So, what are you going to do about it, Thomas?

He closed the big leather book and placed it on the bedside table. 'About what, my dear?' Time was running out. The audit was due shortly. If he could persuade Teuder to let him do it himself, he might be able to juggle the figures.

'About Caseley, of course.'

Thomas removed his spectacles and placed them carefully on the polished table alongside the accounts ledger. He had promised himself it would be once only. But now, with so many demands to meet, he could see no other option. They could count him in. He would tell them tomorrow. Excitement stirred, warming his pallid cheeks.

'Nothing, my dear.'

Margaret's head jerked off the pillow as she glared at him. 'Nothing? You mean –'

'I mean,' Thomas's interruption startled his wife into silence. 'I am happy for Caseley to remain exactly where she is. I never liked Teuder looking over my shoulder, always checking up on me. Since his illness Caseley has so much to do at the yard that she leaves all financial matters to me. For the first time I am my own master, and I like it.'

'What about me? People are talking behind our backs about you being passed over. But because Teuder is sick and you don't have to report to him like a – a – schoolboy, you are happy.'

'You don't understand.'

'No, I don't. I thought that with my encouragement you could make something of yourself, show Teuder that he had underestimated you. This would have been the perfect opportunity. You are content with so little, Thomas.'

'Will you listen?' He fought to contain his simmering rage, terrified of what might happen should he let it loose. 'Caseley is clever, but she's young and too much is being asked of her. Teuder's main interest is the yard. That is where he is directing her attention.'

'How does that help you?'

He hesitated. He had been warned to tell *no one*. But they weren't married to Margaret. They had no idea of the pressures a wife like her inflicted on a man. He *had* to tell her. Not everything, just enough, or she would play the martyr for weeks. Besides, it would show her he was as capable as Teuder of handling complicated business deals. Though obviously he could not give too many details. But the extra money would be a boon. She would welcome that. And when Margaret was happy she was more *accommodating.*

'It allows me to run a little private enterprise. Certain items will be brought to me, and all I have to do is ensure they reach the people who want them. For this service I will receive a commission.

Seeing her expression sharpen he knew he had her. 'How much?'

'That depends on the value of the goods. But the items we have in mind should make the venture well worthwhile.'

'You said *we.* Who –?'

He shook his head. 'No names. I had to promise. I shouldn't even be telling you this much.' He placed a tentative hand over his wife's. 'My only contact is the man who brings me the goods. I arrange transport to their destination. The first consignment arrived yesterday and will be on its way to London on the mail coach tomorrow morning.'

'When will you be paid?' Her expression was avid.

'Within forty-eight hours, provided the buyer receives the package intact.' His voice quivered with suppressed excitement. 'Teuder has done me a favour by bringing Caseley in. Be nice to her, Margaret. We want everything to remain exactly as it is.' His hand crept upward to rest on his wife's large, flannel-covered breast.

She did not move. 'It has been an exhausting day, Thomas. Perhaps by the weekend we may have something to celebrate.' She rolled away, dislodging his hand. 'Turn the lamp out, dear.'

He did as he was told.

Chapter Three

Caseley's dreams were filled with people pursuing her demanding decisions and information she didn't have. Restless, disturbed, she kept waking and listened to the wind rattling the window and causing a door left unfastened in the yard opposite to bang monotonously.

Soon after dawn, unable to remain in a bed that offered neither comfort nor escape, she had got up. Slipping a robe over her nightgown, her hair rippling down her back, she had worked on a reply to the letter from Mexico. She was busy writing at her desk when Liza-Jane brought in hot water.

She dressed in a plain bottle green skirt gathered to fullness at the back waist and a shirt-like bodice the colour of thick cream with a round neck and buttoned cuffs. She brushed her hair until it gleamed like burnished bronze then bundled it into a net secured on her nape with two pins.

Examining her reflection in the ornate mirror she pinched her cheeks to give them some colour. About the shadows under her eyes she could do nothing.

Passing her father's door she heard Ben's voice as he washed and shaved her father.

She ate a boiled egg and a slice of toast, drank the last of her tea, and was dabbing her mouth with her napkin when the door opened.

Unshaven, his hair tousled, with one hand shading his eyes against the sunshine streaming in through the window, Ralph walked carefully to the table and eased himself down onto a chair.

'God, I feel awful.' He supported his head on hands that trembled. His crumpled shirt was unfastened at the neck and wrists and his dark trousers were stained.

'Why do you do it, Ralph?' Caseley asked softly.

'No lectures, Caseley. Not today, especially not now.' He let his hand drop and leaned back. His bloodshot eyes were narrowed against the bright morning and the pain she guessed was hammering at his temples. 'Give me something, Caseley. One of your brews? I can't stand this.'

About to say that he didn't have to, that he wouldn't suffer if he simply left the cork in the bottle, she knew she'd be wasting her breath.

'Please?' He sounded desperate.

'All right.' She stood up. 'I won't be long.'

'I'm not going anywhere.' He sank his head into his hands once more.

She paused in the doorway. 'Could you eat anything?'

He shook his head, clearly regretting the movement as his thin shoulders tensed against renewed pain.

As Caseley entered the kitchen Rosina looked up from the pastry she was making. 'All right, my 'andsome? Want something more?'

'Some lime tea for Ralph. His nerves are in a dreadful state.' She went to one of the large wooden cupboards.

'I bet his stomach don't feel too happy neither. A teaspoon of grated nutmeg on a slice of bread and butter, that's what he need.'

'Maybe later.' Caseley measured a teaspoonful of dried lime flowers into a cup. 'I doubt he'd keep it down right now.' She lifted the heavy kettle from the black-leaded range and poured boiling water onto the flower heads then returned the kettle to the slab with its gleaming brass rail. 'How's your head?'

The housekeeper looked up in surprise. 'My –? She lowered her voice. 'I reckon 'tis me time of life.'

Caseley strained the lime infusion into a fresh cup. 'Odd that they usually happen the evenings.'

'Do they? Well, I never.' Rosina's amazement was beautifully judged. 'Some strange that is.'

Before Caseley could reply, Liza-Jane came in from the scullery carrying a large basket of wet washing.

'I'll just get this put on the line for Mary. Some lovely drying day it is.' She turned to Rosina. 'You was right about Louise Downing.' Her voice held mingled censure and excitement. 'She have got another fancy man.'

'I knew it. Didn't I tell you?' Rosina crowed. 'Is it Jimmy Mitchell? I seen the way he do look at her. 'Tis all Ada Mitchell can do to serve her. But then Ada always look like she's sucking lemons.'

Caseley knew she shouldn't condone gossip. But since her father fell ill she was spending most of each day discussing cargos and destinations with Uncle Richard or ship repairs, labour costs, and wholesale rates for oakum, pitch, Norwegian pine, and English oak with her father. She translated letters relating to his consular work, and relayed his instructions for work at the yard. A little local gossip made a welcome change.

''Tis never right, her carrying on like she do,' Liza-Jane said.

''Tis his own fault.' Rosina sprinkled flour on the pastry board before rolling out a lump of dough. 'If he spent a bit less time with they dead carcasses and a bit more on the live one he's married to, she wouldn't stray. Anyhow, who's the new fancy man? She've kept this one quiet.'

'Because he's foreign,' said Liza-Jane.

Rosina looked up. 'He isn't a Falmouth man?'

Liza-Jane rolled her eyes heavenward. 'He isn't *English.* Leastways, that's what Mary said. Betty Chard told her she seen Louise coming out of the Royal Hotel about ten o'clock last night.'

'That don't mean anything.' Rosina pursed her lips as she pushed the rolling pin to and fro. 'Louise have been seen coming out of stranger places than that at ten of an evening.'

Caseley opened the jar of honey and stirred a spoonful into the lime tea.

'Well, Betty's eldest is a boot boy up the hotel and he says he've seen her in there four or five times in the past six months, and always at the same time as they foreigners.'

Rosina gasped, the pastry forgotten. 'There's more than one?'

Liza-Jane nodded. 'That's what Betty told Mary.

Rosina snorted. 'Get on, 'tis just guessing. What Betty don't know she do make up. That woman is some terrible gossip.'

Biting her lip to hide her smile, Caseley picked up the cup and saucer and returned to the breakfast room. Ralph was where she had left him, hunched forward, elbows on his knees, face buried in his hands.

She felt a pang of sympathy as she set the cup on the table beside him. 'Drink it while it's hot, Ralph. It will help.'

He turned to look at her. Despite the bloating and the stubble his face appeared young and defenceless. 'I can't go on like this.'

Caseley looked at the long sensitive fingers, now grimy and trembling, at the thin body taut with nervous tension and the pain of yet another hangover, at the stained, dishevelled clothing. 'No,' she agreed quietly. 'You can't.'

'What am I to do, Caseley?'

'You have to talk to him.'

'He won't listen.'

'Ralph, you haven't tried.'

He glared at her. 'Of course I've tried –'

'To tell him what you really want? Have you, Ralph? I've heard you rant about what you *don't* want. You've ridiculed all the ideals he grew up believing in. But I've never once heard you explain quietly and reasonably exactly what your ambitions are. Do you even know?'

'How can you say that?' He was deathly pale. 'I thought you understood. Are you turning against me as well?'

'No, of course I'm not. But you're destroying yourself, drinking like this.'

His expression grew sullen. 'Don't preach, Caseley. I'll deal with this my own way.'

She crouched beside him. 'But you're not dealing with it. You're just running away.'

He leaned back. 'You don't understand at all. My whole life's at stake and all you can do is babble on about the demon drink, like some … Methodist.' He spat the word.

Caseley stood up, clasping her hands tightly. 'What about *my* life, Ralph? I've listened and I've tried to understand. I know you are suffering. But I can't do anything to change it. Only you can do that, either by talking to Father and settling it once and for all, or by leaving.'

'Leave? Where would I go? What would I live on?' He grew petulant. 'Why should I leave? This is my home. I'm entitled to be here.'

'Yes,' she agreed. 'And as the only son no doubt when Father dies the house will be left to you, along with shares in the yard, which you don't want. You will be a wealthy man, Ralph. You'll be able to drink yourself to death in style.'

Shaken, he stared at her. 'What's the matter with you? You've never spoken to me like this before. You don't understand at all.' He flung the words at her like stones. 'You have no idea what I'm going through.'

'Perhaps you're right, Ralph. But I have tried. God knows I've tried. Drink your tea.' She turned away.

He caught her hand. 'Don't go, Caseley. Don't leave me. I need someone to talk to.'

His hand was cold and clammy. She held it between her own. 'Then talk to Father,' she urged. 'Or to Dr Vigurs. He'll be in later.'

'Vigurs?' Ralph snatched his hand away, his mouth curling bitterly. 'He'll only lecture me about filial duty and Father's health and the inheritance I ought to be grateful for.' He glared at her. 'Anyway, where are you going that's so important?'

'To do your job.'

She went to her room to collect the books and papers she would need for the day's business, placing them in the leather music case she used to carry them to and from the yard office. She would not think about Ralph. If she did, exasperation and rage would make it impossible for her to concentrate and she needed all her wits about her.

Swirling a hip-length cape of chocolate brown worsted around her shoulders against the morning chill, she went in to say goodbye to her father.

'Dr Vigurs will be calling later.' She moved the bed-table containing his breakfast tray.

'I don't care what he says. I'm getting out of this bed tomorrow. A man could die of boredom lying here.'

Sitting in the armchair while she changed his sheets had exhausted him and he'd been glad to return to bed and rest until his breakfast arrived. But mentioning it would only upset him.

'Shall I bring the newspaper up for you? Or a book?'

'Books? What do I want with books?' he snarled. 'I want the sun on my face and the smell of the sea in my nostrils. I want to be back in my yard and see what's going on. Books!' he grunted in disgust.

She knew better than to argue. She poured out his drops and handed him the glass, watching as he stared at the liquid, clearly debating whether or not to swallow it.

'Dr Vigurs will be impressed by your determination, Father,' she said with studied calm. 'Especially if you are tranquil and your blood is not overheated.'

Teuder grunted then gulped the mixture down. 'What time is he coming?'

'Before lunch, I believe. A nap now will conserve your strength and help you order your thoughts.' Caseley was aware of his gaze as she straightened the bedcover.

'What are you doing about that engine for Guanajuato?'

'I have drafted a letter to Fox's foundry requesting them to send details of engines they think would be suitable, plus shipping costs, to Señor Mantero.'

'Why Fox's? Why not –?'

'Because,' she cut in, plumping his pillows, 'Fox's foundry and engineering works have been operating at Perran Wharf for over twenty years. They've sent pumping engines to tin mines, copper mines, and gold mines all over the world.'

She paused to control the rising tension in her voice. 'I

simply don't have time to make enquiries of all the other possible companies. Anyway, none of them have the freight and transport facilities that Fox's do.'

Making a huge effort she smiled at her father. 'I drafted a reply to Señor Mantero telling him of the company's reputation for reliability and high quality workmanship, and assuring him he will receive Mr Fox's personal attention in the matter.'

Teuder's tired eyes held a glint of admiration as he looked up at his daughter. 'A neat move, girl. Let Fox's do all the work, eh?'

Caseley tugged the bell-pull. 'Aunt Margaret's visit yesterday put me behind.'

'Margaret? What did she want? Poisonous old biddy.' Teuder scowled. 'Was she snooping?'

'No,' Caseley hated lying. But relating her aunt's comments would only upset him and she didn't have time for that. 'She wanted to share some good news. Frances Lashbrooke –'

'Good news? It will be a rare day when any good news that woman wants to pass on doesn't have a sting in the tail.'

How well her father knew his sister-in-law. After a quick knock on the door the maid walked in.

'You can take Father's tray, Liza-Jane. He's going to rest now. Will you bring him some beef tea at eleven? The doctor should be here soon after.'

'Yes, miss.' Liza-Jane picked up the tray. Caseley kissed her father's forehead then followed her to the door.

'Try to sleep, Father. I'll come up and see you as soon as I get home.'

He raised one hand a few inches off the coverlet. 'Has *Dora* left the yard yet?'

'Will moved her round to the quay. He's taking her out

on the morning tide. The account for her repairs was settled yesterday.'

'Where's she bound?'

'Par, to load china clay for Liverpool. She'll bring back salt.'

Teuder's eyelids were dropping. 'I must see him when he gets back. Tell him …'

'I'll try and catch him before he leaves. Sleep well.'

Teuder roused himself. 'Who's sleeping? I'm just resting my eyes until that damn doctor arrives. Don't forget to tell Will.' His eyes closed.

Shutting the door quietly, Caseley went downstairs to the kitchen. She could hear the splash of water and the creak of the wooden mangle as Mary Clemmow wrung out the sheets.

A moment later Mary's head appeared round the door. Greying hair had worked loose from the bun on her nape and floated in wisps about her flushed face as she wiped her red hands and forearms on a threadbare towel.

'Beg pardon, miss, but we need more blue bag. I got enough for today's sheets, but 'twill all be gone by Monday.'

Caseley nodded. 'I'll make sure it's added to the list, Mrs Clemmow.'

Mary bobbed her head and disappeared. Moments later the mangle resumed its creaking.

The scent of cloves and cinnamon made Caseley's mouth water as Rosina lifted a golden-crusted pie from the oven and set it on the scrubbed table beside two others.

'That's one apple, one apple and blackberry, and one plum. They saffron cakes is ready to go in. Fancy anything else do you, my 'andsome? I'll do a slab of 'eavy cake.'

'Thank you, Rosina. As it's the end of the month, be sure to pay both the butcher's and grocer's accounts. Add blue bag to the list. I've left money with the accounts in the drawer of the side-table in the dining room.' Caseley handed her a small key. Experience had taught her never to leave cash where Ralph might see it.

'Put the receipts and change back in there, shall I?'

Caseley nodded. Liza-Jane came in from the passage carrying dusters and polish. 'The wind have broke that low branch on the apple tree. Dragging on the ground, he is.'

'Ask Ben to saw it off, Liza-Jane. And make sure he brings in plenty of coal.

At last Caseley got away. The wind whipped her skirt against her ankles and pushed her along the pavement edging the dirt road. Dust eddies whirled. Leaves and scraps of paper were snatched up, spun then dropped as the gust blew itself out. Puffs of cloud raced across the hazy sky as gulls screamed and wheeled.

Glancing into the grain warehouse as she passed, Caseley saw men loading sacks of oats and barley onto horse-drawn carts. She could hear the *shush* of the mill wheel turning in the tidal pool as water poured through the sluice.

'Caseley!'

Glancing round she saw a familiar figure close the garden gate of an elegant terraced house. Ever fashionable, Tamsyn was wearing short maroon coat over a pink flounced skirt gathered into a bustle topped by a large maroon bow. Her fair hair had been drawn back into a cluster of ringlets. Perched on the front of her head was a small hat with an upturned brim fastened with two pink roses. Matching ribbons tied in a bow hung down at the back. She always looked as if she had just stepped out of the pages of one of the ladies' fashion magazines.

Caseley felt a pang of envy, but it was small and easily ignored. She had neither the time nor the inclination to spend hours on her toilette. Besides, who would notice?

'Hello, Tamsyn. You're looking well. In fact you look radiant.'

'So I should,' Tamsyn laughed. 'That is exactly how I feel.' She gripped Caseley's forearm. 'William and I are to be married before Christmas.'

Caseley laid her hand over her friend's. 'I'm so pleased for you.' She meant every word. Resenting other people's happiness was mean, small-minded, and reminded her of Aunt Margaret.

'You must come to the wedding, Caseley. Papa is holding the reception at the Falmouth Hotel. There is to be an orchestra and dancing –' Her pretty face sobered. 'Oh, I'm sorry. I didn't think.'

'It's fine. Don't worry.'

'I cannot wait to be married. You would not believe how much there is to think about and plan!' Full of bliss, she hurried away towards the town.

Glad for her old schoolfriend, Caseley crossed the road to her father's boatyard, passing beneath the one-word sign over the tall double gates.

Her grandfather had claimed the Bonython name was enough. 'Word of mouth brings us all the business we want. Them that come here know what we do. No point wasting money to have it writ up there.'

In seventy years of building and repairing quay punts and fishing smacks, ketches, and schooners, the sign had never been altered. Nor had Bonython's ever lacked work.

As she passed the blacksmith's shed, the rhythmic clang of hammer on anvil stopped and a cloud of steam billowed out as red-hot metal was plunged into the cooling trough.

'Good morning, Mr Reece, have you seen Will Spargo?'

'Morning, miss.' The brawny smith emerged from his shed. In his huge fist long-handled tongs gripped a bent iron bar dripping water. His scarred and blackened leather apron reached almost to his heavy boots. 'I b'lieve he's down by the slip.'

'Thank you.' Caseley hurried across the yard past a stack of seasoning timber. She breathed in the acrid smell of hot tar coming from the riggers' shed and the sweet scent of fresh sawdust.

Reaching the slip she saw *Dora,* with Will at the helm, already twenty yards off, her sails set as she headed towards the Carrick Roads and the sea beyond.

Caseley sighed. She would jot down a reminder as soon as she reached the office. About to turn away, she saw a two-masted schooner approaching. It was coming in fast – too fast – under a single staysail.

A dark-haired figure stood at the wheel. As she watched he raised one arm then brought it down. A crewman waiting in the bow loosed the staysail sheets. The canvas flapped, spilling the wind, then slid swift and smooth to the deck. The schooner slowed and Caseley saw that the jibboom was broken off level with the bowsprit cap, the guys and bobstay neatly coiled and fastened to the bowsprit.

As the vessel glided alongside, a second seaman and a boy leapt onto the wharf and, whipping ropes around the bollards fore and aft, brought her gently to a stop. The boy let out a delighted whoop and the seaman cuffed him playfully as he jumped back on board.

The man at the wheel smiled, his teeth flashing white in his bearded face. He moved towards the companionway hatch then paused, suddenly still.

The speed of the schooner's approach had held her rooted to the spot, apprehension spiked with curiosity as she noticed the broken spar.

During her recent visits to the yard she had become acquainted with most of Bonython's fleet, except the *Lily.* Loading cod in the tiny harbours around St John's on the Labrador coast, *Lily* had been away for months and was due back in two weeks' time, mid-September.

If the schooner was one of theirs, then who was the man at the helm? The accuracy with which he had judged both the wind and the speed of the hundred-foot vessel proclaimed him a first-class seaman.

But the arrogant tilt of his head and his cool stare stirred unexpected and unwelcome agitation. The yard and everyone in it faded away, leaving just the two of them.

Startled and self-conscious, Caseley turned quickly away, retracing her steps across the yard and out onto the road.

Barely glancing at the overgrown ruins of the Manor, she hurried past the row of four-storey properties with deep windows and pillared porches that housed several of the town's eminent people, including Dr Vigurs.

She would call at his consulting rooms on her way home. She needed to know the truth and her father told her only what suited him.

The breeze whipped the waters of the inner harbour into a sea of white horses. Waves slapped and broke against the sea wall on the other side of the road. Small boats moored to rings in the wall and bollards along the top bobbed like corks on the choppy water.

Gulls flapped and screamed overhead, diving for scraps thrown overboard by fishermen sluicing decks and holds. The clink of caulking irons driving oakum between hull planks rose and fell on the gusting wind. Horses' hooves clopped, cart and carriage wheels rumbled, children squealed and squabbled, hammers clanged in foundries and women packing pilchards in the curing sheds gossiped and shrieked with laughter.

Turning in through the gateway of Bank House she climbed the granite steps. The glossy black door with its polished brass knocker swung open easily on well-oiled hinges. She walked along the tiled hall and up the wide, curving staircase to Bonython's offices on the first floor.

Entering her father's, she removed her cape, her gaze skimming over the glass-fronted bookcases, shelves packed with ledgers, and the small walnut bureau in the corner, its open top covered with neat stacks of papers.

It had been her mother's and usually stood in a corner of the drawing room. She had made Ben bring it down. To see her seated at her father's desk would have offended Uncle Thomas. Working at the small bureau signalled to anyone entering the office that she was simply helping out until her father's return.

Her gaze lingered on the framed letters of consulship approval and appointment. The first signed by Queen Victoria and her Home Secretary, the second by the President of Mexico, Benito Juarez, and his ambassador in London.

She hung her cape on the coat stand and was tucking escaped curls back into their confining net, when the door opened and Uncle Richard waddled in.

Short and plump, wearing black coat and trousers, her father's youngest half-brother resembled an earnest mole. His stiff collar and cravat made his neck appear very short and it merged into shoulders rounded by years of poring over ledgers.

In his early forties, his fair hair was fast receding despite luxuriant side-whiskers. Concentration had furrowed deep grooves in his forehead. Yet he had only to smile for people to realise he was not the dry old stick they imagined. He was smiling now.

'How is the old curmudgeon this morning?'

Laying her music case on her father's desk, Caseley gave a wry smile. 'Determined to be back in the office tomorrow. Dr Vigurs is seeing him later this morning.'

'Irresistible force meets immovable object.' Richard grinned.

'I'm relieved I won't be there. How is Aunt Helen's cold?'

'Improving, though she has not yet recovered her voice. She did manage to rebuke Oliver this morning for some misdemeanour, but a whispered scolding lacks the desired effect.' As he spoke of his wife Richard's habitually fraught expression softened into warm affection.

Brisk footsteps approached along the passage, the door opened wider, and in strode the man Caseley had seen at the helm of the damaged schooner. Instead of the navy reefer jacket, he was wearing a frock coat of fine dove-grey cloth over dark trousers, and in one hand he carried a tall hat with a narrow brim.

Their eyes met, and the impact was like a clenched fist. She looked down at her case trying to hide her shock.

Chapter Four

'Good morning, Captain Barata. Welcome back.' Richard stepped forward, offering his hand. 'A successful voyage, I trust?'

As the two men shook hands, Caseley released a quiet shaky breath, unable to understand her reaction.

'Profitable, certainly. We finished unloading cargo at the Docks yesterday. I picked up a mooring in the harbour overnight and brought *Cygnet* into the yard this morning. She needs a new jibboom and two new jib sails.' His voice was deep and though his English was perfect, a faint trace of accent would have told Caseley of his ancestry even if his name had not.

'I see.' Richard did not sound surprised. 'Do you wish your contribution to the cost of repairs deducted from your share of the profit?' Richard picked up a thick ledger from the desk and riffled through the pages. 'I believe this is the usual arrangement?'

Caseley glanced at the newcomer. Masters did not pay for repairs unless they were also part-owners. She had shares in *Cygnet,* a twenty-first birthday present from her father. Even so impersonal a connection with this man made her uneasy.

'As you will.' A brief gesture disposed of the matter.

Richard looked up from the entry he was making in the ledger. 'Bad weather in the Atlantic?'

'An incompetent master who got in my way.' The cold indifference in his reply sent a shiver down Caseley's spine. 'Where is Captain Bonython? I wish to speak with him.'

Stiffening at his imperious tone, Caseley moved round behind her father's desk so it became a physical barrier between her and the bearded man. But Richard did not appear in the least put out.

'Of course.' His frown cleared as he set the ledger down on top of another. 'You have been two months away. You will not have heard.'

'Heard what?'

'My brother has succumbed to a mild indisposition aggravated by overwork. As you are aware, Captain, it has been his policy to maintain an interest in every aspect of the business.'

'Indeed,' came the dry agreement.

'So to ensure a speedy return to health, his doctor advocated a short period of rest.'

Caseley could not help admiring her uncle's smooth explanation even as she shrank inside at the yawning chasm between what he believed and the truth of her father's condition. She was startled to see Richard steer the visitor towards her.

'Allow me to present Captain Bonython's daughter.'

When he first entered the room his surprise made her wonder if he recognised her from the yard. But he had not mentioned it. Perhaps a woman in a consular shipping office was reason enough for astonishment.

His expression gave her no clue to his thoughts. But the sharpness of his gaze made her wary.

He started forward, a smile lifting the corners of his mouth.

A smile designed to flatter anyone lacking the perception to see the pirate underneath. Why should she think such things? She knew nothing at all about this man.

Yet every instinct was warning her to be wary.

Despite glimpsing her uncle's bewilderment, she remained behind the desk, her fingertips resting lightly on her music case, her chin high.

One dark brow lifted fractionally and she saw a gleam of amusement in his narrowed gaze as he bowed. 'Jago Lantsallos Barata, at your service, Miss Bonython.' His voice was low-pitched and as smooth as dark chocolate.

It was a battle of wills and the force of her reaction overrode polite dishonesty. She cared nothing for his health and she was certainly not pleased to meet him. Remaining silent, she inclined her head briefly.

No longer smiling he turned to Richard. 'Perhaps we could go to your office. There are matters I wish to discuss and I have other appointments.' He started towards the door, irritation crossing his aquiline features when Richard did not immediately follow.

'I fear you do not understand, Captain Barata.' Richard's smile was uncertain as his gaze darted between them. 'I did not introduce my niece out of social convention.'

'I'm relieved to hear it. Apparently Miss Bonython is not sociable.'

'I do not play games, sir,' Caseley said, stung into speech.

He cast a brief sharp glance in her direction. 'Nor do I, madam. You would do well to remember that.'

'Er – what I meant was,' Richard intervened, clearly bewildered. 'She is here at her father's insistence.'

'For what purpose?'

'Miss Bonython enjoys her father's complete confidence. She is more than capable of conveying even the most complex matters to him.'

Caseley felt a rush of gratitude towards her uncle.

'I see.' Coolly Jago looked her up and down. 'It appears I misunderstood. For a moment I thought – a foolish mistake. So, you are a messenger.'

Caseley looked down to hide her wince. As far as Richard and Thomas were aware, that was precisely the extent of her involvement. Anxious to avoid further friction between her father and his half-brothers, she had tried hard to make it appear that she was simply a courier, that it was her father who answered the questions, solved the problems, and made the decisions.

Concerned for his wife's health and busy with his own side of the business, Richard might well have forgotten how long his half-brother had been away from the office.

He relayed his queries to her and the following morning she gave him answers. It was natural he should assume that Teuder was dealing with matters from his bed.

Only she knew it wasn't so. Weakness and delirium had often made it impossible for her father even to hold a rational conversation.

It was totally beyond him to balance materials, manpower, and available berths against deadlines set by owners and agents who wanted repairs done, yet needed their vessels in ports many miles away to collect cargoes won against fierce competition.

One morning four weeks ago, having taken half the night and dozens of sheets of paper to work out the figures, she had gone to the yard and handed the foreman, Toby Penfold, a list of vessels due in for repair the following week, and a countersigned order for materials.

Then she had walked to the office and handed Richard the list of dates, a sheaf of letters to owners and agents, and a page of figures for Thomas to enter in his invoice and accounts ledgers.

When Richard asked how her father was, Caseley

referred to the previous evening's delirious ramblings as 'a slight fever.'

Richard smiled, shaking his head. 'He really is amazing, managing to do all this despite a fever.'

Caseley had opened her mouth to tell him the truth. But he didn't give her the chance.

'Of course, it's the business that keeps him going. It means everything to him. After losing his first wife, then your mother and Philip, it was the yard that kept him sane. A lesser man would have given up, but not Teuder. He put aside his grief and built up one of the busiest shipping agencies and repair yards in Falmouth. There were ups and downs, but he never gave in. Even now he is working from his sickbed. What a man.'

After that, telling him was impossible. That evening she took home with more letters needing immediate replies, an enquiry from the Lloyd's agent regarding preliminary inspection of *Fair Maid* for her A1 classification, and a polite refusal by the Embassy to reimburse the expenses incurred in repatriating two injured Mexican seamen.

The letter stated that information had come to light proving that their wounds had been sustained not, as they claimed, when their ship sank in a storm, but during their attempt to commit an act of piracy. By repatriating them in his capacity as Consul, Teuder Bonython had, albeit unwittingly, abetted the escape of two felons. Therefore he would have to bear the cost.

Finding her father weak but lucid, she had fully intended to tell him what she had done. But then she recalled her uncle's praise for his half-brother. If she revealed her deception she might deal him a blow from which he would not recover.

So she read him the correspondence, soothed him over

the Embassy decision and, as she was writing his reply to the Lloyd's agent, she announced casually that she had done all he'd asked her to the previous evening and both Richard and Toby were delighted to have the matter settled.

She passed him the copies from her music case, hardly daring to breathe. His forehead was deeply furrowed and she could see the effort it was costing him to check the pages that had taken her hours.

What if she had made some glaring error that would demolish her fabrication like a house of cards? What if he thought, as he must, that *he* was responsible? Would he be able to shrug it off as the effect of his illness? Or would it undermine his confidence and erode his belief in himself? If that happened, Caseley knew he was as good as dead. His body might linger, but his spirit would wither away.

As the strain became unbearable and she was on the point of confessing, he sighed and shook his head.

'I don't remember any of this.'

Moistening dry lips, Caseley took the pages gently. 'You had a spell of fever last evening, Father.'

He gave a tired smile and sank back against the pillows. Caseley replaced the papers in her case, relief leaving her shaky.

'I'll do it, girl,' Teuder grunted. 'I'll keep the vultures away and the yard working just like it always has. Truth to tell, there have been days when I just couldn't think straight. The doubts came then. It was all getting away from me.'

Pride shone in his watery eyes as he pointed an unsteady finger at her case lying on the coverlet. 'But I've been running that yard so long I can do it in my sleep. You keep on bringing the work home. I'll be out of this bed soon and when I get back to my yard and the office, no one will know I was ever away.'

That had been four weeks ago. Four long busy weeks, during which she had repeated the deception daily, gaining in knowledge and experience but terrified of getting it wrong and being found out.

She was used to solitude. Ever since the accident her disability had set her apart from her contemporaries. But never in her life had she felt so achingly lonely.

There was no one in whom she could confide, no one to share her anxiety and the crushing burden of responsibility.

Having promised her father she would not reveal the severity of his illness to Thomas and Richard, nor could she reveal the extent of her deception.

Standing behind her father's desk she linked her hands and dug her right thumbnail into her left palm. The pain helped her to focus, gave her strength.

'Yes, Captain Barata, you will find me an adequate messenger.' She lowered her lashes at a sudden sharpening of his gaze.

'Might I be permitted to visit Captain Bonython at home?' His voice was silky smooth.

'Oh no. That is out of the question.' Richard's apologetic smile softened the rejection. 'Even my brother Thomas and I have been dissuaded from calling.'

'Oh?' Jago Barata's black brows rose.

Caseley knew that on no account could she afford to underestimate this man. Formidably intelligent, he was also predatory. She sensed he was listening not just to her words and the timbre of her voice, but to all she was *not* saying.

She made herself relax. Exhaustion was causing her to over-react. Her imagination was playing tricks. For weeks she had kept the severity of her father's illness, and her part in keeping the business going a secret from Richard, Thomas, and Toby. Jago Barata had been in the office only a few minutes. He couldn't know anything. It wasn't possible.

Yet her reaction to him had been instinctive and violent. He represented danger. As a battle raged inside her she managed a contrite smile.

'Perhaps you think me over-anxious, Captain Barata, but my father is very dear to me.'

'I do not doubt it, Miss Bonython.' She recognised genuine sincerity and felt a little of the tension leave her. 'I trust your protectiveness has served its purpose and your father will shortly be well enough to return. He has been away for several weeks?'

'Yes, but we have every hope –'

'When?' he enquired pleasantly.

'It – it is not easy to –'

'But you must have some idea?' He was relentless.

Desperate to be rid of him and free of his probing she blurted, 'A few days.'

'Really?' Richard beamed with pleasure. 'Caseley, that's wonderful. I didn't realise you had definite news of his return.'

Hotly conscious of Jago Barata's steady, speculative gaze, she could not backtrack. 'I – Father wanted it to be a surprise. He – he intended to come in and simply pick up the reins as if he had never been away.' That much was true.

She smoothed damp palms down her skirt. 'Under the circumstances, Captain Barata, no doubt you would prefer to return later in the week and conduct your business with my father in person.' With all her strength she willed him to leave.

Neither his expression nor his shuttered gaze gave any

clue to his thoughts. Eventually he smiled.

'I wish that were possible. But as I mentioned earlier I have other appointments and may not be free at a time convenient to your father. On reflection it suits me better to accept your uncle's recommendation and avail myself of *your* talents – as a messenger.' The pause was brief, but Caseley knew it was deliberate.

He turned to Richard. 'Doubtless there is much requiring your attention, Mr Bonython. I will call in at your office when I have finished here.'

Caseley stiffened. He was dismissing her uncle like a servant. But Richard seemed oblivious, still smiling at the news of Teuder's return.

'Yes, yes, do. I cannot wait to tell Thomas. He will be as delighted as I am.'

'Uncle Richard!' Caseley did not want to be left alone with Jago Barata. He was a threat. But she did not know *why*. She shot a desperate look at her uncle, only to have it intercepted. Realising her nervousness was bound to encourage speculation she reached into her case and pulled out two letters, both unfolded.

'One is for Señor Mantero at Guanajuato, the other for Fox's foundry,' she offered them to her uncle.

'Allow me,' Jago murmured. Taking them from her trembling grasp he passed them over.

Richard nodded. 'I'll see they go in the afternoon post. Sam can take them.'

'I was not aware Bonython's had interests in Mexican silver mines,' Jago said, one hand on the door as Richard disappeared back to his office.

She wanted to tell him to leave it open, but something stopped her. She was afraid for her father and for the tangled web of deceit she had spun to protect him. But the slightest hint of fear would re-ignite the curiosity and scepticism lurking in Jago Barata's slate-grey eyes.

The door closed with a soft click and panic tightened her throat. She swallowed. 'We don't. But as consul my father is frequently asked for information concerning the purchase and shipping of mining equipment.'

'Yes, of course.' One corner of his mouth tilted up. 'Are we not known for our expertise in all aspects of mining? Wherever there is a hole in the ground, a Cornishman will be found at the bottom of it.'

'*You* claim to be Cornish?' The words were out before she could stop them.

One brow lifted. 'My claim is legitimate, I assure you.'

'But your name –' She broke off in confusion, keenly aware it was not simply his name that had convinced her he was of foreign descent. The Cornish were brilliant engineers, fine seamen, and knew more about mining than any other race on earth. They were hardworking, loyal, and self-contained.

Jago Barata might have any or all of those attributes. But he had something else; a patrician arrogance that was as much a part of him as his limbs. She also sensed ruthlessness and a cold implacability that would make him a terrible enemy. Though she brushed the thought aside as fanciful nonsense, her skin tightened in a shiver.

'Surely you know that Jago is Cornish for James?' He was toying with her like a cat with a mouse. 'My maternal grandfather, Joseph Lantsallos, came from Redruth, and my mother's family bible records ten generations born in that area. But you are right, Miss Bonython, I have other blood in my veins. My father's family came originally from Castile. I see you are fluent in Spanish.'

The statement hit Caseley like a slap. 'How –?'

'The letters. The same hand wrote both, a firm neat hand betraying no sign of weakness. Did it take you long to compose them?'

She saw the trap just in time. 'Captain Barata, I am, as you say, simply a messenger. You mentioned having other appointments. If you would care to tell me what it is you wish my father to know, I will detain you no longer.'

He gripped the back of the visitor's chair angled in front of the desk.

'You are not detaining me, Miss Bonython.' His half-smile mocked, and Caseley felt warmth climb her throat and flood her face. 'I am here because *I* choose to be. Shall we sit? The message I have for your father is not unduly complicated but it does deserve your full attention.'

He moved round the chair. 'No doubt you are about to tell me you can attend perfectly well on your feet. That may well be so. However, courtesy does not permit me to sit while you stand and, despite your apparent aversion to introductions, I cannot believe you are entirely lacking in manners.'

Feeling her face flame, she sat on the edge of her father's chair, her back ramrod straight, her hands tightly folded. She could feel herself trembling with anger.

'Your message, sir?'

He settled himself comfortably, crossing one leg over the other. 'I want the post of senior captain. I also want your father's word that if the writ holding my ship in Bilbao is not rescinded in time, I, and no one else, will skipper *Fair Maid* to the Azores in December for the start of the fruit trade.'

Caseley gazed at him in horror. 'No, you can't,' she whispered, completely forgetting she was supposed to be merely a go-between.

'Why?' he enquired calmly.

'The post is not available. We already *have* a senior

captain –'

'Will Spargo,' he broke in. 'He's a good seaman, excellent on coastal trading. But for the Atlantic he is too old.'

'No,' Caseley repeated, her voice rising. 'Will Spargo has sailed Bonython ships all his life. He started as a cook's boy with my grandfather and worked his way up to master. He has earned his rank and the privileges that go with it.'

'Of course he has. I don't deny that. Coastal runs make a fair profit and will bring him home to his family every week or two instead of once in six months.'

'You don't care about Will, or his family,' Caseley cried. 'You just want his job.'

Jago's eyes narrowed. 'Why not? I am the best there is. I have equalled all crossing records and broken several. I have sailed through storm, typhoon, and hurricane without losing a ship or a cargo.'

It was no boast. He was simply stating facts. But Caseley recalled *Cygnet's* broken jibboom.

'A situation due more to luck than judgement if the vessels you command require repair every time you reach port.' Her heart thumped painfully against her ribs.

'So it *was* you,' he murmured. 'What is wrong with your foot?'

'That is none of your business.' He had been fully occupied bringing *Cygnet* in alongside the wharf and she had been many yards away among the sheds and stockpiles in the yard. Yet he had noticed her limp.

'So, you will convey my requirements to your father.' It was not a request.

Before she could respond he stood up. The sunlight caught his close-cropped curls and they gleamed like polished ebony. It cast bars of shadow across the fine material of his frock coat whose superb cut defined the breadth of his shoulders. Tanned by wind and sun his skin glowed bronze against his white collar. He leaned towards her and his clipped black beard reminded Caseley of a picture entitled *Lucifer* in a book of religious stories favoured by Miss Amelia.

'I am offering your father the chance to make Bonython's a major force in international maritime trade. He will want me, do not doubt it.' Caseley stared at him. He smiled. 'So be sure my message is delivered in its entirety. Good day, Miss Bonython. I will see you again. Very soon.'

He gave a mocking bow and strode out.

Chapter Five

A few minutes after Jago Barata left, her uncle Thomas burst in, startling her.

'Is it true? Will Teuder be returning to the office in a few days?'

She had never seen him so fraught. He was usually such a quiet, retiring man. But he must be feeling the strain of her father's absence almost as much as she was.

He had been so helpful, refusing to allow her to carry the heavy ledgers home each evening. Instead he had prepared a weekly balance sheet so her father could see at a glance that all was well. But Teuder had complained bitterly, demanding to see the books. The implied slur on his character and ability had offended Thomas.

Desperate to keep the peace, she had begged her father to accept the sheets. Reluctantly and with much grumbling he had agreed.

'I – I was going to tell you a bit nearer the time,' she stammered. 'We cannot be sure of the *exact* day. It should be soon though.' She had been compelled to tell so many lies, what difference could one more make?

'Then I must get back. Lots to do.' Reaching the door he glanced back. 'Caseley, as soon as you know for certain you must tell me.' He must have seen her surprise at his urgency. 'So we can arrange a small celebration.'

'I don't think he'd want that, Uncle Thomas,' she said quickly.

'No, perhaps you're right. But you will let me know?

‘Yes, of course.’

As he left the offices and turned towards the town centre, Jago reviewed his encounter with Teuder Bonython’s daughter. Caseley: an unusual name for a prickly young woman who apparently cared little for appearance, fashion, or men. With a mental shrug he dismissed her, climbed the five steps, and entered the red brick building that housed the offices of GC Fox and Company.

Only she would not be dismissed. There were hollows beneath her high cheekbones, a wide soft mouth above a stubborn chin, and dark lashes she used to veil emerald eyes flecked with bronze. There was no coyness in her manner. She appeared genuinely reluctant to have anything to do with him. He found that intriguing. As was her refusal to offer her hand.

On his sixteenth birthday, as a gift to mark his entry into manhood, his father had arranged for him to lose his virginity to an attractive young widow. His sensual mouth curved at the memory of Genez. From her he had learned consideration and the exquisite rewards of curbing his youthful impatience. He had believed himself deeply in love with her. With kindness and humour she had convinced him he wasn’t.

In the eighteen years since he had never lacked female company. His striking appearance, punctilious manners, and a background combining wealth and nobility ensured his name appeared on the guest list of every family of rank and many of those with aspirations. But he had avoided emotional entanglements.

His physical needs slaked, he had devoted his energy to his chosen profession, the sea, frequently returning to his ship sooner than planned simply to escape designing mothers. Faced with his lack of interest in their simpering daughters, more than a few hinted at their own availability, colouring his opinion of women and marriage with cynicism.

He had been celibate for a while before starting his liaison with Louise. She was earthy, generous, and honest, shunning many of the pretensions of others in her position. Physically she satisfied him as no woman had since Genez. But she was seeking more than he was inclined to give.

Opening the door he promptly forgot her.

'My apologies for not being here to receive you in person yesterday, Captain Barata,' George Fox said as they shook hands. 'However, I'm afraid there is still no message.'

'I will send a telegraph from the post office,' Jago took the chair Fox indicated. 'Perhaps you can tell me the latest news from Spain?'

'The newspapers –'

'Say very little. They are more concerned with the proposed pilot service around the Lizard, the lack of passenger revenue on the railway, and strike-breakers bound for collieries in the north where mine owners are refusing to employ union men.' Jago crossed one long leg over the other.

'Mr Fox, my ship is being held under writ in Bilbao. You are Vice-Consul for Spain, and I need to know exactly what's happening out there.'

'Yes, of course.' Fox sat down. 'May I offer you some coffee, or perhaps a glass –'

'Nothing, thank you.'

George Fox shook his head. 'The information we receive is garbled and on occasion contradictory. As you can imagine, communication is difficult and the situation changes daily. But it is a bloody war, captain. The *guerilleros* are behaving with appalling savagery. This is no disciplined army supporting the rights of Don Carlos to the Spanish throne. It is a rabble of murderers using the rebellion to satisfy their lust for blood and money.'

'How far have they reached? The last news I had was that Don Carlos had stormed the port of Bilbao, and his brother Don Alfonso was moving south.'

George Fox nodded. 'Don Alfonso's forces plundered and terrorised their way through Aragon and invaded the heart of Castile.' He paused. 'With the capture of Cuenca they managed to come within eighty miles of Madrid. The citizens resisted for two days, but when Cuenca fell –' His voice quavered and he avoided Jago's gaze. 'The mob, for they are little better, was unbelievably ruthless. They took few prisoners. The streets literally ran with blood.'

While Fox struggled to regain his composure, visibly distressed by the terror and wanton destruction convulsing the country whose interests he represented, for Jago this news was infinitely more painful. Spanish blood ran in his veins. Spain was part of his heritage. But his features remained impassive.

'However, there is some good news,' Fox said. 'The siege of Bilbao has been lifted. General Serrano's army defeated the Carlist forces but it was a hard-won victory and the town was a bloodbath. Rumour has it that Don Carlos fled across the border into France. Some are saying the rebellion is ended. But I have my doubts.'

He struck the desk lightly with the edges of his clenched fists. 'Forty years this vendetta has lasted. Two branches of the same family fighting for the crown, and the republican faction adding to forty years of carnage and misery that would never have started if Ferdinand had not bypassed his brother to hand the throne of Spain to his daughter, Isabel.' He shook his head. 'Forgive me,

Captain.'

Waving the apology aside, Jago stood up. 'Your concern does you great credit, sir, and I appreciate it.' He offered his hand and Fox rose to shake it warmly. 'You'll contact me if –'

'I will,' Fox promised.

Needing exercise to dispel his tension, Jago strode along Arwenack Street, heedless of the interest aroused by his dark good looks and proud bearing. Working men, recognising authority, tipped their caps. Men of substance and breeding acknowledged with a nod one of their own caste.

Respectable married ladies glanced at him then averted their eyes, smothering pangs of yearning and their guilt at such inappropriate thoughts. Girls stared openly, then clutched at each other to giggle and sigh. Sullen youths with catcalls on their lips changed their minds as cold grey eyes swept over them and they perceived beneath expert tailoring a muscular physique that owed nothing to padding.

The aroma of freshly baked bread and roasting coffee wafting from a refreshment house reminded him that he'd eaten little breakfast, but his stride did not falter.

The street was busy. Women shopped; errand boys darted to and fro across the dusty street. A hansom rolled past, the driver sitting high at the rear, cracking his whip above the horse's ears to quicken its pace. An argument in the bootmender's doorway had attracted a knot of on-lookers.

The sun was high, but the tall buildings on both sides of the street acted as a funnel for the keen-edged easterly wind. The smells of fish and horse dung competed with rotting vegetables, burning wood, and the gas works.

He crossed the square in front of the church, passed the

King's Head hotel and, a few yards further on, entered the new and beautifully faced post office building. The first rush had eased and he reached the counter with little delay.

'Good morning, Mrs Cox. My mail, if you please?'

The postmaster's wife had a naturally pale complexion, emphasized by the high-necked black bombazine she usually wore. But she was quite pink as she raised one hand in a reflex gesture to untidy, sandy-grey hair that appeared to be on the point of escaping the bun into which it had been loosely gathered.

''Morning, Cap'n. I heard you was back.'

Jago's mouth twitched. There was very little that escaped Mrs Cox, the post office being a clearing house for both local gossip and news brought in by crews of vessels returning from all over the world.

'Staying at the Royal again are you? Only Mrs Sandow up along Woodlane have got a lovely house to rent if you was interested.' She reached up to one end of a large wooden rack that covered half the wall its shelves partitioned into dozens of small compartments, and took down a wad of letters. As she passed them to him under the ironwork grill she leaned forward, her round face close to the heavy mesh. 'She asked me to find a *gentleman.* She said you can't be too careful these days.'

'And you thought of me?' Jago wondered what Mrs Cox would have thought had she seen him cuckolding the town's leading butcher the previous night. He picked up the letters. 'That was kind of you, Mrs Cox.'

''Tis a sad day if we can't help one another.'

'A worthy sentiment indeed. Is Mr Cox in the office?'

'No, Cap'n. He've gone out to meet the steamer to collect the mails. It give'n a break. The post office make'n work from seven in the morning till ten at night. If I wasn't here to help I don't know how he'd do it.'

'Please give him my regards, Mrs Cox.' He bent towards the grill. 'And take good care of yourself. For where would your husband, and all of us, be without you?'

'Get on, Cap'n,' she bridled, her cheeks glowing, one plump ink-stained hand touching the cameo brooch at her throat.

Jago left and climbed the stairs to the telegraph office on the first floor. After sending cables to Farando, his agent in Bilbao, and Ramon Gaudara, his father's representative in Madrid, he returned to the hotel for a late lunch.

At his table, from where he could observe without being too easily seen, he ordered sea-bass with a cream and tarragon sauce, and white wine, remembering with wry amusement the boiled salt beef, figgy duff, and stewed tea he had eaten the evening before he docked.

He flicked though his mail, tossing aside envelopes he recognised as containing social invitations. This left two letters. The first was from a local solicitor informing him that the last will and testament of his maternal grandmother, Sarah Ellen Bray, had been proved, probate granted, and if he would call at the office in Market Street when convenient, the keys to the property could be handed over.

He glanced at the date on the embossed paper. 29th July 1874. It had lain at the post office for over a month. He felt a self-mocking smile curve his mouth. He, who had always travelled light, rejecting the ties imposed by personal possessions, was now a man of property.

He thought of Mrs Cox and her well-meaning attempts to prise him loose from the hotel and establish him in a house like a 'proper gentleman', and wondered how long it would take for the news to reach her ears.

The second letter was from his father. His mother was well, but Elena, the companion who had moved with her from Spain to Mexico, had succumbed to a chronic digestive complaint. The *estancia* was showing a higher profit this year and cattle sales were up. The Indians worked well under the new foreman and the unrest that had cost the estate so much in time and money, had settled down.

Then he came to the heart of the letter. 'There has been another disaster at the Pachuca Silver Mine,' Felipe Barata wrote, his bold scrawl flowing across the pages. 'Fifteen killed and more than thirty injured, such waste! Indian labour might be cheap but owners risk dire consequences from both the law and political vigilante groups if they do not observe basic safety rules.

'As for our own mines, investment in new crushing equipment had proved worthwhile and production has increased. However, the quicksilver for the extraction process has not arrived from Spain this month. I have written to Guadara in Madrid and to Juan at the mine, but have received no replies. I ask you, my son, to find out what is happening. While we are still mining some nuggets at Carmelita, the bulk of our silver is extracted from lead and copper ores and we need the quicksilver urgently. I am enquiring for supplies here, but am not hopeful as competition is too fierce.'

Jago completed his meal with a cup of coffee. How recently had his father written to Gaudara? The letter did not say. Maybe the tide *had* turned in the war and stability would soon be restored. But until then communication would pose an insoluble problem. He would have to allow at least twenty-four hours for Ramon to reply to this morning's cable.

Meanwhile, assuming he managed to find some

quicksilver, all he could do was co-ordinate shipping arrangements from the nearest free Spanish port. He might have to collect it himself, bring it back to Falmouth, then trans-ship it to be sent on to Mexico. Though as he was already committed to an appointment concerning unloading facilities on the wharves and another at his bank, he could not return to the shipping office until the following day.

Immediately an image of Caseley Bonython formed in his mind, her slender neck and the heavy mass of chestnut hair bundled into its confining net. She looked tired and had been as approachable as a porcupine. He brushed the image aside as he would a fly.

Yet for the rest of the afternoon her memory plagued him. Why, he could not understand. Her clothes were plain and understated to the point of making her invisible. And while her low-pitched voice offered a welcome contrast to the usual female shrillness, her tongue possessed a cutting edge that ill-became a young woman. He grew more irritable as they day wore on.

Somehow Caseley got through the rest of the day. But despite valiant efforts to concentrate on the ledgers and papers in front of her, images of Jago Barata kept intruding. Over and over again she heard his cool voice with its subtle, taunting inflections, pictured the wintry gaze that saw too much and revealed so little.

It was late afternoon when she left the office and walked briskly to Dr Vigurs's consulting rooms.

'He can return to the office? And the yard?' Caseley couldn't hide her surprise. Despite his bluster and determination, her father still seemed weak and far from well. But perhaps he had simply been too long indoors, deprived of the sunshine and fresh air he craved.

Dr Vigurs nodded. His portly figure was draped in formal black frock coat, winged collar, and grey striped trousers. Sitting behind his desk he toyed with his pince-nez. 'An hour a day to begin with, and he must keep his drops with him at all times.'

She would be free. Able to relinquish the responsibilities she had been forced to shoulder. But what would take their place? What in her life required a fraction of the intelligence and energy she had discovered as a result of her father's dependence on her? She pushed the thought away.

There was plenty demanding her attention: neglected friends, domestic duties that had been postponed. She would soon fill her days. And she would not be obliged to be civil to Jago Barata. She need not see him ever again.

But as the doctor's gaze met hers, sudden apprehension squeezed her heart. 'There's something else, isn't there?'

'Caseley, what I have to tell you will not be easy to bear. However, you are strong and I know you will be able to accept it and act accordingly.'

I'm not strong. I don't want to hear. I can't take any more. I'm too tired. But not a word escaped as she sat stiff-backed on the edge of the chair and waited.

'You father is still full of grit and determination, and his spirit is as willing as ever.' He paused.

'But?' she prompted softly, a hollow growing in her stomach.

'But his heart has been damaged beyond repair. He will never be the man he was.'

'Are you saying he will be a permanent invalid?'

'Not exactly,' Robert Vigurs replied carefully.

'I don't understand. You are letting him go back to work.'

The doctor placed his hands flat on the blotter in front

of him. 'Given the right conditions your father could live for many months.'

'Months?' she echoed, deeply shaken. 'But I thought – Only *months*? So what are the right conditions? Should he have a special diet? Are there medicines we could buy?'

'The conditions I speak of are not purely physical, they relate to the mind and spirit. But one thing I am sure of. There is nothing more medicine can do for him. Your father's life is in the hands of Providence, and I see little point in demanding he conserve his energy for a future he may not have.'

'That's why you're letting him return to work?' she whispered. 'But the stress could kill him.'

'On the other hand, it might not,' the doctor pointed out. 'And if it does, do you not think he will die a lot happier? He *wants* to go back, Caseley. It serves no purpose to stop him. Indeed it would be cruel.'

Her eyes stung and her throat ached. 'Have you told him?'

'There was no need. He already knows and has accepted it.'

'But –'

'We all die, Caseley. That is the only certainty in this life. You have the hardest task, knowing what you do, to allow him to live his life his way until the end.'

She stood up, swallowing her tears. 'Thank you. I'm glad you told me.'

He came round the desk and took her gloved hand in both his. 'I'm here if you should need me. The drops will ease any pain he may have. As for the rest, there's no way of knowing how long …' He allowed the sentence to hang unfinished in the air.

She nodded, unable to speak. He walked with her to the front door. She had known him all her life. He had brought her and her two brothers into the world. At this moment at least she was not entirely alone.

'It will be a difficult time for you, my dear. Never doubt that your father loves you. But each of us must make the final journey on our own, and your father has already begun his.'

Chapter Six

That night, halfway through his beef with a second glass of claret in front of him, Jago was hailed by a loud voice from the far side of the room.

He looked up to see the mop-headed, reed-thin figure of Luke Dower plunging through the crowded dining room towards him, scattering cheerful apologies as he bumped into chairs and scraped against tables.

'Jago, you old bastard,' he bellowed. 'How's it going, my son? When did you get back?'

'Good evening, Luke,' Jago drawled, raising his glass in salute. Not for an instant was he taken in by the other's expansive smile and bonhomie. 'How are you?'

Luke Dower did his drinking in the waterside inns and public houses. His presence in the best hotel in Falmouth meant a business deal was brewing for which he needed funds. Jago guessed this was no chance meeting.

Luke sat, slammed his glass onto the table, and, with a visibly trembling hand, poured brandy from the bottle he was clutching. 'I'm doing fine. I got a regular run to Portugal, taking out wool and cotton, bringing back wine and lace. Been doing it a few weeks now.'

'I'm glad for you. Last time we met the bank was threatening to foreclose and Trembath –'

'All in the past, my son.' His wide smile revealed stained and broken teeth. 'Old Luke bounced back like he always do. 'Tis looking good.'

Jago finished his beef and pushed the plate away. He

sat back, turning the stem of his wine glass.

Luke hitched his chair closer and Jago noted the greasy shine on his forehead, smelled the stale sweat and tobacco smoke that permeated his clothes. Luke's shirt was grubby and there were spots and stains on his coat and trousers.

'I got a deal you –'

'I don't think so.'

'Wait till you hear. You'd be mad to turn this one down.'

'What is it this time?'

Luke tapped the side of his nose. 'My client has a commodity he wants to dispose of in this country. I bring it over and pass it on to a third party.'

'From Portugal?'

Luke nodded. 'Part of the regular run. No diversions, no problems.'

'No customs duty,' Jago's tone was dry.

'Now why should we give the poor buggers all that extra work? They got too much to do already.' Luke grinned.

'So why do you need me?'

Luke stiffened. 'I never said I did.' He gulped a mouthful of brandy, grimacing as the fiery spirit burned its way down. 'I'm offering you a chance to make some easy money. But if you aren't interested, there's plenty who will be.'

Jago moved one shoulder. 'As you like.'

Luke swallowed another mouthful, wiped his mouth with the back of his hand then leaned forward to confide. 'Look, I shouldn't be telling you this. But I've already got one partner. I'm naming no names, but 'tis a well-known family, solid business background. Would a man like that get involved if it wasn't a sound proposition?'

Jago shrugged. 'That depends on *his* reasons.'

'Look, you and me both know you got to invest if you want to make a profit. My outlet is guaranteed. So instead of me acting as an agent and getting a piddling little commission for handling the goods, it makes better sense for me to *buy* then re-sell. That way I can sell to the highest bidder and control the market.'

'So you're looking for capital.'

'Well, I can't go to the bank, can I?' Luke retorted. 'This is the chance of a lifetime. Turn it down and you'll regret–'

'What is the commodity?'

Luke's eyes flickered sideways.

'You can't expect me to invest if I don't know what I'm buying.'

'You're in then?'

'I didn't say that.'

Luke drained his glass, gripping it with both hands. 'Moidores,' he muttered reluctantly.

'Are you mad?'

'Each one of those coins is worth twenty-seven shillings,' Luke was defensive.

'Have you forgotten the penalty for smuggling bullion?' Jago demanded in an undertone. 'Do you know how many men with schemes like yours died of typhus in Bodmin Gaol last year? You've got work, a regular run. Why in God's name are you risking it all?'

'I don't get an owner's share,' Luke hissed. 'With freightage of two or three pounds a ton to be divided three ways after paying port expenses, wages, and food, there's bugger-all left.' He glanced round again. A look of cunning crossed his face, quickly masked by a wolfish smile.

Curious, Jago turned his head and saw Thomas Bonython weaving through the crowded tables towards them.

Spotting Jago, he hesitated, then came forward, a worried frown creasing his forehead and dragging the corners of his mouth. After a polite nod to Jago, Thomas turned to Luke.

'I must speak with you.' His whisper was urgent.

Luke lurched to his feet and threw an arm over Thomas's shoulders. 'No need to look so tragic, my old son.' He grasped the brandy bottle by its neck. 'Whatever it is we'll sort it out. Let's find a quiet corner. We'll have a drink, and you can tell me what's on.' He winked at Jago, while Thomas twisted his hands together.

'No, I don't think you understand –'

As Luke pushed him through the crush, Jago watched them go, his gaze thoughtful.

A restless night disturbed by dreams of a chestnut-haired girl with shadows in her eyes drove Jago from his bed in a foul temper before six.

Wearing his navy reefer jacket over a clean white shirt and a red kerchief knotted loosely round his throat, he locked his door and left the hotel, heading for the yard.

The wind had dropped and the morning was crisp and fresh. Through opes and alleys leading down to the quays, warehouses and workshops he saw a forest of masts. The water was calmer, changing colour from indigo to sapphire as gold-washed clouds moved slowly across a pearly sky.

By the time he reached the yard his head had cleared and his temper improved. Despite the early hour the yard was busy. Grey smoke belched from the smithy chimney. Two boys called to one another as they staggered with newly cut planks from the sawpit to the dry timber store. A man tended a crackling fire beneath a steaming-box in which planks were being softened and shaped to fit a curving hull.

As he headed towards *Cygnet*, Jago could see pitch bubbling in buckets over fires built within small brick squares and hear the musical clink of caulking hammers. Before he reached the schooner his nostrils flared at the pungent odour escaping from the companionway hatch, fo'c'sle scuttle and ventilators despite their heavy covering of canvas.

'All right, Cap'n?'

He turned and saw the short, stocky figure of the yard foreman coming towards him. Toby Penfold had skin the colour and texture of old leather and iron-grey fluff fringing his skull. His navy-blue Guernsey was darned in several places, as were his paint-smeared work trousers.

''Morning, Toby. When did you start fumigating?'

'Last night. I put four sulphur candles in the cabin, four in the fo'c'sle, and same again in the hold. I'll open her up in an hour. But you won't want to spend time below till tonight. Better still, leave it till the morning. Want something from inside, did you?'

'Nothing that can't wait. I'd rather see those damn bugs killed.'

'The sulphur will do that all right, Cap'n. But give it a week and 'twill be bad as ever. The little buggers nest in they timbers behind the lockers and panelling. There idn no way to reach the eggs, and the sulphur don't touch 'em.' He gave a philosophical shrug.

'How soon can you have *Cygnet* ready for sea again?'

The foreman scratched his head and drew air between his teeth with a slow hiss. 'We should keep her at least two weeks. She's spewing oakum. I got Joe and Henry caulking her now and we'll seal her with pitch.' He shook his head. 'I'd like to replace that there bowsprit with a longer spar and save all the trouble with the jibboom. I know,' he said before Jago could speak, 'you wouldn't have space for extra canvas. But the shroud plates is loose, and 'tis time –'

'Toby.'

The foreman sighed. 'Three days.'

'Thanks,' Jago grinned and Toby shook his head in resignation. 'How far have you got with *Fair Maid*?'

Toby scratched his head again as they crossed the wharf to the dry dock. 'She've had her new felt and metal sheath fitted, and a new mainmast step. Penrose's sent word that her fore, main, and mizzen sails will be ready by Thursday. We already got her squares and topsails and we kept her old foresails and jibs. All her masts, spars, and yards have been scraped and oiled. Standing and running rigging will be fitted by the end of next week.'

The three lofty masts lay in wooden cradles along the dock, the close-grained yellow pine gleaming under its coating of oil. Even without them, *Fair Maid* had the slim lines and pronounced curve at deck level that marked her as a thoroughbred. Her bulwarks were freshly painted and the new varnish on her rail reflected the sun.

As his critical gaze softened in admiration, Jago thought of his own vessel, held for months in the northern Spanish port. What would she look like now? Not wanting to think about the damage she might have sustained during the siege and blockade, he turned to the foreman.

'Has Captain Bonython's illness caused problems in the yard? I didn't know about it until yesterday.'

Pursing his lips Toby leaned back, feet planted wide, resting gnarled knuckles on his hips. 'I can't say it have. We've missed him about the place. But the work's gone on same as always. He's some lucky with Miss Caseley. As for that brother of hers,' Toby turned his head and spat.

'Little twerp should have had his backside leathered years ago. He won't have nothing to do with the yard. He'd sooner be out drinking or painting pictures.'

He glared up at Jago. 'What's it coming to? After he lost his eldest boy, Mr Teuder was some pleased when Ralph was born. Gived that boy everything, he did. Sent him to school and all.' Toby grunted in disgust. 'Fat lot of good that did. Bone idle, he is, and I'd tell him to his face except he never come near the place. Near broke his father's heart. If it wasn't for Miss Caseley I dunno what would have happened here these past weeks. She's some lovely maid. Clever too. Henry's wife had these sores on her legs. Miss Caseley made some herb stuff for her to put on them and they was all gone in a week. Good as gold, she is. The men think the world of her. But though they haven't noticed, 'tis plain to me.'

Trying to reconcile the foreman's description of a warm-hearted, friendly, smiling girl with the defensive hostile creature he had been introduced to, Jago almost missed what Toby had said.

'Noticed what? What is plain?'

Toby shook his head. ''Tis getting too much for her, and no wonder.'

'Looking after her father? Surely –'

'No,' the foreman scoffed impatiently. 'Running this here yard.'

Jago was suddenly very still. 'Are you suggesting –?'

'No, I aren't.' Toby was curt. 'I'm *telling* you.'

'But Richard Bonython said ...' Jago broke off as his initial incredulity gave way to thoughtfulness. 'How do you know?'

'I've worked in this yard since I was a boy. I know the way Mr Teuder do think. The orders I get when Miss Caseley come in of a morning, well, they don't have the stamp of her father.'

'Have there been mistakes?'

Toby shook his head. 'No.' There was a note of surprise in his voice. ''Tis just the feel of it.'

'Have you mentioned this to anyone else?'

''Course I haven't!' Toby was indignant. 'Family business, isn't it? Dunno what I'm telling you for.'

'It will go no further,' Jago promised. 'If you're right, it's my belief she's the only member of the family who knows. I have some personal business to take care of but I'll be back in a day or two. I trust *Cygnet* will be ready?'

As the foreman sucked in a breath, Jago lifted one eyebrow. The foreman threw up his hands.

'I'll do my best, but I can't promise.'

'Your best is all I ask. I may have to go to Spain to pick up a cargo my father needs urgently.'

His thoughts buzzing like a swarm of angry bees, Jago pushed the half-open door wide. Caseley was replacing a file on a high shelf. His gaze swept over her, lingering briefly on the swell of her breast beneath the sprigged muslin blouse. She glanced round, flushing as she recognised him, but the colour quickly drained, leaving her ashen. Her eyes had bruise-like shadows beneath them. Compassion caught him an unexpected blow.

She circled round behind the wide desk, graceful despite her limp, attempting to maintain as much distance as possible between them in the small room. Her back was stiff and she radiated antipathy.

He fought an urge to reach out, tell her she had nothing to fear. Then his habitual cynicism returned, overriding emotion both unexpected and unwelcome.

'Can I help you, Captain Barata?'

Though he had heard her voice over and over in his mind, its musical quality struck him anew despite her icy manner.

He was equally cool. 'I hope so. Does Bonython's have any vessels due to sail for Spain or Mexico during the coming week?'

'You must speak to my uncle Richard. It is he who co-ordinates cargoes and transport.' Her chin rose a little higher. 'As I'm sure you are already aware.' She placed some papers in another folder, picked it up and hugged it in an unconscious gesture of self-protection. She waited, clearly expecting him to leave.

He did not move. 'You do not assist him?'

'No, Captain Barata, I do not. I am here solely to help my father, and his work involves the yard and the consulship.'

'So Richard Bonython would arrange cargoes or shipping to Portugal?' His gaze never left her face.

She shook her head. 'That would be most unlikely. Mr Fox is consul for Portugal so their agency handles all commerce with that country.' There was no hesitation, nothing in her voice but mild impatience. Jago realised that whatever connection Thomas Bonython had with Luke Dower, it was not official business for the company. Surely the man had more sense than to get involved in such a dangerous venture, unless …

'Was there anything else?'

Beneath her coolness he heard a thread of anxiety. It had not been there when she answered his questions. Clearly she wanted him gone.

He had used Bonython's agency to find cargoes for his own vessel for the past five years, ever since deciding to make Falmouth his base for lucrative deep-water runs to the Azores for the fruit trade and the Labrador coast for salt fish.

Teuder Bonython had made him master of the *Cygnet*

after his own schooner, *Cara*, had been seized when he landed in Spain to load a cargo of salt for St John's. He had bought shares in *Cygnet* as an investment and a gesture of good faith. Never before in his dealings with the company had he sensed the undercurrents and tension that existed now.

'Just one more question,' he said smoothly. 'What news of your father? When will he be back at his desk?'

A spasm of anguish crossed Caseley's face and her grip on the folder tightened. 'Probably tomorrow.'

Jago arched one black brow in surprise. 'Indeed?'

'I mentioned his imminent return when you came by yesterday,' she blurted.

'So you did. Yet I had the impression you did not entirely believe what you were saying.'

He saw her flinch. But she recovered quickly. 'I also told you that I care very much for my father. Perhaps I am over-protective.' Her mouth quivered but she controlled it. 'However, the doctor sees no reason to keep him at home any longer. Now, if you will excuse me, I have a great deal to do.' As she looked down at the crowded desk and gathered papers, he sensed desperation.

'Far more, I think, than most people are aware of. At least, that is Toby Penfold's opinion.'

Her head jerked up, eyes wide, and it was obvious that the foreman had guessed correctly. 'How did you –?'

Realising she had betrayed herself, her entire body sagged. She leaned on her hands, her head dropping forward like a blossom too heavy for its stem. 'Was there a mistake? Did I get something wrong?' Her voice was unsteady and full of dismay.

'No. Toby couldn't fault anything. He only guessed because, to use his own words, it *felt* different.'

She nodded without raising her head, merely

acknowledging what he had said.

'Why did you do it?' he demanded. 'What were you trying to prove?

She raised her head and eyed him with a mixture of bewilderment and disgust. 'I have nothing to *prove*, Captain Barata. My father needed my help.'

Jago felt her disdain like a whiplash on raw flesh. Incensed by her defiance, his voice was a deadly purr. 'Then no doubt he is very proud of you. I must congratulate him on having raised a daughter whose gifts, while certainly less common than those of her peers, are plainly far more useful. Good day, Miss Bonython.' He made a mocking bow and turned to leave.

'No.' The word was wrung from her.

He turned slowly. 'I beg your pardon?'

'Congratulations would be out of place.' She laid the folder on the desk with exaggerated care, squaring the corners. 'I only did what was necessary. There is nothing praiseworthy in that.'

He caught the anxiety in her voice and wondered. 'I cannot agree. Such devotion, such a sense of duty and responsibility cannot go unmarked. I shall make a point –'

'No!' She made a heroic effort to control herself. 'It is not your concern, Captain. Please, I – I beg you, don't …' She fell silent under his scrutiny.

'You *beg* me? And with such passion,' he murmured, comprehension dawning. 'I doubt Caseley Bonython has ever begged for anything in her life. Most women seek compliments like water in a desert, but you –'

'Forgive me, Captain Barata.' She drew herself up, her face taut with dislike. 'I should have known better than to request anything of you. I do not wish the matter spoken of because …' She swallowed. 'Because my father did not know what I was doing.'

'I see. May I ask the reason for this deception?'

Caseley hugged herself as if cold. 'To protect him.'

Jago was sceptical. 'From what?'

She half-turned to gaze out of the window. Several seconds passed and he could see her trying to decide how much to tell him. 'No one knew how ill he was, not even the family. He made me promise… he was afraid the business would suffer.'

'I assume from what you're saying that there were occasions when your father was not capable.'

Her eyes flashed splinters of ice. 'Rare occasions, Captain, very rare. I saw no reason then, nor do I now, to –'

'Shatter his confidence? I agree entirely, Miss Bonython. No purpose would be served, especially as he is now sufficiently recovered to take control once more.'

'He never relinquished it,' Caseley shot back.

'No?' He enquired softly. As a tide of dusky rose flooded her face her eyes defied him. But he gave her no chance to reply. 'Still, no doubt you will be pleased to withdraw from this unfamiliar world and return to more feminine occupations.'

'I don't follow you, Captain.' Her gaze was stormy, her tone quiet and controlled.

His gesture encompassed the paper-laden desk, the small writing bureau in the corner, the shelves stacked with boxes, files, and ledgers.

'Surely you are out of place here?' It was unusual for a young woman to accept such a burden of responsibility. Even more unusual for her to acquit herself so well that only one person guessed the depth of her involvement.'

Was that why she disturbed him in a way no other woman ever had? Though neatly dressed, she seemed totally uninterested in her appearance. A sensual man himself, he recognised passion in her of which she was totally unaware.

She irritated him yet he could not get her out of his mind. She didn't fit into any of the categories to which he usually assigned women. That offended his sense of order.

He heard her soft intake of breath.

'Perhaps ladies of your acquaintance are rarely required to use their brains,' she retorted with acid sweetness. 'However I should have been of little help to my father were my only accomplishments the ability to play the piano and discuss the finer points of fashion.'

'Rest assured it had not occurred to me to credit you with either of those attributes. Good day.' He inclined his head, pausing in the doorway. 'You gave your father my message?'

'Of course.' Her eyes were glacial, but the hurt in their depths made him despise himself. That made him even angrier.

'Then I will return tomorrow so we may agree terms.'

'I shall be occupied elsewhere.'

'Did you not hear me? I said *we*. That means your father, myself, and you.'

Her eyes widened. 'But – I am not – It has nothing to do with me.'

'On the contrary, we both know you are deeply involved.' He pulled the door wider. 'I trust you will not fall victim to a sudden indisposition.' Twin spots of colour staining her cheekbones told him the thought had crossed her mind.

'Until tomorrow, Miss Bonython.' He closed the door quietly behind him.

Chapter Seven

Teuder Bonython leaned back in his chair and nodded. 'This is more like it.' He sighed with deep contentment.

Caseley knew the twin patches of crimson on his cheeks were not a sign of good health but evidence of his damaged heart labouring. His clothes hung loose on his large frame, the bones of his face and skull were clearly defined, and his grey-white hair lay flat and thin. But his smile was broad and his watery eyes twinkled.

'I've missed this place. Open that window a bit more. I want to hear the town.'

She did as he asked. A hansom had picked them up outside the front door and dropped them in the courtyard of Bank House. The stairs had seemed endless, but her steady flow of chatter had covered the slowness of their ascent. Even so, by the time they reached his office, he had been breathing heavily.

Hanging up her cape and his hat and coat she had seen pain flicker across his face, and started towards him, but he had shaken his head.

She busied herself around the office, to allow him a few moments in which to recover, and to hide the dampness on her lashes.

If he could pretend then so must she. It would be all too easy to fuss over him and so reveal her deep concern. But he would hate it, and it would be self-indulgent on her part.

'I still say we should have stopped off at the yard,' he

grumbled. 'Dammit, we had to pass the gate. It wouldn't have taken long.'

A knock on the door made Caseley jump. Busy with her father she had managed to avoid thinking about Jago Barata. But now they were in the office, not knowing when he would appear, each footstep in the passage, each knock on the door, stretched her nerves ever tighter.

The door opened and Sam peered round holding a bundle of letters. Caseley hurried forward to take them, fearing the clerk's reaction on seeing the change in his employer. 'Back to normal, eh, miss?'

Caseley managed a smile. 'Back to normal, Sam.'

The clerk withdrew and she placed the letters in front of her father. 'You're needed here, Father,' she said gently. 'I know you'd rather be in the yard. But Toby is following your orders and everything is running smoothly.'

She shivered as fear rasped her nerves. Jago Barata had promised to say nothing about her part in keeping the yard functioning. But could she trust him?

Teuder grunted. 'You open them.' He leaned back in the chair, resting his head. 'Cutting down a tree to build a ship, that's right and proper. A ship has a heart and spirit. But destroying forests to make paper,' he shook his head. 'That's terrible.'

The door opened. Taut as a bowstring, Caseley glanced round then relaxed as Richard bustled in.

'I heard you arrive but I was –' He broke off, his warm smile of welcome fading as he came face to face with his brother for the first time in two months.

'Good morning, Uncle Richard.' Her mouth smiled while her gaze begged. 'We heard voices in your office. I told Father you'd be along as soon as you were free.' She watched her uncle struggle to hide his shock.

'Yes. Yes, indeed. It *is* good to see you once again in your proper place, Teuder.' His sincerity made Caseley's heart swell with gratitude. 'We have missed you, though less than we expected, for Caseley has coped admirably.'

'So I should hope,' Teuder was gruff. 'All she had to do was relay my instructions.'

Caseley lowered her gaze. He didn't intend to hurt. He was simply stating what he believed to be the truth. Dr Vigurs had warned that her father would feel resentful. He had never been ill in his life and equated it with weakness, something to be ashamed of and denied. Compliments on her performance in his absence rubbed salt in his wounded pride.

The door opened again. As Caseley turned, her pulse quickening, Thomas entered. Catching sight of Teuder he stopped.

'My God!'

'No,' Teuder said, droll and impatient. 'Just me. I suppose you've noticed I've lost a bit of weight. Feel all the better for it too. Now we've got that out of the way, I want to know why we're losing Liverpool cargoes to Broad's. Richard, Jimmy Morrison is still our agent up there, isn't he? Find out what he's doing. He's not being paid to let another company steal our bread and butter. Thomas, those balance sheets were pretty enough but I've got a feeling they're not telling me the whole story. I shall do an audit next week and I want the books, *all* the books, up to date and on my desk by Wednesday.'

Seeing both men about to protest, Caseley linked her arms through theirs and drew them out into the passage.

'Try to understand,' she pleaded. 'It's his first day back. He's just settling in.'

'And unsettling everyone else,' Thomas retorted resentfully. 'He doesn't look fit to be out of bed.'

'He's like an old tom cat marking his territory.' Richard's smile was perceptive. He sighed. 'I'd better put a squib under Jimmy Morrison.'

'Stop that whispering,' Teuder roared. 'Caseley, get back in here. There's work to do.'

With an apologetic smile to her uncles, she went back into the office. But as she turned from closing the door her breath caught. Her father was slumped in his chair, eyes closed against the pain that tightened his mouth and scored grooves in his forehead. One hand was pressed to his upper chest. The other clutched the chair arm.

She grabbed the bottle of drops from her case. Biting her lip as she tried to steady her trembling hands she measured out a dose, relieved she had remembered to tell Sam to put a tray with a glass and carafe of fresh water on one corner of the desk. Stirring the mixture she held it to her father's lips.

'This will help.' Her calm voice betrayed no hint of the terror flooding her body. It couldn't be yet. Months, Dr Vigurs had said. *Please not yet.*

Draining the glass he lay back, breathing heavily. Caseley recapped the bottle and moved the tray, watching him.

His breathing eased and he began to relax. His eyelids flickered then opened.

'I'll send Sam for a cab to take you home.' Relief weakened her legs. 'This is your first day back. Best not to overdo it.'

'I'm all right,' Teuder rasped. 'Just give me a minute. I'll be fine.'

'Father, please –'

'Stop your fussing.' What his voice lacked in strength it made up for in irascible determination. 'I'm staying. I didn't ask you to come in today. It was your idea. If there is something you would rather be doing, go and do it. Sam can see me home when I'm ready to leave.'

Caseley turned away. She did not want to stay. But how could she leave him? If he had another attack – if he could not reach the drops – overshadowing it all was the spectre of Jago Barata. If she was not here, if he carried out his threat to tell her father … She had no choice.

She swallowed the ache in her throat. 'There is nowhere else I would rather be, Father. If I seem to fuss it's only because I care. I will try to control it.'

'All right then.' He cleared his throat loudly. 'Let's get this blasted paperwork out of the way.'

Caseley drew the visitor's chair close to the opposite side of the desk and reached for paper and pen. After reading the first two letters and dictating replies, her father pushed the third across to her.

'Here, you read it to me. No sense keeping a dog and barking yourself.'

She saw the drops were taking effect. Now the pain had gone he was becoming drowsy. Settled comfortably in his chair, his fingers linked over his waistcoat and what remained of his paunch, his gaze wandered round the room as she read a request from the owner of a Penzance trading ketch for a new main lower and top mast within ten days.

'Last time I was in Penzance was in '72,' he mused. 'Toby and his son and two nephews came with me in *Ada* to see the Channel Fleet. There was a big sea running but the wind was fair and Toby had every stitch of canvas he could lay hands on up that mast. We were flying.' He smiled at the memory.

'Those ironclads were a sight to behold. Anchored about a mile off the pier head they were. Little steamers were taking parties out for a closer look. *Sultan, Achilles,*

Agincourt, and *Black Prince*, names to stir the heart and put fire in a man's belly. We got quite close to *Minotaur*. Twenty-six guns she had, and five iron masts. That ship weighed ten thousand tons if she weighed an ounce. That was a day to remember.' He nodded, lapsing into silence.

Caseley leaned over the desk and moved one of the ledgers across in front of her father. 'Shall I stop by the yard later and ask Toby if he'll be able to accept Mr Tresawle's ketch? They're very busy at the moment.'

Behind her the door opened. The tiny hairs on the back of her neck prickled and her stomach clenched. She knew without looking that Jago Barata had entered the room.

She tried to hide panic she could neither explain nor control. Laying her notepad and pen carefully on the desk she rose and turned, her face carefully expressionless.

'Good morning, Captain.' Her voice was calm and clear despite the sensation of standing on shifting sand.

'Good morning, Miss Bonython.' His coolness matched hers. Then taking her completely by surprise, he caught her right hand and raised it to his mouth, brushing her knuckles with warm lips that sent tiny flames along every nerve.

Her breath stopped in her throat and she snatched her hand back, furious at the scalding blush. Clasping her hands, she rubbed her knuckles, not caring what he thought, desperate to erase the sensation of his mouth.

One black brow arched and his eyes gleamed. Then he walked past her to greet her father, extending his hand across the desk. Teuder leaned forward to grip it with both his.

'Good to see you again, Jago. How did it go?'

Standing to one side, Caseley watched Jago as he gave a brief account of cargoes and ports of call during his two-month absence. Not by the flicker of an eyelash had he betrayed the shock he must have felt at her father's changed appearance. Perhaps after what she had been forced to tell him, he had prepared himself – but for a moment her dislike and mistrust were pushed aside by gratitude.

It didn't last.

'So, that is the past. Let us look to the future. Your daughter told you of my proposition?'

'She did.'

Caseley looked away. She had reminded her father of Will Spargo's years of loyal service and prior claim, urging him not to give way to Jago Barata. He let her finish then demolished every objection.

'You can't afford a soft heart in business, girl. I know Will's value, and I'll see he don't lose by it. But Bonython's can't afford to miss this chance. If I don't make Jago Barata chief captain, Broad's or Fox's will.'

'Let them,' Caseley cried. 'We don't need him.'

'Don't be so bloody daft, girl.' Teuder had been testy. 'You don't give an advantage to your rivals. Has your sense gone begging? Seems to me you've taken against him, though for the life of me I can't think why. How many times have you spoken? Once? Twice?' He had shaken his head in disgust. 'Dear life!'

What could she say that he would understand? He was talking competitors and potential profits. All she had was intuition.

'He's a pirate.'

Clearly startled, her father had nodded, admiration stealing across his tired features. 'Could be you're right. But then so was I. We're the ones who run risks. We push hard. We take what we want, and pay for it,' he added. 'But we get things done and build something that will last long after we've gone.'

It was the first time he had mentioned a future in which he had no part. It had cost her dearly not to react.

'I'd be a fool to turn him down. I have faults a-plenty, but I'm not stupid. He's half Spanish. He speaks the lingo. He can negotiate new contracts and markets that will put Bonython's leagues ahead of our competitors. Not just in Spain, but South America. And we need 'em, make no mistake about that. The railways are taking a good part of our freight, and road hauliers are developing their own transport networks at competitive prices. We have to develop our foreign trade. That's where the future lies.'

'Don't you agree, Miss Bonython?' Cool and ironic, Jago Barata's voice jerked Caseley back to the present.

She looked up at him and the amusement in his grey eyes told her he was well aware her thoughts had been far away.

Her skin burned but she did not shrink from his gaze. 'I'm afraid I wasn't listening, Captain.' His mouth twitched at her candour. 'If you'll excuse me, I will leave you and my father to discuss your business privately. It is not my concern so –'

'Indeed it is,' Jago interrupted.

'I don't understand.'

'Then allow me to explain.' A smile still hovered at the corners of his mouth, but his eyes were as hard as granite. 'I made your father a business proposition. I believe he is about to accept it. However, there is something I wish to add.'

'I'm not looking for further inducement, Jago,' Teuder grunted. 'I reckon we'll both do well out of the arrangement.'

'We will. This is no inducement. I am making a request. No, a demand,' he amended without taking his eyes from Caseley.

She stared back, her breath and heartbeat quickening as apprehension crawled along every nerve.

'Demand, is it?' growled Teuder. 'Go on then.'

Jago rested one lean hip on the edge of the desk. 'My maternal grandmother died some months ago and has left me a property along Greenbank.'

'Nice houses, they are,' Teuder said. 'You planning to sell it?'

'No, I plan to live there. Though it is structurally sound it has been empty for over a year. My grandmother was ill for several months before her death and stayed with relatives in Redruth. The garden is a wilderness and the house needs completely redecorating. As I am away at sea much of the time a task of such importance must be handled by someone I trust.'

Caseley still didn't understand why he had insisted she stay.

'I want Miss Bonython to take charge.'

She felt her eyes widen as she stared at him. He didn't mean it. He was having a joke at her expense.

Teuder frowned. 'You want *Caseley*?'

Jago nodded. 'Such a task needs someone with an eye for colour, style, and flair.'

Flinching at his irony, she gritted her teeth as a wave of fury and embarrassment broke over her.

Her father shrugged. 'I'm bound to say I've never noticed any talent in her for such things.'

'Nevertheless, I want her to do it.'

'No,' Caseley said. 'It's impossible. I have too much to do at home.'

'Get on, girl,' Teuder scoffed. 'Rosina can run the place with one hand tied behind her back. She's got Liza-Jane and Ben, and Mary Clemmow.'

'Father,' Caseley stepped forward, pleading. 'There is

still so much to do here. This is only your first day back.'

'Miss Bonython,' Jago cut in. 'I do not expect you to devote the whole of your time to my house. An hour or two each day to supervise however many workmen you deem it necessary to employ will be sufficient. I have no desire to interfere with your other commitments.'

'See? You're making ponds out of puddles again. I'm not saying you haven't been useful. But I can manage without you for a couple of hours a day.'

Caseley tried. 'Father, you're only just getting your strength back.'

'And wasting too much of it arguing with a stubborn young miss who should show a bit more gratitude,' he snapped.

'Gratitude? For what am I supposed to be grateful? I did not ask, nor do I want –'

'Don't try my patience too far,' Teuder warned.

'Perhaps it is merely a question of confidence,' Jago said, his voice smooth, his gaze implacable. 'Miss Bonython, I have no doubt you possess talents that would be a source of considerable surprise to those who feel they know you so well.'

Shock drained the blood from her head leaving her dizzy. She reached blindly for the chair back and gripped it. It was blackmail. Either she agreed or he would tell her father how she had run the yard well enough to escape detection by everyone except Toby.

But if she gave in now, where would it end? How many more demands would he make? What choice did she have? Another attack like this morning's could finish her father.

Now she knew why Jago Barata had wanted her here. Yet his request – demand – made no sense. He had accused her of lacking any sense of style or fashion. So *why* was he entrusting her with his house?

'Come, Miss Bonython,' he drawled. 'I have never yet seen you lost for words. Many women would consider such a request an honour.'

Caseley raised her head. Though she dared not say the words she longed to hurl at him, she made no effort to hide her contempt. He totally ignored it.

'But you must not feel overwhelmed. A simple yes will do.'

'Goddammit, Caseley. What's the matter with you?' Teuder snapped. 'I've never known you so contrary. A deal is a deal, and if Jago's agreement is dependent on you refurbishing his house then I want your word, and an end to this wilful selfishness.'

The injustice stung and she had to swallow twice before she could utter a sound. 'As you wish.'

'That's settled then.' Jago leaned over to shake Teuder's hand. 'With your permission I shall call for your daughter this afternoon and take her to see the house.'

'Please do not trouble yourself, Captain,' Caseley said quickly. 'If you will leave the key and the address, I can manage perfectly well alone.'

He held her gaze for a moment then bowed. 'Until three, Miss Bonython.'

As his footsteps receded down the passage, Teuder rubbed a hand over his face. 'Where were we? Ah yes. Tresawle's ketch. Check the dates in the ledger, Caseley. See if we can fit him in.'

Chapter Eight

The ground and first floor sash windows of the stone-faced house were multi-paned oblongs. Those on the top floor were square. Shallow granite steps led up to an open porch with a flat roof supported by two granite columns.

Reluctantly, Caseley followed Jago up the path as the driver turned the cab in the road and bowled back towards the top of High Street.

Rosebeds on either side of the mossy flagstones were choked with weeds. Summer sun and salt-laden winter gales had flaked paint from the window frames and the heavy front door. The house looked neglected and sad.

Catching a movement, Caseley glanced sideways. In the house next door a lace curtain twitched and was still. She looked down at her feet, wondering if it belonged to anyone who knew her or her family. She had not been near this end of town for several months.

'At last,' Jago muttered as the lock finally yielded. Withdrawing the key he opened the front door. The top half of the inner door had panels of stained glass surrounding a frosted panel, which maintained privacy while admitting light when the front door was open.

'Your first job,' he said over his shoulder, 'will be to have all the locks and hinges oiled.'

Caseley barely heard him. The wide hall was laid with terracotta tiles patterned in cream and green. Their colours were muted by dust that covered smears of long-dried mud trodden in by many feet.

The paintwork was dull and scratched. The wallpaper showed scrapes and tears and in some places had peeled away from the wall. Cobwebs hung like grey lace over the gas mantles. The glass globes were dusty and flyblown and one was cracked.

Her first impression was one of decay. Yet, against her will and in defiance of her expectations, Caseley liked the house. Now empty and neglected, once it had been filled with the laughter and chatter of a large family. Echoes remained and welcomed. It occurred to her that here she would never feel lonely.

Abruptly shutting off the thought, she was relieved that the gloom hid the betraying colour in her cheeks. She turned to see Jago watching her with an arrested expression on his face. His grey eyes gleamed like a cat's.

'It is fortunate you enjoy a challenge, Miss Bonython. You certainly have one here.' He opened a door to her left and gestured for her to enter, following close behind. 'At least I shall be spared the expense of dust covers,' he remarked as they surveyed the empty room.

His footsteps were loud on the dusty wood floor as he crossed the dim room to the window and folded back the wooden shutters. Several moths fluttered from faded curtains of crimson plush.

'I loathe that colour.' Brushing dust off his hands he returned to the hall.

Caseley followed him through the door opposite into another bare room. The opened shutters revealed lumps of soot from the chimney lying scattered over the blue and white glazed tiles in front of the grate.

The lace casement curtain fixed across the sash had frayed at the edges and along the bottom. Cobwebs stretched from the gas-lamps on either side of the fire to the mantelshelf. Lighter patches on the wallpaper showed where once pictures had hung, and a newspaper, yellow with age, lay in a corner.

'Why did you say that?' Caseley directed the question at Jago's broad back as they entered the large kitchen after a quick glance into another empty room that faced the back yard.

He glanced over his shoulder. 'Say what?'

'That I enjoy a challenge. You know nothing about me.'

The kitchen was large and airy with a Cornish range on one wall above which was suspended a wooden frame for drying or airing clothes. Beneath the window was a stone sink with a wooden draining board. An oblong wooden table stood in the centre. The terracotta floor tiles were covered in dust and muddy footprints.

'You're wrong, Miss Bonython. I know a lot about you.' His voice floated out from the walk-in larder. 'Before you accuse me of invading your privacy,' he closed the door and turned to face her, 'what I have learned comes from my own observations. Until we were introduced, I was not aware Teuder Bonython had a daughter.'

Why should he have known? Her father and uncles would have had no reason to mention her. 'What about Toby? You must have asked him –'

'My only question was if your father's illness had had any effect on the yard. The rest he volunteered.'

Strangely, it did not occur to her to doubt him. She turned away. Toby hadn't intended it, but she felt betrayed. She crossed to the door that led out to the yard and washhouse. Jago followed.

'Toby Penfold thinks very highly of you. He says the men do too. Though judging by your behaviour toward me, I cannot imagine why.'

She swung round, a stinging retort ready on her lips. But seeing his mocking smile and the glint in his eyes she realised he was deliberately trying to provoke her. *Why?* If she asked him he would probably deny it. In any case, she did not care. Her chin rose.

'Do not make sport with me, sir.' As his eyes narrowed she swallowed her anger and shrugged. 'I have known those men and their families since I was a child. They have my affection and my respect.'

'And I do not?' His tone bantered, but beneath it lay something darker.

'You have given me little cause –' she broke off and took a deep breath. 'My opinions are of interest to no one but myself.' Despite her determination not to react, his goading unnerved her. Why was he doing it? What did he want from her? She walked past him back into the hall.

'Are you ready to see upstairs?' When she nodded he gestured for her to lead the way.

The carpet had been removed and the wide staircase rang hollow beneath their tread. Caseley hesitated on the landing. Jago simply waited behind her, so she pushed open the right-hand door.

The rails and knobs on the huge brass bedstead were tarnished and dull. A few feathers were all that remained of the mattress and pillows. Hearing him come in, she focused her gaze on the floor, the planks scarred where heavy furniture had been dragged across them.

The tiny fireplace with its black-lead surround was framed by green and white porcelain tiles decorated with a flower pattern. Old newspapers had been stuffed into the chimney and grate.

'This was the room my grandparents shared all their married life,' he said, looking round. 'All their children were born in that bed. Perhaps mine will be.'

Abruptly Caseley crossed to the window.

'Are you not fond of children, Miss Bonython?' His voice followed her and she could feel his ironic gaze between her shoulder blades.

'I have no experience of them.' She gazed across the harbour towards the village of Flushing basking in the afternoon sunshine.

'But you would like children of your own, would you not?'

Beneath her enfolding cape, Caseley cupped her elbows, unsettled by his questions. 'Captain, we are barely acquainted. Such talk is not proper.'

'Not proper?' he mocked. 'Since the moment we met your attitude and behaviour towards me has been barely civil, let alone *proper*. You are in no position to invoke convention now. I merely asked –'

She whirled round, hands clenched at her sides, her face burning. 'Why are you doing this?'

His features tightened. 'Such innocence,' he mocked. 'Such wounded vulnerability.' Two strides brought him to within inches of her. She flinched from the tension he radiated, the anger he was fighting to control. His eyes glittered and she saw her own image reflected in them, pale but holding her ground.

'You give me no peace.' With a muttered oath he turned away, rubbing one hand across the back of his neck.

'Then why am I here? You don't like me. I irritate you and make you angry. So why –'

He looked at her over his shoulder. 'Your father and I have an agreement.'

'Which need not include me. You had no right to demand my involvement. Why do so when you must know dozens of women who would be only too pleased to refurbish your house for you, and remain afterwards to –' She broke off as horror washed over her.

She had never, *ever* behaved like this. Though he brought out the worst in her, her wilful, wayward tongue had handed him the ammunition with which to shoot her down.

'I beg your pardon, Captain Barata.' Seeking refuge in formality, she clasped her hands tightly. 'It is not my habit to be –'

'Rude and ill-natured?' he supplied, his eyes gleaming with amusement. 'But that is precisely why I wanted *you*, Miss Bonython. I need not lose a moment's sleep wondering how to get rid of you once the job is completed.'

Caseley caught her breath as the arrow found its target. 'You will not release me from this – this charade?'

'Agreement,' he corrected.

'Blackmail,' she flung back. 'As we are dispensing with convention, let us be completely honest. You used blackmail to get me here.'

'Yes, I did,' he said calmly, surprising her. 'Now tell me you hate the house. Tell me that the task of making it a comfortable, welcoming home neither interests nor appeals to you.'

'I –' she stopped. She moistened dry lips, willing herself to say the words. If she did, would he let her go? Unlikely. He would twist them to suit himself. And he still held the trump card: his threat to tell her father.

But those were not the reasons she remained silent. She could not say she hated the house, because she didn't. It was a happy house. With care and thought it could be made beautiful.

Now she had seen it, the challenge fired her imagination and offered a much-needed respite from the pressures she faced at home and in the office. To say she hated it would irreparably damage something she had sensed as they moved from room to room, something fragile and precious. She turned away.

'This will not be spoken of again.' It was an order. 'You are here, that is enough.'

She looked out of the window at quay punts ferrying provisions out to two barques and a brigantine moored in the middle of the river

'To do it properly will cost a lot of money.'

Jago came to stand beside her. 'I expect it will.'

'Perhaps you should give me a figure, a limit.'

'Are you a spendthrift?'

She glanced at him briefly. 'No.'

'Do you intend to cheat me?'

'No!'

'Then it's unnecessary.'

'Naturally I shall keep accounts, and all the invoices will be retained for your inspection.'

'As you like.' His disinterest was plain.

'Captain Barata, you are not taking me seriously.'

He turned towards her. 'Are you concerned that I cannot afford it?'

'No, of course not.' But the warmth climbing her throat to her cheeks betrayed her.

'Forget about the money. I have enough in the bank here to cover the initial work and by the time I return from Spain I shall have the rest.'

Caseley risked a sidelong glance. He had the look of a man who had just made a far-reaching decision. But the harshness of his chiselled profile discouraged questions.

He turned to her. 'Shall we look at the remainder of the house?'

After climbing the flight of narrow stairs that led to the

servants' bedrooms and the attic, they returned to the landing and entered the second front bedroom. It was a mirror image of the first, except that it was empty.

Once more Caseley was drawn to the window. A brig laden with granite was coming down-river from Penryn. Passing ships moored in the King's Road she headed out towards Trefusis Point and the Carrick Roads, and on into Falmouth Bay. As they watched, the main staysail and flying jib were hoisted. Caseley sighed.

'I believe it is common for wives and daughters of owner-skippers to sail with them on occasion,' Jago said. 'Did you and your mother ever accompany your father?'

'We did once. But I was very young and remember little about it. Ralph, my brother, was away staying with friends, and Father took Mother and me up to Southampton.'

'You have not been to sea since?'

Caseley darted an uncertain glance at him. 'Why do you ask, Captain?'

'You gaze at those ships with such yearning. Is the sea in your blood? Or do you simply seek escape from all the problems besetting you?'

His gentleness startled her. She had grown used to being defensive, prepared for battle, trusting neither him nor her own reactions. But for the moment at least, they appeared to have a truce.

'You make me sound like a coward.' She tried to smile.

'You are many things, Caseley Bonython. But not a coward, never that.' The smile in his deep voice sent a quiver through her. 'So, answer my question.'

She looked out of the window. 'A little of both. The past months have been so … full.' She shrugged lightly. 'I am a little weary.'

'Is there no one you can turn to? No one from whom

you can seek help or comfort?'

She shook her head. 'My grandparents are dead. My closest female relatives are Aunt Helen and Aunt Margaret. Aunt Helen is a dear, but she has a young child and does not enjoy good health. Aunt Margaret –' she looked up at him. 'Have you not met Uncle Thomas's wife?'

'Not that I recall.'

Caseley sighed. 'If you had, you would remember. Aunt Margaret has fixed ideas about everything and does not approve of me.'

'That I can understand.' Jago's tone was dry. 'What about your mother?'

Caseley looked down at her hands. 'My mother is dead.'

'When and how?'

Though taken aback by his bluntness, it did not offend her. She told him about the event that had shattered her life and of which she seldom spoke.

'My father – it was too painful for him. His first wife and son had died of diphtheria, you see. He and my mother – I remember them as very happy together. He was so proud of Ralph, my elder brother. And as the youngest and the only girl I was indulged.' She smiled at memories.

'He bought me dolls and loved to see me in pretty dresses. But Ralph was his favourite. A son to replace the one he had lost. An heir who would inherit –'

'Never mind your brother,' Jago was impatient. 'What happened?'

'An accident. A stupid, senseless accident.' Caseley wrapped her arms across her body. 'Mother had hired a pony and trap to take me out for a birthday treat. She loved to drive herself. But when we went out as a family, Father wouldn't let her. He and Ralph used to take turns while Mother and I rode in the back.

'She took me round Castle Drive. It was a beautiful spring day. The sun was shining and there was a breeze off the sea. The hedges were full of primroses and red campion. Bluebells lay like a carpet among the trees. We could see the fishing fleet out in the bay. The outer harbour was busy with ships entering and leaving Falmouth, their masts crowded with canvas. I remember seeing the steam ferry coming past St Mawes Castle.' She paused for a moment as images crowded back, still vivid.

'We had just rounded Castle Point when two fighting magpies flew out of the hedge right in front of us. The pony took fright. It reared then started to bolt. Mother wrenched on the reins. One wheel hit a fencepost and the trap turned over. We were both thrown out onto the road. The pony trod on my foot and crushed it. Luckily the coastguard was doing his round and saw what happened. He got help and they pulled me away and managed to calm the pony.

'I couldn't understand why Mother didn't come to comfort me. My foot was already swollen and hurt dreadfully. My new dress was dirty and torn and streaked with blood from all the grazes. She just lay there by the hedge, not scratched at all, just very pale. Then someone said her neck was broken.'

Caseley had not realised she was crying until Jago turned her towards him. He wiped the tears from her cheeks with gentle thumbs then cupped her face between his hands.

Her vision was blurred. As scalding tears spilled over her lashes, her breath caught in her throat, and her heart stuttered, missing a beat.

He was gazing at her with a dark intensity that made her tremble. She sensed a battle raging in him and felt herself grow hot. His rough hands so gentle on her face made her crave more. She wanted his arms around her; wanted to be held. The need, the hunger, terrified her. She gripped his wrists and drew his hands down.

'Forgive me – I am not usually so weak.'

He released her. Turning away she fumbled for her handkerchief, quickly wiped her eyes and swallowed the painful ache in her throat. 'I have not spoken – tried not to think – Telling you brought it back. I miss her.'

'There is no shame in grief,' he said quietly. 'And no one could ever call you weak.'

She looked round, pushing a loose curl back from her damp forehead. 'But –' she stopped as one dark brow rose, daring her to argue with him.

'Who took care of you?'

'Rosina, Mrs Renfree, our housekeeper. She was widowed young and has lived with our family since I was a baby. She's been wonderfully kind to both Ralph and me. As I grew up Father insisted I take responsibility for running the household. I couldn't have done it without her help. But it changed our relationship. She said that was as it should be. But –' She stopped, shook her head.

'You were lonely.'

She looked up quickly. How had he known? How had he heard what she hadn't said? She gave a tiny nod.

Holding her gaze he rested one elbow on the sash and linked his fingers. 'I am my father's only son. He has always been ambitious, for himself and for me. He has family connections in Mexico. So after he had made enough money from his business interests in Spain, he bought into silver mines there. He also breeds and sells pedigree cattle.

'I remember as a small child being placed on a pony and led around his estate in Castile. He told me that one day it would all be mine. But I did not want it. I wanted to go to sea. The day I told him was the day I grew up. I saw part of him die and knew I was responsible.

'But I also knew I had to carve out my own destiny. For a long time we both suffered. He considered me ungrateful. I was angry that he did not understand my need to be my own man, the man he had raised me to be. The family took his side.' He shrugged.

Caseley stared at him. This arrogant, demanding man was admitting loneliness? She felt a rush of empathy. 'And now?'

He moved away from the window. 'Now, there is great affection, and even greater respect. Each of us has a star to follow. We must be true to ourselves or risk the consequences.'

'My brother –'

'I know about your brother. He is older than you, yet still a child. When he finds the courage to be honest with himself then he will become a man.'

'You sound – hard.'

'Perhaps. I am not a patient man. But I demand no more from others than from myself.'

'Not everyone is as strong as you.' She was amazed at her own temerity in speaking so openly to him.

'We are all capable of far more than we imagine.' Reaching out he caught her hand. 'You, for instance: who would have suspected such strength, such capability?'

Acutely aware of the latent strength in his warm fingers, struggling with the emotions his touch aroused, she took refuge in tartness. 'You certainly have an unusual way of paying a compliment.'

He laughed softly, his teeth very white against his dark beard. He studied her face, his gaze growing shuttered as his amusement faded and she grew hot under his scrutiny.

Releasing her hand, he turned once more to the window.

'Has your father spoken to you of his intentions?'

She struggled to adjust. His moods changed swiftly and without warning. 'I don't understand. What intentions?'

'You know he is dying.' Though the words were blunt, his tone was not unkind. She was about to deny it, to say what she so wanted to believe, that her father had many months of life ahead of him. But the awareness in Jago's eyes stopped the words before they reached her lips. She nodded, unable to speak.

'Does *he* know?'

'Yes.' She cleared her throat. 'But we have not spoken of it. He wants everything to continue as before.'

'So he has not told you what he plans to do with the yard?'

She shook her head. 'I assume he will leave it to Ralph –'

'Who does not want it,' Jago pointed out.

Caseley shrugged helplessly. 'I don't *know*. I don't want to think about it.'

'You must.'

'Why?' she cried. 'What is it to you anyway? Why should you care –' she stopped abruptly as dread gnawed a hollow inside her. 'Unless –'

'Unless?'

'You want the yard. You have shares in *Cygnet*. You want Will's job as senior captain. But why this?' She flung her arm wide in a gesture that encompassed the house. 'How does this fit into your plan?'

'It doesn't.'

'Then why ask me such questions? Why drag *me* into your dealings with my father?'

Tension shimmered between them as he gazed at her,

slate-eyed and tight-lipped. Abruptly, he turned away. 'Why indeed?' he muttered in harsh self-mockery. 'Come, I will see you home.'

Caseley walked quickly from the room before he could touch her. Even his formal gestures of politeness, his palm cupping her elbow, a handshake, set her heart pounding and heightened her confusion. Rather than ask herself why, it was safer to avoid all contact.

'We can get a cab from the Greenbank Hotel,' he said as he locked the front door.

A middle-aged woman wearing a blue and white printed cotton day dress and a straw hat stood in the tiny front garden of the house next door. She held a pair of scissors and was snipping the dead heads off some roses. Caseley guessed she had been behind the twitching curtain.

''Afternoon,' the woman said with a bright smile.

'Good afternoon,' Jago replied pleasantly. Caseley merely nodded.

'Moving in, are you?'

'Not just yet,' Jago said before Caseley could open her mouth. 'There's a great deal to be done first.'

The woman nodded. 'Been empty for a while, it has. Still, it's some lovely family home.' Her sharp eyes flicked between them. 'Plenty of room for children. I got four so I know what I'm talking about. Now they've built that there new sewer, we're having one of they proper flushing water closets. Always had a privy up the garden before. But 'tis no joke in the winter. Nor when the children are ill. All that to-ing and fro-ing is enough drive you mad. I expect you'll be having one put in?'

'I expect so,' Jago agreed, and placed a hand in the small of Caseley's back. 'Please excuse us. Nice to have met you.' He flashed a charm-filled smile and the woman simpered like a dewy-eyed girl.

Caseley walked quickly down the path. The warm pressure of Jago's hand on her waist was too possessive. She had not the sophistication to ignore it. Nor could she control the rapid pounding of her pulse.

'Why did you do that?' she hissed as they reached the pavement and were out of earshot.

'Do what?' he appeared surprised but removed his hand. 'I was under the impression you wished to leave.'

'I was – am. I didn't mean that,' she retorted. 'Why did you allow that woman to think that you – that we –' she felt heat in her face and wished she hadn't said anything. 'You know what I mean.'

'Does it matter what she thinks? I feel no obligation to explain myself to her. Do you?'

'No. But –'

'Then why worry? We both know the truth. Why should we concern ourselves with the opinions of people who don't matter?'

Caseley said nothing as her thoughts whirled like windblown leaves. Maybe he was right. How could they explain without causing even more speculation? Besides, what was the truth? Certainly there was no attachment between them. Though no longer strangers, they were not friends. She irritated him. He infuriated her.

Her life and his were becoming inextricably tangled. Her father claimed there were good reasons. Jago would not explain his. And she – she didn't know what she felt.

He was silent, abstracted, as they rode back to the other end of town. Her thoughts fluttered like a cage full of birds. Yet despite the tension that vibrated between them, this afternoon had subtly altered their relationship.

The direction her life was taking seemed fraught with danger. But it was outside her control and there was no turning back.

'When do you intend to begin work on the house?' His abrupt question made her start.

'I – I hadn't thought,' she blurted in total honesty.

'I would like to move in this year.' His tone was dry. 'Hotel life has lost its appeal. May I suggest you start tomorrow?'

'I can't. I haven't had time to –'

'I will go to the bank in the morning. Aside from oil for all the hinges, you will first require a plumber and a mason. The house is already connected to the main water supply so the installation of a proper bathroom with a geyser for hot water, an overhead shower above the bath, and a new water closet should have priority, don't you agree?'

As she'd had no idea where to start, Caseley was relieved. 'Where should the bathroom go?'

'Where would you propose?'

About to tell him it was none of her business, she caught the warning glint in his eye and decided not to risk antagonising him. She closed her eyes and tried to recall the layout of the house.

'That small room behind the main bedroom on the first floor?' She turned to him. 'Then the waste pipes could go down the wall into a drain at the side of the house and join up to the new sewer.'

'I see I shall be free to devote my attention to other matters.'

The implied compliment warmed and terrified her. 'What about the tradesmen?'

He shrugged. 'You have lived in the town all your life. You should know who best ones are, and who to avoid. Your task is to organise the work and the people to do it. I will arrange the finance.'

'But – the wallpaper, curtains, furnishings – what colours ...'

'I leave that to you,' he waved a dismissive hand.

'No. I cannot take that responsibility. What if you hate the things I choose?'

'Why should I?'

'Because,' her chin rose, 'because I have no taste, no sense of style.' She tried to suppress anxiety and deep lingering hurt with anger. 'You implied as much when you pressed my father into agreeing this arrangement.' She shook her head. 'None of this makes sense. You say you want only the best. So why pick me? Why –'

'Enough!' His tone made her flinch. 'I do not plan to abandon you entirely. I shall follow progress with great interest.'

'I do not doubt it. Waiting for my first mistake. What then? More taunts? More derision?'

'God give me patience,' he muttered. 'Cruel tyrant that I am, I did not wish you to feel I was watching your every move. I wanted you to have time to –' He controlled himself with an effort. But Caseley's heart sank as she saw his expression harden. 'Surely there is nothing unusual in what I ask? Do not all women consider men totally without judgement in such matters?'

'But ... I am not ... This is *your* house, *your* money.'

'Precisely. Mine to do with as I please.' As the hansom rocked to a halt, Jago leaned towards her, his eyes gleaming. He tilted her chin, making her burningly aware of their closeness in the confined space. 'And it would please me very much,' he said softly, 'if you would do as you have been asked, accept that I trust you, *and stop arguing*.'

Chapter Nine

Still wearing his nightshirt, his clothes over his arm, Thomas crept across to the door. Hearing the bedsprings creak he tensed.

'Thomas?' Margaret's voice was thick with sleep. The bed creaked again as she sat up. 'What time did you get in last night?'

He turned the doorknob, still clinging to hope of escape. 'Don't let me disturb you, my dear.'

'I'm awake now, so you can stay right here.'

Reluctantly, he released the handle and turned back, dropping his clothes on the ottoman at the foot of the bed.

'Well? I'm waiting.' Margaret's mouth was tightly pursed as she removed her bed cap and began to unplait her hair.

'I told you I would be late.' His attempt to placate succeeded only in sounding defensive as he pulled on his trousers before taking off his nightshirt. 'It was business.'

'At that time of night?'

'People have commitments. They aren't always available during the day.' His hands trembled as he buttoned his shirt.

'I was worried sick. You know what this town is like at night. All those lewd women. They don't even wait for darkness. Shameless, they are.'

Thomas glanced up. 'You were afraid I had been kidnapped by lewd women?' He felt a trace of wistfulness.

'There's no call to be vulgar. I heard something

shocking yesterday. You should have been here so we could discuss what to do.'

The roaring in his head made Thomas sit down suddenly on the ottoman, his back to his wife. His heart was racing and perspiration beaded his forehead and upper lip. *He had been found out.*

No, he hadn't. Teuder had not done the audit yet. When he did there would be nothing to find. It had taken him until midnight but he had altered the books so the losses did not show. Now the money was back in the bank, all the figures balanced.

He sucked in a shaky breath. Everything was fine. Colenzo would not say anything. The man was a shark. But as long as the repayments arrived on time he'd keep his mouth shut.

Could Luke have let something slip? Brandy and bitterness might have loosened his tongue, made him careless.

Dare he risk continuing? But if he didn't, how would he be able to repay Colenzo? Why had Luke been talking to that arrogant half-breed, Barata?

'Thomas, you're not listening to me,' Margaret nagged. 'It's a disgrace. Lord knows what people will think of us now that Caseley has got involved with that – that person. I don't know what Teuder is thinking of to allow it.'

Straightening her voluminous nightgown she stood up. 'Where *is* that girl? She knows I must have my warm water in the mornings. You have no idea what I have to put up with, Thomas. Then you stay out half the night –'

'Shut up, damn you!' His voice teetered on the edge of desperation.

'Ohhh,' Margaret collapsed onto the bed, one hand flying to her mouth. 'How could you speak to me like that? Here I am, worried out of my mind –'

'What about *me*?' Thomas turned on her. 'Don't you ever think about *anyone* but yourself? What does it matter who Caseley takes up with? You have a daughter of your own. If you must worry, then worry about her.'

'I am!' Margaret wailed. 'It's her I'm concerned for. Can't you see what might happen?'

The violence had drained away, leaving him spent and shaking. 'What are you talking about?'

'Teuder must know. In fact he must be encouraging this – liaison between Caseley and Captain Barata –'

'Who?' Thomas croaked. '*Who* did you say?'

'I wish you'd listen. Barata, Jago Barata. You must know him. He's one of Teuder's captains, master of the *Cygnet*. Thomas, what if Teuder is planning a match between them? God knows, Caseley hasn't much to recommend her. But then that man is not like us. He probably doesn't have the same tastes we do, or the same idea of beauty for that matter.' Margaret's pursed and bitter mouth indicated that as far as she was concerned, Jago Barata had no taste at all. 'If Teuder sees this man as the only hope of a husband for Caseley, he might do something foolish.'

'No,' Thomas whispered. Shock and fear were paralysing his ability to think.

'Caseley is twenty-one, and lame,' Margaret went on. 'Any man prepared to wed her will seek a sizeable dowry. Ralph has no interest in the business. What's to stop Teuder leaving the yard to Caseley? If he does that and she marries Jago Barata, what will become of us then, Thomas? You, me, and Charlotte?'

'You might have it all wrong. I've met Barata. He doesn't look like a man who could be bought.' Thomas recalled cool grey eyes and lightning appraisal. He had felt his soul stripped bare and his guilt exposed. Glancing back as they left the dining room he had seen the speculative gaze following Luke and himself.

'Three times that man has been into the office to see her. Even Richard noticed and you know how blind he is. Mrs Cox in the Post Office told me that Captain Barata has acquired a house up along Greenbank. She expected me to know all about it seeing that Caseley is my niece, and he was seen entering and leaving the house accompanied by a young woman with a limp and reddish-brown hair. That's Caseley all right. So what's going on?'

'I don't know.' Thomas felt panic churn like acid inside him.

Caseley glanced up as her brother entered the dining room. He was freshly shaved, his hair neatly combed. His shirt was crisp and his coat and trousers had been brushed and pressed. Though pale, his eyes red-rimmed, he looked better than he had for days.

'Hello, Ralph,' she smiled. 'You're up early. Would you like some breakfast?'

'Just coffee.' He shuddered. 'I don't know how you can face food at this time of day.'

'I don't know how you manage without it,' she replied lightly, pouring his coffee as he sat down opposite.

'What are you doing?' He indicated her notepad, pencil, and other pieces of paper beside her crumb-strewn plate.

'Trying to work out the best order for jobs to be done.'

'Now Father's back at work –'

'Not for the business. The list is for Captain Barata's house.

'Ahhhh.'

She ignored the inflections in her brother's tone and continued writing.

‘How is it coming along?’

‘Faster than I expected. Mr Endean was due at a house in Florence Terrace but a family bereavement meant the work had to be postponed. So he was able to come right away. The inside plumbing should be finished by the end of the week. When the plaster has been made good and the other repairs completed, the decorators can begin.’

‘My, my,’ Ralph raised his cup in mocking salute. ‘You have been busy.’

‘Sometimes I feel it’s running away with me,’ Caseley admitted. ‘I had no idea how much there was to do. Which is why getting it all in the right order is so important.’

‘What does the good captain think of progress so far?’

Suppressing a pang, she riffled through the papers, pretending to search for something. Though he had promised not to watch her every move, she had expected a visit, braced herself in anticipation. But he hadn’t come.

Ignoring the surprise and unease shown by the plumber and other tradesmen she consulted hadn’t been easy. She had met the same reaction in shops when she enquired about materials.

The salesmen were polite but evasive, making it clear that ‘the gentleman’s approval must by confirmed by his visit in person before an order could be accepted.’

The second time this happened, Caseley gathered her courage, stood her ground, and asked to speak to the manager. Quaking inside, she informed him that she alone was responsible for the purchases she wished to make. The order was of considerable value, and she expected to pay at the end of the month like any other respected customer. If he was unable to meet her demands, she would take her business elsewhere.

Lavish apologies for the misunderstanding and thinly disguised curiosity had accompanied offers of assistance to locate anything else she might require. She had longed to tell someone about it, to share the experience and laugh at her own bravado. But there was only one person directly concerned, one person who would understand.

'Captain Barata has not visited yet. But I'm sure he will be impressed. Mr Endean takes great pride in his work. He's also very quick and keeps the man and boy who work with him busy all the time.'

'Doesn't it worry you? I mean you hardly know the man. I'm talking about Barata, not Mr Endean.'

She shrugged to hide the doubts that were her constant companions. 'He and Father made the arrangement.'

'So you said. But you must admit it's rather odd. He's expecting you to do something that would cause most *wives* to hesitate. Why *you*?'

'I have no idea.' She rose and carried her cup to the sideboard. That question had kept her awake night after night. All too aware of her many defects, she could not fathom the reasoning behind Jago Barata's demand. They struck sparks off each other every time they met.

To cope with the loss of her mother, her father's absorption in the business and her brother's unhappiness, she had always striven for calm, balance. But from the instant she and Jago Barata met, she had been buffeted by violent emotions.

She loathed his arrogance and cutting irony. Yet he stirred yearnings that no self-scolding or rationalisation could banish. He could be cruelly derisive yet moments later reveal an understanding that left her breathless.

He was a man of the world in the widest sense: of dual ancestry, well educated, widely travelled and independently wealthy, leading life on his own terms. What could she ever be to him apart from briefly useful?

'Why me?' She raised slim shoulders. 'I don't know.

Captain Barata is very busy. He needed someone to organise and oversee work on the house. It was my misfortune that I happened to be there at the time.'

Even as she spoke, innate honesty made her conscience prick. Certainly she had felt like that to begin with, but now? She gazed up at the overcast sky. The cloud, thick and low, promised rain before the day's end.

'Father approved the idea and it was agreed between them.'

'But you have no experience.'

'I know, and so I told them.' Returning to the table she leaned over to gather the papers together. 'It didn't make the slightest difference. They are very alike in their stubbornness.'

Ralph pushed back his chair and stretched out his legs, regarding his sister with a mixture of curiosity and admiration. 'Aren't you nervous? It must be costing him a bundle. What if you make a pig's ear of the whole business?'

'Thanks, Ralph.'

'You know what I mean.'

She nodded, hugging the bundle of papers to her chest. 'I admit I was terrified at first. But Mr Endean has taken me under his wing. He put me right on several matters. I've got the best mason in town in George Tallack. He'll be starting in a couple of days. He and Mr Endean have worked together many times. I think Mr Endean may have persuaded him to take this job. I know he's usually very busy. I still get butterflies in my stomach about the furnishings. Colours and textures are such a personal choice. But Captain Barata trusts me.' She shrugged, trying to ignore the combined thrill and chill that tingled through her.

'I don't know how you fit it all in. Aren't you

exhausted?'

'I expected to be. But now Father seems so much better – You should have seen his face when Toby and I took him round the yard yesterday afternoon. The men gave him such a welcome. He roared at them for wasting time when they should have been working, but there were tears in his eyes. Dr Vigurs was right to let him go back.'

Seeing his shuttered expression she moved quickly on. 'Even though the house is in a far worse state now that when I first saw it, with holes in the walls and dust everywhere, it has a lovely atmosphere. It will be beautiful when it's finished.'

'Take care, Caseley,' he cautioned. 'Don't put your heart into it. It's not yours, nor ever will be.'

'I'm fully aware of my limitations. But I can't – won't – do less than my best.'

'Listen, I didn't mean –'

'I know, and it's all right.' She didn't want to hear his awkward apology, knowing that she lied. Deep in her heart she wondered what it would be like to be mistress of the house. She banished the thought. She did not need that in order to walk through the rooms, touch the furniture she had chosen, see the colours she had blended to create harmony and welcome.

Besides, being mistress of the house would require that she also be Jago Barata's wife, a thought that terrified her as much as it admittedly intrigued.

She flashed him a bright smile. 'So why are you up early looking so smart?'

He stood up, shooting his cuffs. 'I am off to work.'

'What? Has Uncle Richard –?'

'I'm not going to Bonython's. It's not for me, and never will be. I am waiting on Mrs Edwin Lashbrook to make preliminary sketches for a portrait. But I need to go into town first to pick up one or two things.'

'You're going to paint *Frances*? But how – when –?'

'I wasn't commissioned directly,' Ralph admitted. 'Jason Blamey was going to do it. But he cut his hand on a broken bottle – of linseed oil,' he added as Caseley frowned. 'Anyway, Frances wanted the portrait done at once and Jason recommended me.'

'Ralph, I'm so pleased for you.' Caseley limped around the table and clasped her brother's hands. 'I know how much you want to paint. If this portrait is a success it could mean more commissions. Who knows where that might lead? You have a wonderful talent and this is a great opportunity.'

She made herself stop. She wanted to tell him not to waste it as he had wasted so many others. Not to seek solace in alcohol if he could not immediately achieve the perfection he sought. But saying such things might create doubts in his mind.

'I'll show them.' His eyes glittered. 'The doubters, the gossips, Father. I'll show them all.'

'I know you will.' Reaching up she kissed his cheek.

Grinning, he squeezed her fingers before crossing to the door. He paused, listening. 'He's on his way down.'

'Have you told him?'

Ralph shook his head.

'Why not? He would be pleased for you.'

Her brother regarded her with a bitter smile. 'Poor Caseley. You try so hard. I know you mean well but surely you've learned by now that nothing I do will ever please Father? I am doubly damned. I don't want the yard and I am not Philip.' He walked out.

She heard him say good morning, heard their father's gruff voice demanding to know where Ralph was going, and when did he intend to start accepting his responsibilities, behaving like a man. But the words lacked heart and hope. They were uttered out of habit and were answered by the sound of the front door slamming.

Jago Barata packed with an expertise born of practice. His white shirt was open at the neck, the sleeves rolled halfway up his forearms. Two canvas bags lay on the bed. Into the smaller he placed the clothes he would need while in Spain, plus toiletries. The rest of his belongings went into the larger bag.

A flurry of telegraph messages between himself and Ramon Gaudara over the past three days had established that Guadara had received Felipe's letter and reached Juan at the mine. The quicksilver was being sent to the port of Santander for him to collect. Now the blockade had been lifted, Bilbao was chaotic as all the shipping companies sought desperately to clear the backlog of waiting cargoes.

Though the fighting had not reached the mine area, it had been impossible to move anything in or out.

Packing reminded him of how little he possessed. When he left his father's house and travelled to Bilbao to begin his career at sea, he had arrived there with several bags and a chest.

Sailing with Basques whose reputation as seamen was renowned throughout the world, he had learned quickly. His love of the sea in all her many moods, coupled with technical skill, a sixth sense regarding the weather, and nerves of iron, soon gained him a reputation that rivalled those of his teachers.

Realising that light was the only way to travel he had sold everything but basic necessities. He moved from ship to ship, line to line, always seeking the best, oblivious to discomfort or length of voyage, caring only for the captain's skill and what he could learn.

Having worked his way up from ordinary seaman to mate, he sat the examinations necessary before he could captain a ship in foreign waters. Two years later he had his own command, a small two-masted schooner sailing out of Bilbao, carrying oranges, lemons, salt, wine, and brandy. The ship was his home and cabin space so limited there was simply no room for personal possessions.

It was on that schooner he had first come to Falmouth. Now he owned a house here. Since his parents had moved to Mexico he had no personal ties to Spain. Here, at last, he had a home of his own and an opportunity to put down roots.

He dropped the shirt he was rolling onto the bed and flexed his shoulders, stretching his arms high and wide then running both hands through his hair. Tension lay like a yoke on the back of his neck as he looked out of the window.

Below in the busy street carts and cabs delivered goods and passengers. Two women wearing short capes and beribboned bonnets entered the grocer's opposite, where signs advertised provisions, patent medicines, pure Ceylon tea, and coffee roasted daily on the premises.

To the left was a boot and shoe shop, the wares displayed on hooked poles resembling strange trees. Next door the Supply Stores invited inspection of Devenish's Celebrated Dorset Ales in casks or bottles at popular prices, fine wines from the wood, and choice ginger wine.

Alongside was the second of George Downing's butcher's shops. Short and rotund, George stood by the window display between two pig carcasses suspended on steel hooks from an overhead rail. A blue and white striped apron covered the front of his starched white coat and a straw boater was set at a jaunty angle on his balding head. Jago's frown deepened. Why did he want a house?

A house was a tie, a responsibility, and he valued freedom. He came and went as he pleased, limited only by wind and tide.

Yet had not the impersonal anonymity of hotel rooms begun to pall? After eighteen years of criss-crossing the oceans, was it not time he had somewhere of his own to come back to?

Thinking of the house brought Caseley to mind. What infernal impulse had goaded him to insist on her help? Correct in her guess that others would have jumped at the chance, her reluctance had intrigued and irritated.

His accusation that she gave him no peace was the naked truth. Since their first meeting he had been haunted by her. Why?

She was not beautiful. Her cheekbones were too pronounced, her chin too firm, her eyes too large, and her mouth too tempting. Her hair might have the healthy shine of a polished chestnut but its springy waves and curling tendrils were untameable. She had no sophistication.

A flash of insight needled him. Enticing, amusing, worldly women had passed over the surface of his life without leaving a ripple.

Caseley Bonython touched him as none of them ever had. Straight-backed and slender, she had a presence that made her limp irrelevant. The way she held her head, the way she seemed so often poised for flight, reminded him of a gazelle.

She was defiant, quick-tempered, and impulsive. She was also intelligent, courageous, and loyal. Amusing though her anger and dislike of him had been, it had also jolted him. Not given to introspection, he found examination of his own behaviour disconcerting.

Often pursued, he was now the pursuer. He could not comprehend what drove him, for she threatened his whole way of life. Drawn to her, he deliberately kept his distance except to goad her, as if antagonising her might destroy in him the need he perceived as weakness. But his conscience wracked him and the guilt became anger directed, perversely, at her.

Picking up the rolled shirt he pushed it into his bag. He needed to get to sea again. The whisper of the night wind, the hiss of the bow cutting through the water, and the vastness of the dark sky glittering with patterns of stars would clear his head.

Though this room would be let in his absence the manager had promised to look after his spare bag until he returned. He had considered taking it up to the house and immediately dismissed the idea. Once he left possessions there he would have committed himself. He was not sure he wished to do that.

For three days he had stayed away. He had plenty to keep him busy. But too often his thoughts strayed. To Caseley. To Caseley in his house.

Anger and self-disgust burned in his gut. He should never have forced her to do it. Doubtless she would have her revenge by stuffing the place with grotesque furniture and ugly useless ornaments. The house would be desecrated with clashing colours and suffocating designs. There would be frills and fringes and lace and his money would have been wasted.

Yet the thought that, despite hating him, she would create a comfortable welcoming home was far more unsettling.

The door burst open and Louise whirled in. Slamming it shut she leaned against it, her voluptuous breasts straining against the orange material of her tight-fitting jacket.

'Why didn't you tell me?' Her eyes were bright with

accusation and excitement. The tiny hat, a confection of straw, feathers, and ribbon, tilted forward on her high-piled hair, sat slightly askew. 'Why did I have to hear it from Amy Cox?'

After a moment's utter stillness Jago continued pushing the last few items into the larger bag.

'Good morning, Louise.' His tone was cool. Brief fury swiftly contained. 'I thought it was understood that *I* would arrange our next meeting.'

'I know, Jago. But when I heard, I didn't know whether to believe it or not. I *had* to –'

'What exactly have you heard?' Drawing the cords tight to close the neck of each bag he knotted them, lifted both to the floor by the door, then scanned the room to make sure nothing had been forgotten.

'That you've bought a house up Greenbank. Is it true?'

'No,' he said evenly. 'I have not bought a house.'

'But Amy said –'

'Mrs Cox might at least make sure her information is accurate before she spreads it around the town.' Weariness tempered Jago's irony. 'The house was a bequest in my grandmother's will.'

Louisa's face lit up and she launched herself at him. 'Oh, Jago, that's handsome. I know you never liked me coming here. You was worried about people seeing us.'

'Seeing you, Louise,' he corrected. 'I am answerable to no one. But your husband is at this moment in his shop opposite the hotel entrance.'

'If he's got a customer, he wouldn't notice the Queen herself,' Louise scoffed. 'But we won't have to worry no more now, will us? I just wish you'd told me yourself. It hurt awful hearing it from that old gossip.' Wrapping her arms around his neck she pressed close to him, moving sinuously. 'You was keeping it for a surprise.' She rained kisses onto his cheek, his bearded jaw, and finally his mouth. 'God, I've missed you,' she breathed.

He lifted his hands to break her hold. 'I have to go, Louise. I'm due at the yard. *Cygnet* sails tomorrow.'

'Be gone long, will you?' she murmured between kisses. Feeling his body's response to her provocative movements she drew her head back to give a roguish smile.

'Can't go yet, can you, my lover,' she drew the tip of her tongue along her upper lip.

His hands tightened. Images of Caseley tumbled through his mind like windblown leaves. He shuddered and ran his hands down Louise's back, pressing her hard against him. This he understood. This posed no threat.

Chapter Ten

Caseley finished the letter she was writing, addressed the envelope, then passed both across the desk for her father's approval and signature. Her thoughts strayed to the house on Greenbank.

Recalling her conversation with Ralph at breakfast she realised that in only a few days her life had taken on new purpose. But it was very different from the crushing obligation to keep the yard running smoothly. She found she was constantly thinking about colours, textiles, and furniture that would enhance the best features of each room.

The ladies' magazines Aunt Margaret had bought in a bid to 'sharpen up your fashion sense, my dear,' had been retrieved from the cupboard and pored over for their soft furnishing advertisements. She had ignored glances heavy with significance that Rosina exchanged with Liza-Jane, more concerned with working out colour balances.

'Pull yourself together, girl.' Her father shattered her reverie. 'If that's the last of the letters you may as well go.'

Caseley started. 'I'm sorry. Was there something else you wanted me to do?'

'No,' he grudged. 'It's all done for now. I suppose you'll be going up to Greenbank?' His pale gaze was shrewd and Caseley felt warmth creep into her cheeks as she stood up and placed her chair neatly against the wall.

'Not immediately.' Was he implying that she spent too

much or too little time at Jago Barata's house? She wasn't about to ask.

Lifting down her short cape from the hook on the back of the door she swung it around her shoulders. 'I have some shopping to do first. Would you like me to walk you home?'

'I would not. I'm going to the yard. Sam is coming with me. I shall be better for some fresh air. It gets stuffy in here. All this damn paper. You be on your way.' He paused. 'Coming on all right, is it?'

'I think so.' She fastened the cape, put on her hat, and picked up her music case. Instead of business letters and ledgers it now contained colour charts, lists of building and plumbing materials, and invoices. 'It's difficult to tell at the moment. I'll know better when it's finished.' *Then it will be too late.*

It was one o'clock before she reached the other end of town. She had visited all the furniture repositories, comparing styles, quality, and price, making copious notes. So much was needed: a dining table and chairs, a sideboard, a sofa and armchairs, at least two small tables, a clothes press for each bedroom, a blanket chest, a dressing table, stools or chairs for the kitchen.

Then there were all the soft furnishings: curtains, rugs, cushions, bed linen, towels, tablecloths, and napkins. She had not even started on crockery, cutlery, glassware, and kitchen utensils.

She was tired and hungry, and the burden of choosing what was right for the house *and* its enigmatic owner had begun to weigh heavily. For an instant she was tempted to ignore the display in the large window of Joseph Roskruge's Drapery Emporium and simply order curtains for every room in the crimson plush he loathed. It would serve him right.

But pride triumphed over her brief dream of vengeance. Pausing to take a deep breath, she entered the shop, hearing the bell tinkle over her head as she pushed open the door.

Half an hour later she left carrying a package containing samples of curtain material in jade velvet, maroon and ivory regency stripe, and an oyster-coloured fabric with a silken sheen and a subtle pattern of leaves.

Restored by a cup of hot chocolate and a toasted teacake at Alice Teague's refreshment house on Market Strand, she climbed the steep length of High Street. Reaching the brow of the hill she could see the river. The water looked cold and grey reflecting the heavy sky, and the wind had a keen edge.

After announcing her arrival to Mr Endean, for whom she had had a second key cut, she went back downstairs. Removing her cape she hung it over the newel post and went into the drawing room. She unwrapped the fabric samples and stood against the back wall, trying to visualise the room fully furnished.

Each day she became more concerned that the décor complemented the rooms, enhancing their proportions and emphasising the light.

The chesterfield she had seen in Prout's, with its buttoned upholstery of dark green velvet, would look equally well with the regency stripe or the oyster curtains, and perhaps two rosewood balloon-back chairs. A small rectangular sofa table could stand where she was now, and another in the corner holding a jardinière. But for the right-hand wall behind the door, which would be more suitable, the mahogany bureau or a bookcase?

She caught herself. What did it matter which she chose? Once finished she would see none of it again.

The knowledge was painful, but she had to keep it at

the forefront of her mind. Doing the job to the best of her ability was one thing. But she must not become emotionally involved. She must not *care.* Jago Barata had made his reason for selecting her abundantly clear. *'I need not lose a moment's sleep wondering how to get rid of you once the job is complete.'* She was simply the means by which his property would be made habitable without any involvement from him other than paying the bills.

Caseley left the empty room and walked down the passage to the kitchen. It was better that he had stayed away. The urge to ask his opinion, his preference, would have been too strong to resist.

She looked down at the three pieces of material she still held and shook her head in bewilderment. How could he show so little interest in what was, after all, *his* home? Did he really not care? Was that why, without a qualm, he could delegate such a personal matter to a virtual stranger?

But surely no mere stranger could have divined her loneliness? He had even spoken of his own. The fact that he had done so had shaken her more than the revelation itself.

He had trusted her. And for a few precious moments she had opened like a flower to the warmth of his understanding. He recognised that she felt the loss of her mother more keenly now than in her childhood.

He had spoken of her family with brutal frankness, demanding answers as if by right. For two people who had known each other barely a week their arguments had had a startling intimacy.

Her father, her brother, and her two uncles were the only men she knew well, though she had seen more of Toby and Will Spargo in recent months. But nothing had prepared her for the impact and complexity of Jago Barata. She doubted anything could.

The crash of the doorknocker echoed through the house. Caseley returned to the hall and saw the plumber's lad on his way downstairs. 'It's all right, Ross. I'll answer it.'

He continued on down. 'I got to go uplong and tell Mr Tregaskis he can bring the bath and all down now. Mr Endean's ready for 'em.' He waited at the bottom of the staircase.

The outer door was opened back to the wall and through the coloured glass Caseley could see a woman silhouetted on the step. A neighbour perhaps? Bringing an offer of help or a cup of tea as a cover for curiosity? She opened the door and Ross slipped out, ducking his head politely before disappearing down the path.

The visitor was plainly startled. Caseley's gaze skimmed the high-piled hennaed curls crowned with a chic feathered hat tilted forward over one eye, a vivid orange jacket decorated with gold frogging and cut a little too tight, and an orange and black taffeta skirt with a cascade of flounces reaching to the dusty granite step.

'Good afternoon, Mrs Downing. Can I help you?'

Louise quickly retrieved her control. But the smile that stretched her painted mouth did not reach eyes as hard as sapphires and bright with suspicion. 'You're Caseley Bonython.'

Caseley gave a brief nod. In a close-knit town like Falmouth everyone knew everyone else by sight if not by name.

'Father better, is he?'

'Yes, thank you.'

'You're some long way from home. What you doing up here? Friend of the captain, are you?' Her tone was light, artless, but her gaze was as sharp as a blade.

'No,' Caseley replied after a moment's hesitation.

Friendship meant the gentle warmth of long acquaintance, empathy and loving attachment. Not friction, wariness and flaring tension. 'Not exactly. I am doing a job for him.'

'What job is that?'

Caseley was taken aback by both the impertinence of the question and the inquisitorial tone in which it was asked.

'Forgive me, I don't wish to appear rude, but my reasons for being here are not your concern.'

Louise's eyebrows arched. 'Me and the captain is friends. Very *close* friends. So whatever is going on in his house certainly does concern me. Told me all about it he did, this very morning.' She nodded sharply, daring Caseley to doubt her. 'Now if you'll just move aside, I'd like to come in and look over the place. I don't think Jago would be very pleased if I was to tell him you kept me standing out here.'

Without a word Caseley stepped back and Louise swept past her into the hall. As she closed the glass door, her fingers froze on the knob as she recalled Rosina and Liza-Jane gossiping. *Foreign*, Liza-Jane had said. *It wasn't just once that Louise Downing had been seen leaving the Royal Hotel after ten in the evening.*

Caseley closed her eyes, hearing the echo of Jago's voice. 'For some reason hotel life has lost its appeal.' The pain was so sharp, so piercing, that for a moment she couldn't breathe.

'What's going on up there?' Louise jerked her head towards the stairs at the sound of a hammer falling to the floor, male voices, and footsteps moving about.

Caseley's throat was so dry she had to cough before she could speak. 'Captain Barata is having a bathroom installed.'

Louise poked her head round the drawing room door

then walked all the way in.

Had Jago sent her to the house? But why would he do that? There was nothing to see yet. Perhaps it had been her idea to come. Clearly she had not expected to see Caseley, which was odd. Surely Jago would have explained what she was doing here? He must have realised that if Louise came to the house it was likely they would meet. Perhaps he did not care. Perhaps he considered it none of her business. It was his house and he could open his door to whomever he chose. Certainly Louise was making no effort to hide their relationship.

'What's this here job you're s'posed to be doing then?' Louise demanded over her shoulder as she wandered across to the window, inspecting the chipped paintwork and peeling wallpaper with distaste.

'Overseeing repairs to the house and selecting suitable furnishings.' Had she jumped to the wrong conclusion? Could Liza-Jane have meant someone else? The desperate hope shrivelled and died. Had Louise not just announced their '*very close friendship*'?

Why this stupid pain? Only for a few brief minutes had he treated her with anything other than amusement or impatience.

'A room this size will take some filling up,' Louise frowned. 'Still, I can see a nice china cabinet over by that there wall.' She tapped one gloved finger against her chin, cupping her elbow in her other hand. 'And a sofa covered in dark red brocade with a valence and chairs to match. A big round table with one of they chenille cloths with a bobble fringe round the bottom would fill up the space a bit, and a fire screen, and some ornaments on the mantelpiece. I fancy one of they glass cases with dried flowers or stuffed birds in. I could have this place looking handsome. A bit of pretty paper on the walls, something with a nice bright flower pattern, would look just right in here.' She glanced at Caseley. 'What are you smiling at?'

'I wasn't smiling,' Caseley replied truthfully. Louise's vision was so close to the revenge she had planned she should find it amusing. But she didn't. Nor could she have done it, not to this house.

'I dunno what he asked you for,' Louise sniffed. 'Got an eye for colour, I have. Everyone say so.' Her hard gaze defied argument. 'Why *did* he ask you?' Her critical gaze flickered over Caseley's simple blouse and skirt and her expression was one of open scorn.

'I have no idea, Mrs Downing.' Only bitter stubborn pride held Caseley's voice level and stopped her snatching up her cape and running from the house. 'Captain Barata arranged it with my father.'

Ralph had warned her not to put her heart into it. She had heard his words and truly believed her commitment was only to the task. It had taken the arrival of Jago Barata's mistress to rip the blinkers off. In her secret heart she had hoped that by creating a beautiful and tranquil home for him he might see her in a different light.

Hot with shame and embarrassment she allowed herself no respite. What a *fool* she was. Clinging to the few moments' conversation they had shared upstairs, she had hoped, so wanted to believe, that it had forged the first tenuous strand of friendship. How could she have been so naïve, presumptuous, *stupid*? She was useful, nothing more.

Had he been referring to Louise when he said that once a determined woman gained access to a man's house it was difficult to dislodge her? That would explain why he had insisted on her instead. After all, she posed no threat.

It was doubtful he had ever regarded her with anything other than irritation or pity. She cringed inside, recalling how gently he had wiped away her tears. He'd have done as much for a child.

She had revealed so much, betraying her grief and uncertainty. He had crushed her defences like eggshells, making her aware of her vulnerability, attracting and terrifying her at the same time.

Despite her denials she had dared to dream foolish dreams and, like Icarus, had been scorched by flying too close to the sun. But no one would ever know. She'd had years of practice at hiding her feelings. She straightened, holding herself tall and proud.

'Show me the rest, then,' Louise commanded.

'Certainly, Mrs Downing.'

When they returned to the hall after looking into every room on the ground floor, Louise suddenly remembered another engagement and left in an excited rustle of skirts and clicking heels.

Caseley closed the glass door. She would write to Jago and tell him she would not be doing any more work on the house. His 'close friend' Mrs Downing had, during her visit, shown such interest and offered so many suggestions, he might prefer to enlist *her* services in preference to someone who had not wanted the job in the first place.

He could hardly argue with that. Given his total lack of interest, Louise Downing's choice of red brocade sofa and flower-patterned wallpaper would suit him as well as the more restrained decor she had envisaged.

Returning to the drawing room and settling herself on the bare wooden seat in the bay window, she took pen, ink, and paper from her case. She would write the letter now and leave it at the hotel on her way home.

She wrote quickly and when she had finished laid the paper aside to dry while she re-corked the ink bottle and put away her pen. After reading it through once more, satisfied that it was businesslike and revealed no emotion whatever, she folded it carefully and slid it into her case. She would buy an envelope at the stationer's next to the old Town Hall.

Louise Downing appeared not to care who knew of her relationship with Jago Barata. But he had never given any hint that he had a mistress. Perhaps he considered it none of her business. Indeed it wasn't. But she would not leave an unsealed letter in a public place for any prying eyes to read.

Did Mr Downing know? Surely he could not, for what man would accept such behaviour from his wife? Yet according to Liza-Jane, Jago was not the first lover Louise had taken. So how *could* George Downing have remained in ignorance?

Caseley felt confused and revolted. Did the sacrament of marriage mean nothing to any of them? She remembered Jago's cruel smile as he taunted her about the bed upstairs. Louise Downing's manner had been one of defiant pride and possessiveness.

That he might be the 'fancy-man' Liza-Jane had spoken of had never occurred to her. It lessened him in her eyes even as it crystallised the yearning she had felt for him. She understood Spanish, tide tables, and balance sheets, but not men, especially a man like Jago Barata.

It no longer mattered. When she left the house in a few minutes she would have severed her connection with him. Now her father was back in the office and had Sam to accompany him to and from the yard, she could take time off and stay away from places where her path and Jago's might cross.

She needed time to regain her balance, put all the upheaval behind her. She had been intimidated, bullied, and blackmailed. Yet the touch of his hand on her flushed and tear-wet cheek, his rare gentleness and insight, the sheer power of his personality, had awakened deep and powerful emotions.

She felt a frisson of fear remembering his voice, flat and cold, delivering his ultimatum. Why had he sent Louise Downing to the house? Why put her in charge of the refurbishment and not his 'close friend', who clearly believed *she* should have been asked?

Whatever his reasons, his threat to tell her father of her deception had made refusal impossible. But two could play that game. She would make public his relationship with Mrs Downing –

No, she wouldn't. In any case, the threat had no power because according to Liza-Jane it was common knowledge already.

She put on her cape, tossed the material samples onto the window seat, and picked up her case. She could not leave without saying goodbye to Mr Endean. He was visibly disappointed when she cut short his description of blue and white porcelain tiles she might like for the bathroom walls. Excusing herself, she ran downstairs, eyes stinging, biting hard on her lower lip to stop it quivering.

The first drops of rain were already falling as she hurried along the high pavement. But no matter how much distance she put between herself and the house she had only to close her eyes to recall every detail of every room.

Her hat had no brim and the slanting rain, blown by the wind, raised little puffs like smoke as it hammered onto the dusty road, darkening it and turning it to mud. It soaked into her cape and skirt and ran cold down her face, mingling with her tears. In front gardens flowers bowed their heads, and trees dripped as their leaves were washed clean.

The heavy clouds parted and the rain eased as Caseley reached the stationer's. Pausing on the step she dried her face with a wisp of lace handkerchief. She bought an envelope, slid the letter inside, and sealed and addressed it, hotly aware of the tremor in her hands and the assistant's curiosity.

By the time she reached the Royal Hotel a watery sun was shining. People had left doorways in which they had taken shelter and the street was becoming busy again.

She walked up the steps and into the noisy crowded foyer. The smell of wet clothes and tobacco smoke caught in her throat. She eased her way through to the desk. Waving to attract the attention of one of the uniformed messenger boys she handed him the envelope.

'Please see that Captain Barata receives this as soon as possible.' She dropped a coin into his other hand.

The boy touched his cap with a forefinger. 'Yes, miss.' He tucked the envelope into a long rack on the wall beside the board on which numbered hooks held keys.

Turning away, Caseley fought her way to the door. It was done. She had regained control of her life and salvaged a little dignity. There would be a price to pay. But she refused to think about that now.

Rosina met her in the hall. 'Soaked, you are,' she scolded, taking the sodden cape and holding it at arm's length. 'Get up they stairs and change while I make you a nice cup of tea. How didn't you get a cab instead of walking all that way and getting drenched?'

'I had some errands.' Caseley removed her hat and pushed wet curls back from her forehead.

'So how's it coming on then?' Rosina's expectant smile faded. 'What is it, my bird? What's wrong?'

Caseley shook her head, fighting for control. 'I –' she cleared the thickness from her throat. 'I shan't be doing any more up there, Rosina.'

The housekeeper's jaw dropped. 'What d'you mean? Why not? I know it haven't been easy, but 'twas far better than working in that there office all day and bringing more home to work on half the night. I can't believe the captain don't want you up there no more. Not after all he done to get you there in the first place.'

Caseley started towards the stairs. 'Who knows how Captain Barata's mind works, Rosina.'

'What happened?' Rosina's face puckered in concern.

'I knew he didn't like me much,' Caseley's throat ached. 'But to send Louise Downing –' She swallowed hard then shrugged. 'It's not important.' She tried to smile. 'Father will have to be told and that won't be easy.'

'*Louise Downing* was up the captain's house? What's the woman thinking of? You *sure* he knew she was there?'

Caseley shrugged again. 'Apparently he told her about the house this morning. It's none of our business, Rosina.'

She started up the stairs. If only she could go away. But that was impossible. She could not leave her father, especially now. Nor would it make any difference. She could not out-run her thoughts.

'I'll get you that tea, my treasure,' Rosina called after her. 'Oh, afore I forget, your father's in the parlour. He said he want to see you soon as you come in.' She dropped her voice to a whisper. 'He can wait till you've changed and got something hot inside of you. White as a sheet you are. Go on now, bird.' Muttering indignantly, she hurried away to the kitchen and Caseley continued up the stairs.

Having changed her clothes for a full-sleeved bodice of pale green sprigged cotton over a plain skirt of pine worsted, her hair held back in two combs and falling loose in heavy waves down her back, she approached the parlour.

The hot tea had soothed her tender stomach and restored some colour to her cheeks. She reached for the doorknob. *She* would tell her father about the figures she had pretended were his. But not yet, not until she was certain there was no alternative. First she had to tell him she would no longer be a party to his agreement with Jago Barata.

She knocked lightly and went in. Her father was in his usual chair beside the hearth. The fire was lit and despite the heavy, dark overcrowded furniture, the glowing coals made the room feel cosy.

'You took your time,' he grumbled, resting his head in the angle between the high padded back and winged side.

'I got caught in the rain,' she apologised and started forward. 'Father, there's something I –'

'It will have to wait.' With the impatient gesture of one bony hand he scooped up an opened package from the scalloped-edged round table beside his chair. 'This arrived in the afternoon post.' He pulled out a folded sheet of paper and an envelope sealed with red wax imprinted with a signet.

'It was addressed to me as consul for Mexico, it's from a group of Spaniards with interests in both countries. They want the documents in the sealed envelope taken by hand to Spain and placed into the hands of Canovas del Castillo, leader of the royalists.'

Caseley was horrified. 'Father, you can't. You've been ill. You're not strong enough for such a journey. Anyway, why were the documents sent to you? Why not to the Embassy in London, or direct to Spain?'

'If you'll hold your tongue a moment, I'll tell you.'

She flushed. 'I beg your pardon.'

Teuder Bonython sucked in a breath. 'When these men heard that certain members of the royalist party were trying to safeguard their own futures by dealing in secret with the rebels, they sent similar packages, one direct to Spain, the other to the Embassy in London. Both these packages contained false information. Their suspicions proved well-founded when that information was offered for sale to the rebels. Knowing their usual routes of communication are compromised they have approached me. It is a great honour, Caseley, proof of their faith in my integrity.'

'I understand that, Father. Truly I do.' Crouching by his chair she placed her hand over his. 'But you must see it's impossible for you to go? Can you not confide in Mr Fox? He is Vice-Consul for Spain –'

'And as such is bound by oath to serve whichever government is in power. Spain is currently a republic. So how can he honour his pledge *and* handle documents that might assist the restoration of Queen Isabel's son, Alfonso, to the throne?'

'How do you know what's in the documents?'

'When Jago was describing the situation in Spain he spoke of del Castillo, though he was not complimentary.'

The mention of Jago's name sent an uncomfortable tingle along Caseley's nerves. 'Does he know about this?' She indicated the package.

'No one knows. And no one must find out. Secrecy is vital. I've told you only because I have no choice.'

'Father –'

'Will you stop fussing and listen!' His face suffused with angry colour. 'I *know* I can't go, Goddammit. I'm too weak.' His head fell back. 'Besides, if I'm to die soon I want to be here, not in a strange country torn apart by bloody civil war.'

'Oh, Father.' Her eyes filled at this acknowledgement that his time was running out.

'None of that,' he muttered. His hand rested briefly on her bent head. 'I cannot go to Spain, Caseley. So you must.'

Chapter Eleven

Her head jerked up. 'Me?'

'Yes, you.' Her father was impatient. 'There's no one else I can trust.'

'When –?' Her voice emerged as a dry croak.

'I'm trying to tell you.' Wincing, he pressed the heel of his hand against his chest.

She jumped up. 'Where are your drops?'

His eyes were closed, his forehead trenched with lines of pain. 'I want brandy.'

Catching sight of the small tray standing on a table in the corner she rushed across, and with shaking hands poured water into the glass then picked up the medicine bottle.

'No, I can't be doing with fog in my head. There are things you need to know. Pour me a brandy. Please, Caseley?'

He never *asked.* Demands, orders, instructions, she was used to those. She had never heard him plead.

He tried to smile, but it was no more than a twitch of purple-tinged lips. 'Humour an old man. I'd as soon spend what time is left to me in my right mind.'

Replacing the medicine bottle on the tray she took a small bunch of keys from her skirt pocket, went to the chiffonier, and unlocked the doors of silvered glass. The neck of the bottle clattered against the glass as she poured. Her father was facing death and sending her away.

She handed him the spirit and watched as he swallowed

half of it in one gulp, his lips peeling back from his teeth as he shuddered. Replacing the bottle she re-locked the doors.

It was three years since, in an effort to curb Ralph's drinking, her father decreed that all money and alcohol in the house be kept under lock and key. It had not worked. Ralph still got drunk. Only he did it in town, on credit, pawning his belongings, mortgaging his allowance, or at the expense of his friends.

Her father sighed deeply. The harsh grooves in his face softened as he relaxed. 'You sail tomorrow morning. Officially you are going on my behalf to sign a new trading agreement with Señor Miguel Spinoza, for whom we will carry iron ore. I had Thomas work out the figures with our attorney this afternoon. The contract is perfectly legal. A telegraph message has been sent to say you're on your way.'

Caseley wrapped her arms across her body. Despite the glowing fire and the warmth in the room, she was chilled to her bones.

'But *where* am I going? And how am I to get there?' She had arrived home fighting a tangle of emotions and working up the courage to tell her father about actions she had taken on his behalf, only to have all of it brushed aside as irrelevant.

Now, with no warning or time to prepare, she was being sent to Spain on a matter of vital importance and secrecy.

'I spoke to Toby this afternoon. *Cygnet*'s repairs are finished. Jago is sailing her to Santander to collect a cargo. You will sail with him.'

The room went dark. With a noise like rushing water in her head, feeling as though she might shatter into a million fragments, Caseley reached blindly for the back of a chair.

She collapsed onto it as her knees gave way. Her father was still talking.

'... Should take three or four days, depending on the weather. I've always said there are worse storms in the Bay of Biscay at the end of summer than in January. Still, you'll be safe enough with Jago.'

She closed her eyes. *Safe*? Only an hour ago she had planned never to see him again, to lick her wounds in private. That they were self-inflicted, the result of her own gullibility and foolishness, did not make them hurt less.

Now she had to spend at least a week on a boat with him. A week that would allow neither respite nor escape. Having received her letter he would know she was aware of his relationship with Louise Downing.

She had deliberately kept it brief. But he was astute. What if he had seen through the polite formality to the anguish beneath? She had been so naïve. How would she survive a week of barbed shafts delivered with careless skill and lethal accuracy? She couldn't. It was impossible.

'You might show some interest!' Her father's bellow made her jump and her head flew up. 'I don't expect you to understand how much it would have meant to me to go. All these years I've been consul, authenticating signatures, signing crews on and off, arranging sightseeing tours for visiting dignitaries, and acting as agent for trade contracts. All these years of routine, then this comes along.' There was hopelessness in his headshake.

'I've always been a practical man, happiest at sea or in the yard. Now I'm too old and sick to go to Spain myself.' He thumped one fist on the arm of his chair. 'And I can't trust my son to go in my place.'

For the first time Caseley began to comprehend the enormity of his disappointment. Immersed in her own problems, she had not realised how deeply her father had been hurt by Ralph's rejection of the inheritance that was more than merely a business.

The consulship was a position of trust and prestige, a public honouring of moral and financial integrity. Though not hereditary, in the case of a family business the post often passed from father to son. But there was no chance of Ralph retaining it.

Hard-pressed to cope with all her father demanded of her, plus the intolerable strain of keeping secrets from him, she had not looked beneath the surface, hearing only his complaints, orders, irascibility.

He made a weary gesture and closed his eyes. 'It's not you I'm railing at, girl. But what was the point of it all?'

Pushing herself out of the chair, Caseley knelt in front of him. He had little time left. He had seen two wives and his elder son die. Then all he had worked for, all he had built and nurtured had been tossed aside by his remaining son. She was under no illusion. She could never take the place of the sons he had regarded as his stake in the future. But she had a choice: to give the knife a final twist, or do this one last thing for him.

He would never know what it cost her. But in going to Spain she would not be haunted by the anguish of 'if only' and 'too late'. She licked paper-dry lips.

'I won't let you down, Father. The documents will be delivered as safely and secretly as if you had taken them yourself.'

Opening his eyes, he gazed at her. 'If only you had been a boy.'

Patting his knee, she rose to her feet. She was less than a son to her father and less than a woman to Jago Barata.

'What was it you wanted to tell me when you came in?'

She turned away to put his brandy glass on the table. 'Nothing important.' She offered her arm. 'Shall we go and have dinner?' Her stomach was a small hard knot and the thought of food made her feel queasy. 'I expect there are other things I should know. Who will meet me? How will I know him?'

Later, she bathed and washed her hair in the slipper bath in front of her bedroom fire, refusing to think about the lack of facilities aboard the schooner. Rosina laid skirts, blouses, and underwear on the bed.

Shrouded in a white cotton nightgown, Caseley perched on a padded footstool beside the fire, her head tilted as she brushed her hair.

Rolling each item of clothing to minimise creasing, Rosina paused, a smile dimpling her plump cheeks. 'I'd give good money to see Louise Downing's face when she hear about this.'

Caseley glanced up. 'About what?' She swung her hair to the other side and resumed brushing.

'You and the captain sailing to Spain together. She'll be mad as fire. Still, 'tis time he come to his senses.'

'We're not sailing *together,* Rosina.' Caseley's cheeks were burning. She was too close to the flames. 'We both have business there. There's no more to it than that. He doesn't even like me.'

Rosina snorted. 'Don't you believe it, bird. I'll fetch clean towels for you to take.'

When the last item had been neatly tucked into the leather portmanteau, Rosina had gently rubbed Caseley's upper arm. 'Be all right, will you?'

She nodded. She would keep out of his way. When he was in the cabin she would go on deck. When he was on deck she would stay below.

'I'll be fine.' She crossed to the shelf to choose a book.

She hadn't expected to see him again, and wished it

wasn't necessary. She had defied him. He would be angry.

Dawn had just broken when she left the house next morning. Her sleep had been restless and her eyes felt hot and gritty. But the cool air was fresh after the rain. It rippled over her face like silk, sharpening her senses.

The smell of frying bacon wafted from a nearby house on the stirring breeze.

She looked both ways before crossing the muddy road. But apart from a brewer's dray laden with casks turning into the yard of the Dock Inn, there was no traffic and few people. She closed the tall gate behind her and walked through the quiet yard towards the quay and slip, her bag bumping against her leg. Passing the sawpits and the golden dunes of sawdust, the silent sheds and the timber pool, she saw *Cygnet's* tall masts.

The jibs and topsails were loosed, the foresail set and the huge fore-and-aft mainsail partly hoisted. Gulls screamed mournfully as they wheeled overhead. The breeze sang in the rigging and made the shrouds slap against the masts.

Her hull protected from the rough stone quay by cork and rope fenders, the schooner floated on the rising tide, held only by a single rope at bow and stern. Smoke rose from the curved chimney of the cooking shack bolted to the deck behind the foremast.

Her footsteps faltered and she stopped. Where was everyone? 'Hello?' She cleared her throat and tried again. This time her voice was at least audible.

A head popped out of the cooking shack. She beckoned and the skinny boy glanced round to make sure it was him she was waving at before he crossed the deck to her, wiping his hands on a grubby cloth.

'Yes, miss?'

Caseley smiled at him. 'What's your name?'

'Laity, miss. Martin Laity.'

'I'm Miss Bonython. Will you help me aboard?'

Startled, the boy's glance jumped from her bag to the companionway hatch and back to her. 'Aboard *'ere*, miss?'

'Yes.' Caseley tamped down impatience. 'If you will take my bag, I'll get over the side by myself.'

The boy glanced round again then backed away. 'I'd better git the cap'n.'

'Please take my bag first.' She hefted it onto the gunwale. Taking it reluctantly, the boy set it on the deck.

Caseley gauged the distance between the vessel and the quay. Though it wasn't far, Jago could at least have put out a ladder or a gangplank. Was he deliberately trying to make it difficult for her? He must know this was the very last place she wanted to be.

The gunwale was several inches above the quay. Gathering her skirts in one hand, Caseley placed one foot on it and held out her hand to the boy. She would not think about the gap between quay and ship, and the cold grey water slopping between the two. Flushing crimson, he grasped her fingers, steadying her as she jumped down. She winced as she jarred her damaged foot.

'What's going on?'

She stiffened at the familiar deep voice, and kept her gaze lowered as she shook out her skirt and picked up her bag, giving the boy a brief smile.

'Thank you, Martin.' She could feel her face burning as she met Jago's eyes. 'I had a little difficulty getting aboard.'

'Get back to the galley, Martin,' Jago dismissed him without a glance.

Caseley braced herself, waiting for him to mention her

letter.

'Aye, sir.' The boy scuttled away.

His expression unreadable, Jago folded his arms, his skin brown against the rolled-up sleeves of a white shirt. A red kerchief loosely knotted around his throat emphasised the blackness of his beard.

'Now that you are on board, perhaps you will tell me why. We are due to sail shortly.'

Had he simply accepted her decision? While she longed to believe that, she couldn't because it would be totally unlike him. Not saying anything now could only mean he was saving it for later.

'Did my father not tell you?'

'I haven't seen your father.'

Though her promise made it necessary, lying to him was far harder than she expected. She moistened dry lips. 'There is a trade agreement that must be signed –'

'Then I suggest you give it to me and return home.'

Caseley stared at him. Why was he pretending not to know what she was talking about?

'I can't give it to you. If you didn't speak to my father then Toby must have told you.'

Jago frowned. 'Told me what?'

Caseley swallowed, her parched throat making an audible click. 'That you have a passenger for this trip.'

Jago nodded. 'Yes, I was told. He's already aboard. He arrived last night.'

'Who did?'

'Antonio Valdes.'

Caseley was totally confused. 'Who is Antonio Valdes?'

Jago's expression darkened. 'The passenger I am taking to Spain. Why are *you* here? Sam could have brought this trade agreement down. Is it money? Do you need more?

The bank has my instructions. You have only to speak to Mr Buller. As for the house, this is neither the time nor the place for such discussions.'

Money? The house? He was talking as though *he had not received her letter.* The deck heaved beneath her feet. His last words brought back vivid memories of Louise Downing's visit and her own awakening to the true situation. But he was right in one respect. This was not the time to talk about his house or anyone connected with it.

She raised her chin. 'As far as I am concerned, Captain, there is nothing *to* discuss. Obviously there has been a misunderstanding. My father told me he left a message with Toby that you were to expect a passenger.'

'Yes. Antonio Valdes.'

'No.' Caseley was firm. 'Whoever this person is, and whatever his reasons for wanting a passage to Spain, he is *not* the passenger my father meant.'

'No? Then who –?' He broke off, his gaze darting to the heavy bag clutched in her white-knuckled hands. '*You*?' She gave a single nod. 'Why?'

'I started to tell you.'

'Ah yes. Trade contracts.' Hands on his hips he studied her but before he could speak, a man appeared behind him. He had fair hair, a narrow face, and wide-set eyes that sharpened as they saw her.

Distracted by his sudden emergence, uncomfortable beneath his intent scrutiny, she turned back to Jago, lowering her voice. 'Perhaps you had better explain the misunderstanding to Señor Valdes. No doubt he will be able to find another berth within a few days.'

As the newcomer approached, Jago swung round. 'If you will kindly go below, Señor Valdes, Martin will bring your breakfast. I will join you shortly.' Politely phrased it was nonetheless an order.

The man stopped. Slightly built, he wore a superbly cut dark coat and ochre waistcoat over grey check trousers. His linen was spotless and a garnet pin glowed in the folds of his cravat. Caseley guessed him to be a few years older than her but younger than Jago. Surprise and displeasure crossed his face.

'Forgive me, Captain. It was not my intention to intrude.' His voice was heavily accented and betrayed a pique at odds with his apology. Bowing, he returned to the companionway.

Caseley looked at Jago. 'Why didn't you tell him?'

He leaned towards her. '*I* am master of this ship,' he said softly. 'I am not obliged to explain my decisions.'

'Your point is taken, Captain.' Her heartbeat thudded so loud and fast she feared he might hear it. 'If you have decided Señor Valdes can remain aboard then so be it. But my father and I have a prior claim in ownership. I am here, not through choice, but on his instructions in a matter of some urgency. So if you will show me to my cabin, you need delay your departure no longer.'

He masked it quickly but she saw shock. 'You cannot sail with me.'

Why was he doing this? Her father had told her it was all settled. 'On the contrary, Captain, I can and I must. The error was yours, not mine. I am undertaking this voyage in my father's name because he is not well enough.' Her voice nearly faltered but she caught it in time. Anger bubbled up lending her strength. 'Were he standing here you would not attempt to force him ashore.'

'Were he here, the situation would not arise,' he retorted.

In the tense silence he rubbed one palm across his beard. 'Will you not consider another vessel?'

Feeling his rejection like a slap she took a breath then

shook her head. 'That is not possible. I need to –' Recognising the audacity of his suggestion she stopped. 'Why should I? This confusion is not *my* fault.'

'So you are determined to stay?' His tone implied a warning but against what she had no idea.

'Believe me, Captain Barata, it gives me no more pleasure to be here than it gives you to see me.'

He studied her for several seconds, frowning slightly. 'Are you aware of the conditions?'

She nodded. 'My father warned me we might encounter rough weather.'

'I was not referring to the weather.'

'I do not expect all the comforts of home, Captain.'

His gaze was thoughtful. 'Once we leave, I will not turn back.'

She glanced towards the town. Once the ship sailed she would be on her own with no one to whom she could turn for advice if anything went wrong. *She had survived the past two months. She could survive this.* She thought of her father.

'I told you.' Her voice sounded thin and strained. 'I have no choice.'

'For trade agreements.' He was openly sceptical.

'They are very important.'

'They must be.'

Uncertain, she glanced at him. Their eyes locked. She wanted to look away but his steady gaze held her fast. She was acutely conscious of his physical presence, his stillness. The grey eyes were no longer cool but questioning.

The yearning she had fought so hard to deny surged over her like a breaking wave and she fought to retain her balance, barely aware of holding her breath.

Seeing his expression change, sensing his retreat

behind a barrier as solid as a wall, she remembered Louise. Louise who had age-old eyes, a full-lipped mouth, and a voluptuous figure, who spoke possessively of Jago, regularly visited him at his hotel, and now laid claim to his house.

Her lashes lowered. She was grateful for the pain. Where was her pride? Could she so easily forget how cynically he had used her? She raised her head, drew herself up.

'My cabin, Captain?'

He regarded her for a moment longer, then leaned forward to take the bag from her nerveless fingers, anger flashing across his face as she flinched. Silently he gestured for her to precede him. She stopped as they reached the double doors of the companionway, now latched back.

He pushed the sliding top further open to reveal a spiral staircase with perforated brass treads and a wooden handrail that curved out of sight.

Misinterpreting her hesitation he went ahead of her and waited halfway. 'It's not as steep as it looks. You'll soon get used to it.'

She glanced over her shoulder in one last agonising instant of doubt, glimpsing the little tower atop her father's house. The breeze was like cold breath on her neck and suddenly she was afraid.

She thought of Ben helping her father wash and dress for the day while Rosina prepared breakfast and Liza-Jane worked through her morning chores. Maybe Ralph was awake and thinking about the portrait.

There was no going back. Placing one foot on the top stair, she gripped the teak rail and followed Jago down.

He pointed to a door at the bottom of the companionway. 'This is the mate's cabin. Do you know

Nathan Ferris?'

Caseley shook her head. 'We've not met. I believe he lives over at Feock with his wife and children.'

Jago merely nodded and opened a door facing forward. 'This is my day room.' He stood back to let her pass.

A salt-stained and grubby canvas bag stood against an upholstered bench seat. The cabin narrowed towards the stern. Though not large, it was light and airy thanks to a large skylight that had a brass oil-lamp suspended below it.

Panelled in wood, the cabin had two shelves edged with thin rails at the aft end. The lower one held rolled charts. The upper was crammed with books, a tin of oil, and several small tools. A barometer and a clock were set into the panelling above them.

A table between the two upholstered bench seats was hinged to fold down and provide more floor space. A small stove stood on a stone slab in front of the forward bulkhead with a coalscuttle and basket of kindling beside it.

Jago dropped her bag on the table. Pulling back the dark curtain on the far side of the stove he stepped aside.

Caseley saw the space had just enough room for a bunk and a small cupboard with a hinged lid on top, which she guessed would contain a small removable washbasin, and a single door below. A reefer jacket lay on the grey blankets and she glimpsed a canvas bag beneath the bunk.

Without a word he crossed the cabin, pushed open a sliding door on the locker above the seat, and beckoned her forward.

Aware of his mocking gaze, Caseley looked in. The sea-berth was six feet long, just over two feet wide, and contained a thin mattress, several folded grey blankets, and a pillow covered in blue and white striped ticking.

She remembered enough about the layout of a schooner to realise this was not a deliberate attempt to embarrass or frighten her off. The crew slept in the fo'c'sle; the master and mate had cabins aft. There was no extra accommodation. These vessels were built for carrying cargo, not passengers.

She turned to Jago. One dark brow rose but he did not speak. Nor did he smile. Was he expecting accusation? Complaint? A hasty retreat?

Caseley cleared her throat. 'If you are offering me a choice, I'll take the sleeping cabin, thank you.'

He gave a brief nod. She thought she saw fleeting approval but dismissed it as wishful thinking.

There was a tap on the door and a man poked his head into the cabin. 'Ready to warp out, skipper.' Catching sight of Caseley, his eyes rounded, darting from her to Jago.

'Thanks, Nathan.' Jago opened the door wider. 'Miss Bonython, allow me to introduce *Cygnet's* mate, Nathan Ferris.'

'How do you do, Mr Ferris.'

The mate was visibly surprised as Caseley extended her hand. She saw Jago's mouth twist and recalled their first meeting and her refusal to acknowledge their introduction.

Nathan quickly wiped his hand down the side of his trousers before taking her hand and giving it a single careful shake. 'How do, miss. I seen your father down here yesterday. Not looking too bad, is he?'

'No, he is much better,' she agreed, feeling Jago's eyes on her. What else could she say? People saw what they wanted to see. Even when they guessed the truth they would cling to the old adage about life and hope.

'Take you topside, shall I, miss? We're casting off d'rectly and –'

'That won't be necessary,' Jago broke in. 'Miss Bonython is sailing with us.'

The mate blinked. 'Ah. Right. Well. If you'll 'scuse me, miss, I'd best get on.' He touched his forehead in salute. 'Soon as we're under way I'll move my stuff down the fo'c'sle, skipper. 'Ammer can rig me 'ammock.'

Jago clapped the mate's shoulder. 'I'm much obliged, Nathan.'

The mate nodded and left.

Caseley looked at Jago in relief. But before she could speak, he shook his head.

'No. Señor Valdes has Nathan's cabin. You will remain here.' She opened her mouth to protest, but he didn't give her the chance. 'While you are aboard I am responsible for your safety.' His tone implacable, he reached for the door handle.

Caseley burned with fury and indignation. Everyone aboard would face the same dangers should the weather turn wild. So he was simply making her pay for insisting on sailing aboard *Cygnet.*

She should have known better than to expect consideration. He had made it clear from the moment they met that as far as he was concerned she deserved none. But with him in it the cabin felt very small.

Unexpectedly he turned. As her chin lifted his mouth curved in a caustic smile. 'For what it's worth,' he spoke quietly, 'our enforced proximity will be no easier for me.' He left, closing the door behind him.

Caseley pressed her palms to her hot cheeks. Never had she felt so wretchedly out of place.

Through the open skylight she could hear orders being shouted, the squeak of ropes through blocks, and the rattle of steering gear. She leaned against the doorjamb, her fingers pressed to her trembling lips as she tried to swallow the lump that threatened to choke her.

Her father was depending on her. At worst the voyages out and back would take ten days. Given good weather it might only be a week. Then she would be free of Jago Barata.

The cabin was stifling. She needed air. Quickly wiping the wetness from her cheeks, she walked out, closing the door behind her. She refused to think about the coming night and the ones to follow. Gripping the handrail she climbed the companionway and stepped out onto the deck.

Already clear of the quay, *Cygnet* was swinging round, her bow pointing towards Trefusis. She saw Jago at the wheel. He ignored her, gazing forward to where Nathan and two other men were hauling on ropes, setting the two huge fore and aft sails and sheeting home the square topsail. Even the boy Martin was involved, darting to help wherever he was needed.

The bow came into the wind then with a crack like a pistol shot, the sails filled, and the schooner surged forward.

Caseley moved to the starboard side and stood close to the mainmast rigging. *Cygnet*'s raking stem cut through the choppy water like a knife as they passed the north arm of the docks and headed out towards Black Rock and the English Channel.

The sky was a pastel wash of lemon, pale green, and turquoise. Slivers of high thin cloud were edged with rose. With the breeze cool on her face and the deck moving beneath her feet like a living creature, she watched spellbound as the rising sun peeped over the headland behind the St Anthony lighthouse, unrolling a carpet of liquid gold before them.

When she looked back for one last glimpse of the town, it was already out of sight.

Chapter Twelve

Dazzled by the sunrise, Caseley watched Nathan and the two crewmen trim the sails. Hauling in and loosening ropes, winding them in figures-of-eight around two-pronged wooden pegs with speed and dexterity, they ensured that each sail drew its dull share of wind.

'Jimbo!' Nathan bawled at a stocky figure in the bows. 'Coil they jib sheets down clear for running. Likely the skipper'll gybe when she's clear o' the Point for a broad reach down past the Lizard.'

Jimbo raised a hand in acknowledgement. Where the bight of rope fell from a peg he laid it in a wide circle on the deck. He added several more turns finishing with the loose end. Quickly flipping the whole coil over, he neatly overlapped both sides of the centre into a figure-of-eight with an extra loop in the middle.

If the sail had to be loosed in a hurry, once the rope was free of the peg it would rise from the coil with no risk of knots or tangles.

As the men worked swiftly round the deck tidying all the loose ropes, she wondered why they were lifting them off the deck and hanging them over stanchions or on the gunwale. Then Martin hauled a bucket of seawater in over the side. As he sloshed it over the deck and began scrubbing with a short-bristled broom, she realised she had not heard Jago issue one word of command.

'The captain runs, how you say, a tight ship, no?'

The soft voice so close to her ear made her jump. She

turned quickly.

'Antonio Valdes,' he introduced himself and bowed his head without breaking eye contact. 'It is an unexpected pleasure to have the company of such a beautiful young lady.' His brown eyes were soft and languid, his smile admiring. 'Tell me I am not dreaming. I see this apparition before me, with hair as rich as cinnabar. Does she have a name?'

Suppressing a smile, Caseley offered her hand. 'I am no ghost, Señor Valdes. My name is Bonython. Do tell me, what is cinnabar?'

Instead of shaking her hand he raised it to his mouth. Ignoring the convention that a gentleman stopped short of actual contact, he touched his lips to her knuckles.

When Jago had done the same, his touch had stirred new and powerful emotions in her. This felt impertinent.

Firmly withdrawing her hand, she saw surprise and speculation in his gaze. She realised he would take advantage of the slightest encouragement. Yet his lavish compliments were balm to her bruised heart.

He leaned on the gunwale beside her. 'Cinnabar is the red ore from which quicksilver comes.' He paused, smiling as he studied her. 'Is there beneath those lovely tresses a silvery spirit that slips through the fingers, unwilling to be captured?'

His tone was light, bantering. Though she lacked experience in the art of flirting, Caseley recognised the skill in others. Perhaps Antonio Valdes was merely seeking to relieve a tedious voyage in a socially acceptable manner with no offence intended. But unease riffled over her skin like a cat's paw of wind on still water.

'My hair has been compared to many things, sir.' She recalled childhood taunts of *carroty*, *conker*, and *radish-head.* 'Though of a more mundane nature.' Before he could comment, she deliberately shifted the conversation away from herself. 'Are you involved in mining?'

'No, though there are quicksilver mines where I come from. Also coal, iron, and zinc. But I would not have you think that is all Asturias can offer.' He smiled into her eyes, his narrow face enthusiastic. 'Along the coast are small fishing settlements at the foot of sheer cliffs. Behind these, maize grows on rolling hills. We do not have frost, so dates ripen in the sun and oranges scent the air with their blossom. In the west are the mountains, wild and rugged and capped with snow.'

'You paint a vivid picture, Señor.'

'It is a vivid country, Señorita. Oviedo's cathedral has one of the finest church towers in Spain. It is the burial place of ancient Asturian kings. But most of the people live in small villages. Beside each house there is another, very tiny. This is ... *horreo* ...'

'A granary?' Caseley supplied.

His eyes narrowed briefly then he laughed. '*Sí,* a granary. You speak Spanish?'

'Very little.' Her response was pure instinct. There was no logical reason to deny her fluency in the language. But the warmth in his smile had not reached his eyes. Her wariness returned. 'Do go on.'

'The granaries are built on four legs to protect the maize of each household from rats and mice. The mountain ham of Asturias is famous through all Spain.' His smile faded. 'Forgive me. I think I am boring you.'

'Not at all,' Caseley said with perfect truth. 'I enjoy learning about other countries. Reading books is never as informative as listening to someone who lives there. What is so special about the ham?'

Once again something about his warm open smile disturbed her. She glimpsed hints of satisfaction and smugness that made her wonder if she had been manipulated into asking the questions. But what would be the point? Besides, she *was* interested. Why pretend otherwise?

'It has a unique flavour,' he said. 'The ham is laid in the snow high in the mountains so the sun may cure it. The cold snow stops the meat spoiling. It becomes a beautiful dark red in colour. Sliced very thin it is almost translucent. To eat it with ice-cool melon,' he bunched the tips of his fingers and kissed them, 'is a wonderful experience. Now, beautiful miss, you must tell me about yourself. Where is your home?'

'In Falmouth.' Caseley saw him look over her shoulder. As she started to turn, Jago spoke.

'A few moments of your time, Miss Bonython?' He did not even glance at Valdes. Cupping her elbow, he indicated that she should precede him aft.

Valdes straightened from the rail with languid grace and bowed to her.

'I enjoyed our conversation, Miss Bonython. Captain.' With a brief nod he made for the companionway and disappeared down the stairs.

'Well, Captain Barata?' Caseley matched his coolness. 'You have my attention. What do you want?'

'Martin needs to finish swabbing the deck. You and Señor Valdes were in the way.' He guided her towards the stern. 'You also risked getting your head knocked off.' Without waiting for a response he turned to Nathan. 'I'll take the helm. Make ready to gybe.'

'Aye, skipper.' Stating their course, the mate relinquished the wheel and hurried forward, shouting orders to Jimbo and Hammer.

Watching the smooth, sure movements of the crew as they hauled in the two booms to which the fore and aft mainsails were laced, Caseley forgot her anger.

Jago turned the wheel slowly, watching the sails to see when the wind left them. 'All right, boys,' he shouted, and spun the wheel. Nathan released ropes on the port side and the huge booms swung across. One passed right where she had been standing.

Jimbo and Hammer hauled in the starboard sheets and, as the sails filled, made them fast. Heeling slightly, *Cygnet* leapt forward on her new course. The two crewmen went forward to trim the jibs and staysail and Jago checked the compass suspended just inside the day room skylight as Nathan returned.

'Keep her steady on this heading. If the wind holds we should make Ushant before sundown.'

'Only a hundred miles, skipper?' the mate grinned. 'Slowing up, are 'e?'

Caseley waited for the explosion. But to her amazement it never came.

'If you'd had my lay-over,' Jago snorted, 'you would not smile so readily.'

'Need a wife and family, you do,' Nathan advised.

Jago's laugh was brief and humourless. 'You married men want to see everyone else enslaved.'

She might as well have been invisible.

The mate's grin widened. 'Well, if 'tis a prison to have a warm bed and a woman to match waiting for me after every trip, I aren't in no hurry to break me chains.'

Jago shrugged. 'Who needs marriage for that?'

Caseley's heart was wrenched. He certainly didn't. Not when he had someone else's wife waiting for him.

'Git on.' Nathan shot him a dry look. 'If you think 'tis the same, you got a lot to learn.'

'Mind your tongue,' Jago growled, his expression severe. But as he cupped her elbow once more she saw the glint of laughter in his eyes and envied them their comradeship.

'Nathan and I have faced death together on several occasions,' he said. 'Our lack of formality –'

'Does not indicate lack of respect. I'm aware of that.'

He nodded. 'You and your housekeeper share a similar rapport.'

He remembered.

'I will show you around the ship.'

'That is kind of you, but –'

'Kindness does not enter into it. If we are to complete this voyage quickly, the crew needs to concentrate on their tasks without concern for passengers. If you are in the wrong place at the wrong time you could endanger both them and yourself. Besides, despite your brave claim about not expecting the comforts of home, surely even you require certain amenities?'

Caseley felt a blush scald her face as he indicated an oblong wooden hut. Almost his height, it was set across the deck.

'This is the wheel shelter,' he announced, then opened a door in the side. 'This is the lamp store and paint locker.' Caseley peered in, wrinkling her nose at the strong smell of oil, varnish, and turpentine. 'There is a door on the other side into our lavatory. Though it's a basic bucket-and-chuck-it, there is a proper wooden seat. As we don't usually carry passengers there's no lock. To avoid embarrassment I suggest you tie a piece of cloth to the door handle when –' he made a small gesture leaving the sentence unfinished.

Torn between wishing she had never set foot on the boat, and gratitude that he had anticipated her needs, all she could do was try to match his cool matter-of-fact manner.

He pointed to the teak rubbing boards fixed at hip and shoulder height to the front of the shelter behind Nathan.

'They give some support during the long watches. The wooden grid is to stop the helmsman losing his footing on a wet deck.'

'Does the rain make it slippery, then?' she asked, determined to be seen to be taking everything in her stride.

He threw her an oblique glance. 'Large seas breaking inboard are a greater concern.'

Caseley swallowed as her imagination instantly conjured terrifying visions.

He guided her forward. His hand under her elbow was warm. It offered strength and comfort; reminding her of the soul-baring moments they had shared in his house. Before she had opened the door to Louise Downing who had shattered every foolish dream.

Passing the companionway he knocked his knuckles against a large covered tank with a copper dipper attached to it by a line. 'Our fresh water. And this' he pointed to a cask harnessed to the tank, 'contains salt beef. Bread, fruit, and condensed milk are stored in a zinc-lined cupboard below the sea berth in my day room and apportioned daily. Vegetables are kept here in the galley shack.'

Looking in, Caseley saw Martin crouched in front of the black cooking range, shovelling coal through a hole in the flat top. Pots and pans surrounded a small stool. One pan contained a sharp knife and a huge ladle. A curved chimney pipe rose from the back of the stove and belched thick smoke into the air.

As they reached the mainmast, Caseley gazed up in awe.

'One hundred feet from keel to masthead,' Jago said. 'The foremast is five feet shorter. Cargo hatches.' The large wooden covers were almost hidden beneath coils of rope, buckets, a wooden ladder and a small rowing boat mounted on a cradle.

In front of the foremast the two crewmen were sitting on the deck, binding frayed ends of rope with fine cord. Both nodded respectfully at Jago and glanced sideways at Caseley, eyes bright with curiosity.

'Hammer, Jimbo, this is Captain Bonython's daughter.'

The men scrambled to their feet, grinning at Caseley's surprise.

'You're twins,' she blurted.

'Yes, miss.' Jimbo touched his brow with a stubby callused forefinger. ''Ammer's eldest by ten minutes, but we don't fight over it. He got the beauty,' his finger strayed to a puckered scar running down his cheek. 'But I got the brains.'

'And a quick tongue,' she smiled. His grin widened.

Jago's grip tightened. 'This is the fo'c'sle, the crew's quarters.'

Caseley peered through the small, whale-backed hatch with a latched door and ring handle now hooked open to reveal a steep ladder.

'It looks very dark.'

'Since I had the skylight installed, the crew get as much light and fresh air as I do.'

'You make it sound like a luxury.'

The twins had abandoned any pretence of working and were watching, open-mouthed.

'The point I was making, Miss Bonython, is that much of my work is done in my day room. All theirs is done on deck, and they eat in the mess.'

'That's right, miss,' Jimbo began, but was instantly silenced by Jago's glare.

Caseley could feel the anger radiating from him and wished she had not spoken so hastily.

The schooner's bow rose and fell, parting blue-green masses of water and tossing it aside in hissing waves of white foam that left streaks in her wake.

'We'll go below.' Jago was abrupt, hustling her aft along the canting deck and down the companionway. 'The mess is through there, next to Nathan's cabin. You'll see it later.'

She turned to face him in the small space. 'Why have you brought me down here now?'

'So that you can move your gear into the sleeping cabin while I mark the chart and write up the log.' Opening his day-room door he pushed her gently inside and closed it behind them.

'But – but you haven't moved your things out yet,' she stammered, nervous of disturbing his possessions, knowing she was an unwelcome intruder.

'We do not carry servants.' His tone was cold. 'You insisted on coming, so while on board you will pull your weight.'

'That's not what I meant.' The implied criticism stung. 'I was not trying to avoid doing anything, and I certainly don't expect to be waited on. It's just – I'm not used to handling other people's belongings.'

'If *I* don't object, I see no reason why you should.' Bending over the table, he picked up a ruler and pencil and studied the chart.

Caseley glared at the broad, white-shirted back. She had never met anyone who stirred so many conflicting emotions. Compared to Jago Barata, Aunt Margaret was a novice.

'Leave my bag under the bunk,' he said without looking round. 'There's no room for it out here. Just change the pillows and blankets over. We do not run to sheets or lacy counterpanes. But as you said, you are not expecting home comforts.'

Caseley refused to be drawn. She could feel his antagonism. It seemed to come and go. But as she had no idea what provoked it or how best to react, silence seemed the safest course.

She remade both bunks, noticing with relief that though the blankets were coarse, they were clean. After pushing his bag to one end under the bunk so she could fit hers in, she straightened up. Brushing her hands down her skirt, she stood, uncertain, in the narrow doorway. Seated on one of the bench seats, Jago was apparently engrossed in the notes he was making in a leather-bound book resting on the chart.

Caseley cleared her throat. 'Unless there is anything else you wish me to do here, Captain, I thought I might help Martin in the galley. He –'

'No,' Jago looked up. 'You will not interfere with the running of this ship.'

'I have no intention of *interfering*, as you put it. I simply wanted to help. Martin –'

'Is a member of my crew, and perfectly capable of carrying out his duties by himself.'

'I wasn't suggesting –'

'Can we drop the subject, Miss Bonython?'

'I cannot win. If I don't help, I'm lazy. If I try to, I'm interfering. There's no pleasing you, is there?'

'That remains to be seen.' He leaned back, turning the pencil in his fingers, his expression was enigmatic, his eyes unreadable. 'What is the present state of the house?'

The question stopped her breath. She should have known he would ask. Of course he would want some idea of what had yet to be done. A band of tension tightened round her skull. Moistening her lips she steadied herself against the sleeping cabin's door-frame.

'Mr Endean has almost finished. When I left yesterday he was about to install the bath and hand basin. The inside repairs will be complete by the end of the week. After that,' her throat closed forcing her to swallow. 'After that, you may arrange for the painters to start.'

'I, Miss Bonython?' He slid from the bench and rose to his feet. 'That is *your* job.'

She looked at him. She had hoped, how desperately she had hoped, that he would behave honourably. Instead he was playing with her.

'Not any longer.'

He frowned. 'We have an agreement.'

'Had.' She folded her arms, recognised the move as defensive, and quickly unfolded them, clasping her hands instead. 'Under the circumstances you cannot expect me to continue. Nor can you want it.'

'What circumstances?' His apparent puzzlement was too much.

'I told you once before, Captain. Now I'm telling you again. I will not be made sport of. You must find your amusement elsewhere.' In spite of her anger, she kept her voice low. The skylight was open and their voices would carry. Their business was private. She would not be responsible for it becoming gossip.

'You received my letter. You know full well Mrs Downing will make it impossible –'

He took a step towards her, his expression ominous. 'What letter? What has Mrs Downing to do with the house?'

'Everything!' Caseley flung at him. 'Why this pretence? Surely you are not concerned for my sensibilities? After all,' fury and bitter hurt spilled over despite her resolve to remain calm. 'I am only the hired help. Or I was,' she corrected immediately.

Jago seized her shoulders, his face thunderous. ‘I don’t know what you’re talking about. I never received any letter.’

Caseley brought her arms up as a barrier between them. ‘I took it to your hotel. One of the boys put it into the rack behind the reception desk. I saw him. You *must* have received it.’

‘When did you take it there?’

‘Yesterday afternoon.’

‘Apart from an hour ashore to arrange an outward cargo, I have been on board *Cygnet* since yesterday morning. I did not return to the hotel last night and no mail has been delivered to me here.’

‘Oh.’

‘Why should you imagine Mrs Downing has any connection with my house?’

‘Imagine?’ A harsh, painful laugh tore from Caseley’s throat. ‘I did not imagine her arrival on the doorstep. Nor did I imagine – She was very specific about –’ She could not go on. Hot colour suffused her face and throat. She lowered her lashes to veil the anguish her pride refused to let him see.

‘Louise Downing went to the house yesterday?’

‘You should know. You sent her.’ Caseley bit hard on the inside of her lower lip to stop it trembling.

‘Is that what she told you?’

‘Yes – no – but she intimated –’

‘What happened? Why did you feel it necessary to write this letter I never received?’ He radiated tension.

Caseley tried to pull away, but his fingers tightened, biting into her flesh. They would leave bruises.

‘Tell me,’ he demanded.

She could not meet his eyes. ‘M –Mrs Downing announced herself as a “very close friend” of yours. She left me in no doubt that she did not approve of my presence in the house, or of me working for you. That being so, I thought it best to withdraw and allow her to take over.'

'Oh you did, did you? You've got the devil's own cheek.'

Her head jerked up. '*What?*'

'You appear to have overlooked the fact that it is *my* house. *I* decide who will work on it. How dare you involve Louise without consulting me.'

'I didn't –' Caseley gasped.

'Had I wanted her to have anything to do with it, I would have asked her.' His eyes were fire over ice.

'But she said –'

'I don't give a damn what she said. You should not have let her in.'

'*I* should not –?' Caseley's voice rose to a squeak. 'I couldn't stop her. She was there at your invitation.'

'She wasn't.' He was grim.

'She said – she said you would be angry if I didn't let – ' she stopped. It was pointless to continue. 'Anyway, she *wants* to do it.'

'And you don't?'

'I never did. You know that.'

'I know the *idea* did not appeal.' His tone softened slightly. 'But now you are seeing it change and come to life, are you still so set against it?'

She did not reply.

'Look at me, Caseley. Tell me.'

'I –' Her throat was parched. The lie would not come. 'That is not important.'

'It's the only thing that matters,' he said quietly.

'To you.' He did not understand at all. How could she have thought him intuitive, aware? He saw nothing, cared for nothing but his own selfish desires.

'I want you to finish it.'

'No.'

'Why not?'

She raised her eyes to his. 'I've given you my reasons.'

'Louise will not come to the house again. You have my word.'

Pride stiffened her spine. 'It's your house. You can please yourself whom you entertain, or involve –'

His breath hissed. 'You –' He yanked her towards him and her eyes flew wide as she saw his fury. 'Who in God's name do you think you are? What gives you the right to –' He stopped suddenly, eyes narrowing. The speculative gleam in their smoky depths made her tremble inside. 'Unless ...'

Bracing her fists against the hard wall of his chest she pushed with all her strength.

'Caseley?' He sounded stunned.

'Let me go,' she panted, struggling violently. 'I hate you!'

A rap on the door froze them both.

'Yes?' Jago snapped.

Martin's voice came through the wood. 'Dinner, Cap'n.'

'We'll be right there.'

Seizing her chance, she pulled free. He made no effort to hold her. She was shivering yet perspiration pricked her temples and upper lip. Her heart pounded against her ribs. She rubbed her arms, the flesh tender where his grip had crushed it.

'After you,' he said solemnly, gesturing towards the door.

'I'm not hungry.' Her voice was husky and unsteady.

'I told you once, and I'm telling you again, while you

are on board you are under my protection. You will not go hungry. Nor,' he forbade the idea even as it occurred to her, 'are you going to disrupt the routine of the ship by having your meals served in here. Now, will you walk to the mess, or must I carry you?'

She lifted her chin. 'And who will protect me from *you*, Captain?'

One dark brow rose. 'What makes you think that will be necessary?'

Wrenching the door open she stormed out of the day room, wanting to scream with frustration. How did he always manage to twist her words?

As she entered the mess, Jimbo, Hammer, and Martin scrambled awkwardly to their feet bumping against the wood table and making the spoons clatter against the enamel plates. It cost effort, but she smiled.

'Where shall I sit?'

'Beside me,' Antonio Valdes said from behind her, indicating two places on the bench opposite the twins. She sat down and he slid in beside her.

Jago took his place at the head of the table and ladled out steaming stew from a large iron pot with a ring handle and lid, serving the crew first in order of rank.

Antonio Valdes looked astonished, then annoyed, as Jago poured meat and vegetables onto his plate. He muttered something in Spanish but seemed unwilling to issue a challenge.

Caseley was served last. She murmured her thanks and the meal began.

Chapter Thirteen

There must have been conversation, but no one addressed her directly. By serving her last Jago was making it clear that despite her financial interest in the vessel, the crew's welfare took priority. Antonio Valdes took it as a personal slight. She did not. Besides, she had other things on her mind.

Barely tasting the food, she chewed and swallowed, her thoughts fluttering like a jarful of moths.

The sound of her name on Jago's lips had jolted her. Had he been anyone else she might have ignored it, or told him that such familiarity had no place between them. How could she do that? He was like no one else she had ever known.

Recalling the look on his face as comprehension broke through his scowling anger, embarrassment dewed her skin so her shift clung uncomfortably. It hadn't occurred to her that her weary remark might be construed as jealousy. Only when she saw his expression change did she realise how it must have sounded.

About to protest, she had imagined the sardonic twist to his mouth, his dark brows lifting in mocking disbelief. What exactly was her grievance: his use of her first name? Or that he recognised a truth she had denied even to herself. Anything she said would only convince him he was right. Yet in his eyes her silence served the same purpose.

Still, though he might *assume*, he could not be certain.

To say nothing and keep her distance was her only hope of hiding her fear and shame. There was something pathetic and ridiculous in yearning for a man to whom marriage meant nothing, who already had a mistress, who was contemptuous of those who condemned him, and whose regard for her extended only as far as her usefulness.

A touch on her arm jerked her out of her thoughts. Antonio Valdes's fingers lingered as she turned. Hammer and Jimbo had risen from the table and were listening as Jago gave them quiet instructions. Martin was on his way out of the mess carrying the empty cauldron. The table was cluttered with dirty plates and cutlery.

'Señorita, tell me,' he coaxed softly, 'what has caused your cheeks to take their colour from winter snow instead of summer roses? If a man is responsible,' he paused, 'I will kill him for you. To mar such beauty with sadness he no longer deserves to live.'

Caseley forced a smile. 'Your gallantry does you credit, señor,' she said lightly. 'Indeed, you are correct. It is a man who occupies my thoughts. A man about whom I care deeply.'

Hammer and Jimbo had gone but Caseley was aware of Jago pausing to listen. She ignored him but could not control her stuttering heartbeat.

'And he does not return your affection.' Antonio made it a statement.

Though she held her smile steady, Caseley knew a moment's anguish. For all his lavish compliments, Antonio Valdes did not *expect* anyone to love her.

As if realising he had made a slip, the Spaniard gazed into her eyes. 'What a fool he must be.' His voice was vibrant, his frown intense.

He had given her the perfect opportunity to offer a reason for her preoccupation. It meant accepting Antonio's true evaluation of her appeal rather than the extravagant compliments he poured over her like rich cream. But what did that matter? Was it not the truth?

'On the contrary, señor,' she corrected, 'my father loves me very much.'

From the corner of her eye she saw Jago's mouth twitch and with a murmured, '*Touché*,' he too left the mess.

'Your *father*?' Antonio repeated.

'He has been ill, and I worry about him. I fear that on occasion my concern outweighs my manners. If I have been a poor table companion, I trust you will forgive me.'

He seized her hand, pressing warm, moist lips against her knuckles. 'Lovely señorita, there is nothing to forgive. Such devotion must be admired. Come, let us go up on deck. There is little air down here, and though the furniture is adequate …' his shrug expressed disdain.

Caseley hesitated, unsure of committing herself. More than anything she wanted to be alone, to rest and think. She slipped out of her seat and as they reached the bottom of the stairs, glimpsed Jago in the day room seated at the table writing in the log. She would find neither peace nor privacy in his company.

'I should enjoy a spell on deck. My father warned of rough weather, so we should make the most of the sunshine.'

'I sincerely hope your father was wrong.' Their feet rang on the brass as Antonio followed her up the stairs. He moved two coils of rope and a bucket further along the cargo hatch, clearing a space for them both to sit.

Caseley looked up at a brilliant blue sky scattered with puffball clouds, enjoying the warm breeze on her face. 'Are you not a good sailor, Señor Valdes?

'Alas no.'

'Then to risk such discomfort you must be anxious to return to Spain.' She was simply making conversation, being polite while half her mind was with the man downstairs.

'I am. Are you aware of events in my country, señorita? The battles? The terrible loss of life?'

Caseley nodded. 'I have read newspaper accounts, but I doubt they describe the true extent of the people's suffering. You have my sympathy, Señor Valdes.'

'We Spaniards are renowned for many things: our wines from Jerez, the windmills of Castile, Seville oranges, the Pamplona bullfights, and even Andalusian flamenco. But it is our fierce pride and religious fervour that sets the Spanish character above all others.'

Caseley considered his statement arrogant, but courtesy would not allow her to argue. Yet though she had not observed anything remotely religious about Jago Barata, other than his occasional blasphemy when she irritated him beyond bearing, and though he was only half-Spanish, he certainly possessed his full share of arrogance.

Antonio smiled, revealing small even teeth. 'I, however, have avoided such excessive rigidity of character. I am altogether more … flexible. A trait my beloved family finds unsettling. But we do agree that it is exhausting to belong to a country which last year had four different presidents.'

'Four?' she echoed in surprise.

'Yet at this moment we do not have even one. Our last president, Castelar, was ousted in a military coup and now General Serrano is back in power.'

'At school I was taught that Spain is a monarchy.'

'Indeed it was, until six years ago when Queen Isabel abdicated.'

'I thought a king or queen reigned until they died. I

cannot imagine Queen Victoria abdicating.'

'The lives of the two queens have little in common,' Antonio said. 'The forty years of Isabel's reign saw the worst scandals and excesses in Spanish history. My people have always been tolerant of small weaknesses in our royalty. But Isabel's behaviour went far beyond the forgivable. At times the court resembled a brothel. Even when the king was alive there was public doubt over who fathered certain of her children.'

Caseley turned her head away, shaken that he would repeat such scurrilous gossip to her.

'Once the junta had got rid of the queen,' he continued, oblivious to her discomfort, 'they declared that due to Isabel's appalling immorality the Bourbon family had forfeited all rights to the crown. When General Serrano was made regent everyone believed it would be the dawn of a new era.'

His tone held cynicism Caseley did not understand. 'Wasn't it?'

'Appointing General Prim as prime minister, Serrano decided Spain would remain a monarchy, but a limited one, with the real power invested in two chambers …'

'Like our Parliament?'

Antonio nodded. 'However, this provoked a revolt among those who were disgusted with the monarchy and wanted Spain to become a republic.'

'But how could the country remain a monarchy if the royal family was no longer permitted to reign?' Caseley was astonished that a queen could behave in such a manner, and a country could be squabbled over.

'Serrano made Prim offer the throne of Spain around Europe.' Once more bitterness curled his mouth. 'But no one wanted it. Eventually he persuaded Amadeo, the second son of King Victor Emmanuel of Italy, to accept it.

Amadeo might even have been a good king for my country.' Antonio shrugged.

'Might have been? But he *accepted* the crown.'

'Yes, he did. But the day Amadeo arrived in Spain, General Prim was murdered.'

As she caught her breath, Antonio spread his hands. 'Amadeo could not speak our language and no longer had a mentor to help him unravel our tangled politics. After two years he gave up the struggle and abdicated.' Antonio lifted one exquisitely tailored shoulder. 'So General Serrano is back in power for a second time. But he has lost patience and now rules as a dictator. Thus my country is relieved of a freedom it could not handle.'

Caseley thought she detected a note of approval. But the impression was fleeting as his tone changed to one of frustration.

'Yet still there is no peace.'

'Why not?'

'Though there are those who support the republic, many of the Spanish people find it totally abhorrent. We are a Catholic country and the monarchists consider the present system a godless regime. But even if the clamour to restore the monarchy gained sufficient power, how are we to choose between two men who both claim to be the rightful king, and who both have armies of supporters?'

'*Two*? But how is that possible?'

Antonio took a breath. 'Over a hundred years ago, Philip V, the first Bourbon King of Spain, passed a law that said no female could succeed to the Spanish throne. Many years later this law was reversed. But the reversal was never made public until Isabel's father, King Ferdinand, announced his wife's pregnancy and declared that boy or girl, the child would be the next sovereign of Spain.'

'Yes,' Caseley nodded, 'and so she was.'

'Indeed. But under the *old* law, Ferdinand's brother, Don Carlos, would have inherited the throne. He and his supporters distrusted the new liberal ideas of Ferdinand and his queen, and were furious with what they considered sacrilegious interference with Divine Right. So the vendetta began. Now Carlos's grandson, also named Carlos, claims to be the legitimate heir to the throne. Meanwhile the Royalists want Isabel's son, Alfonso, to rule.'

Hearing Alfonso's name reminded Caseley of the package, her reason for being aboard *Cygnet*. Trepidation made her tremble inside as she recalled the documents, wrapped in the disguising contract and sealed inside another envelope, hidden among her clothes.

Concerned about her father, desperately anxious to fulfil what might be his last request, and burdened with the realisation of her feelings for Jago, she had pushed the package deep into her bag and out of her mind.

In her possession was something that could have a profound effect on the future of Spain. In the hands of either faction the package would be explosive. But which side was right?

She was only a courier. As soon as she handed the package over, her job would be done and she could go home.

'I fear I have bored you,' Antonio broke into her thoughts.

'Not at all. I appreciate you taking the time to explain.'

'So now you understand it will be easier.'

Caseley wasn't sure what he meant. 'Your people must be suffering greatly during this unrest.'

He moved one shoulder in a careless gesture. 'It is the price of progress.' His gaze sharpened. 'But the instrument of change is within reach.' He smiled. 'Now let us talk of other things. You were telling me about your father.'

'Was I?' Caseley could not remember doing so.

'He sounds a most accomplished man. The name of his shipping agency is not confined to Cornwall. Juan Rodriguez speaks most highly of him.'

'You know Señor Rodriguez?' Caseley asked eagerly. 'I have corresponded with him on my father's behalf and found him charming.' The wine merchant's letters with their courteous old-world phraseology had created in Caseley's mind an image of a tall, silver-haired man of proud bearing and the impeccable manners of a grandee.

'Not personally,' Antonio admitted after a moment's hesitation. 'But his views were passed on in conversation.'

'Oh, I see.' How foolish of her to assume that simply because he was Spanish, Antonio Valdes might know people with whom her father did business.

'Managing such a thriving concern would be demanding even without the added burden of illness,' he gushed. 'Then there are his consular duties. I have heard you are of great assistance.'

Startled, Caseley caught herself. Showing concern would convince him she had something to hide. She softened her dismissive gesture with a smile. 'You flatter me, señor. '

'And you are too modest, señorita. A young woman helping her sick father in such masculine domains as shipping and politics? How could that pass unnoticed?'

Her unease increased. 'My help – such as it was – consisted of paperwork relating to cargoes. It simply released my father from routine matters during his recovery.' What was Antonio Valdes's interest? Where had he obtained his information? Had he learned it from Jago?

Perhaps he had asked who she was and why she was aboard. The thought of them discussing her father or herself was unnerving. She had never pictured Jago as a gossip. In fact the idea seemed impossible. But was it? He had no reason to consider her feelings. Indeed, up to now he seemed to have made a point of *not* doing so.

She realised she was very much alone. As her skin tightened in a shiver she was overwhelmed with relief to see Nathan approaching. Hammer had taken over the wheel.

'Skipper says to come for tea, miss.' The mate sketched a salute. 'You an' all, sir.'

Caseley stood up at once, clinging to the hatch cover for support as she shook out her skirt. Though a command rather than an invitation, it provided escape from a conversation she suspected was more than polite interest. 'There is no hurry,' Antonio protested. 'Let us ignore this tea and take our meal at a more civilised hour.' He patted the hatch beside him.

His warm smile did not disguise his irritation and Caseley was surprised at his thoughtlessness. She remained standing, gently rotating her crippled foot to ease its stiffness.

'Señor, I understand it is the custom in Madrid to take one's evening meal at ten or even later. In English cities dinner may be served at any time between seven and nine. But in Cornwall our habits are different. On board ship tea is not simply a drink. It is the last meal of the day. I'm sure it will be possible to get a mug of cocoa later in the evening when the watch changes. But a seaman's main meal is served in the middle of the day, not at the end.'

He spread his hands, palms up and lifted his shoulders. 'I must submit to this barbaric arrangement or starve?'

Caseley gave a brief nod. 'It would appear so.'

He sighed. 'Then I will come.' He stood and offered his arm.

Though reluctant to take it, she knew it would be foolhardy as well as churlish to refuse. The deck was rising and falling as the schooner cut through the darkening water, and after sitting for so long she had pins and needles in her foot. Yet she knew her instincts had been right when he rested his other hand on top of hers.

'We will talk again, beautiful señorita. We have much to discuss, you and I. Like a flower of many petals you hide yourself.' His voice was husky, his smile intimate. 'But I will pluck those petals one by one.'

Fear trickled, ice-cold, from the nape of her neck to the base of her spine. Pulling her hand free she gripped the handrail and started down the stairs. The intense stress of the past few days had made her over-sensitive. Why else would his words, spoken in such vibrantly romantic tones, sound like a threat?

As she reached the bottom of the stairs with Antonio close behind, Jago emerged from the day room. His cool grey gaze flicked over them both, but it was Caseley he addressed.

'Martin has put hot water by the stove should you wish to wash your hands.'

'Th – thank you.' Caseley stammered in surprise.

He nodded without expression and would have walked on into the mess had Antonio not put out a languid hand to stop him.

'And I, Captain?'

Jago turned his head slowly, looking at the Spaniard's fingers on his shirtsleeve. Only when Antonio had removed them did he raise his head.

'You may do as you choose, Señor Valdes. There are buckets on the cargo hatch and an ocean all around you.'

He nodded briefly and moved on.

Caseley glimpsed barely concealed rage in Antonio's shrug. Excusing herself, she entered the day room and closed the door.

Lifting the lid on top of the cupboard to reveal the basin, she picked up the bucket. It was only a third full but given the movement of the ship, she feared more would end up on the floor than in the basin. Imagining Jago's reaction to that, she set the bucket down again, fetched her soap and towel, and knelt to wash her hands.

Jago need not have agreed to Antonio making the voyage on *Cygnet.* After his initial mistake in believing the Spaniard was the passenger he'd been expecting, he could have refunded whatever Antonio had paid for the trip and referred him to Fox's or Broad's to arrange another berth.

So why had he insisted Antonio remain aboard? It wasn't for the money. Jago was a wealthy man. Given the animosity between them, what reason would be strong enough to force each into the other's presence? The matter had to be urgent.

Antonio had admitted needing a fast passage to Spain. Why? Was it connected with the unrest? Or was it that, like Jago, he had business interests that were under threat? What had he meant by saying that now she knew it would be easier?

Checking her appearance in the mirror, she tidied her hair. She was becoming far too inquisitive. This was a result of listening to Rosina and Liza-Jane gossiping.

Pierced by homesickness she pictured the kitchen: Rosina, red-cheeked from the heat of the range, bustling about getting tea, Liza-Jane holding the doors open for Ben as he brought in the coal. She thought of her father dozing by the fire. Was he all right? Would Ben remember to give him his drops at bedtime?

Fretting was pointless. There was nothing she could do. Placing the bucket between the stove and the cabin door she returned to her bag and lifted out a cloth-wrapped parcel.

When she slipped into her seat the men had already begun eating. For once she was glad Jago Barata set his own rules. Nathan pushed a plate of thickly sliced bread spread with butter towards her, interrupting what he was saying to point to a jar of jam.

''Tis raspberry, miss. Susan, my eldest, made six pound of it this year from our own bushes.'

'Thank you, Nathan.' Realising there was no serving spoon and unwilling to embarrass him she dipped into the jar with her knife.

'Tea, miss?' Jimbo held the battered iron kettle over the mug in front of her. Remembering her father's tales of tea the colour and consistency of tar, she hesitated. But longing for a hot drink overcame her doubts.

'Yes, please.' Dark brown and steaming, it wasn't as bad as she feared. Without a word, Jago placed a jug of condensed milk in front of her and her spirits rose. Lifting the bundle from her lap she set it on the table and opened the cloth.

'These were baked yesterday –'

'Saffern *and* a hevva cake,' Jimbo gasped in awe. 'I 'aven't tasted saffern cake for months. Bless your 'eart, miss.'

'I'll cut 'n,' Nathan insisted as Jimbo reached for the knife. 'Leave it to you and we'll only get half a dozen slices. By your leave, skipper?' he added quickly, glancing at Jago who nodded. His gaze met Caseley's, and his barely visible nod suffused her with warmth. Quickly she looked away. Aware that cake was a rare treat, she had brought it for the men not to win his approval.

'You won't want none, Mart.' Jimbo shook his head at the boy, who was staring round-eyed at the two cakes. One was deep yellow-gold and studded with currants and lemon peel. The other was a square slab just over an inch thick, full of dried fruit. The top was crunchy with sugar and scored in a criss-cross pattern.

'I do too want some,' the boy yelped, blushing as everyone grinned and he realised he had fallen for Jimbo's teasing yet again.

The cakes were sliced and everyone took a piece with a decorum Caseley found touching.

'Cap'n, is it all right if Nathan finish what he was saying 'bout that boat from Peru?' Martin asked.

Jago gestured to the mate. 'Carry on, Nathan.'

The mate washed down the last crumbs of his cake with tea. 'Well, knowing 'twas a long trip home and the captain's mortal remains wouldn't keep, the mate had the body stuffed with *guano* –'

'Excuse me,' Antonio broke in. 'What is this *guano*?'

'Bird shit,' Jimbo said, 'begging your pardon, miss.'

Caseley swallowed and simply nodded, hard-pressed to hide her smile. After a bewildered moment, Antonio's eyes widened and he studied the slice of saffron cake on his plate.

'They buried the coffin three foot deep in the hold,' Nathan continued. 'When the ship reached Falmouth, they dug 'n out and he looked as good as the day he died. Smelled a bit ripe, but you can't have everything. Anyhow, they took 'n over to St Ives where he come from, and buried 'n there in the churchyard like he always wanted.'

''Tis the lime,' Jimbo announced. 'Keep a body in lime for years you could.'

'Know about that, do you, boy? Got a few in your garden, have you?'

'Jimbo, tell 'em about Captain Evans,' Martin nudged the stocky seaman. 'Go on.'

Jago poured himself another cup of tea.

'Well, Hammer and me wasn't on board ourselves, but our cousin Arfie was. He swore 't was God's honest truth. See, Captain Evans was master of *Odette*, a tea-clipper out of China. He took sick with some bug out there. The cap'n I mean, not Arfie. Anyhow, he died. Cap'n's wife was with 'n and she said she wasn't going to have 'n buried in no heathen country. He had to be brought home. Well, you know what the heat is like out there. He wasn't going to be very sweet after three weeks at sea.' A master storyteller who relished his audience's attention, Jimbo paused.

'The cap'n had always run a dry ship. Both he and Mrs Evans was teetotal and they never allowed so much as a drop of liquor on any vessel under his command. But there was only one way missus was going to get her man home for burying all in one piece, so to speak. She had to have 'n put in a barrel filled up with alcohol.'

His grin gleeful, Martin wriggled on the bench.

'That's almost poetic,' Jago mused.

'Pickled,' Nathan guffawed. 'And the poor soul wasn't even alive to enjoy it.'

'Ah, but that isn't all,' Jimbo said quietly, his eyes dancing as everyone turned to him once more. 'Mrs Evans couldn't understand how the crew was so cheerful, specially after they was caught in a typhoon four days out. She asked the mate and he told her that though the cap'n was gone the whole crew was uplifted by his spirit. That was God's honest truth too. When *Odette* reached port and the barrel was opened, the cap'n's body was fresh as a daisy. But there wasn't a drop of alcohol left.'

After a moment's stunned silence, the small mess erupted in laughter. Shocked, Caseley couldn't suppress her giggles. Excusing herself, she returned to the cabin for her paisley shawl and, swirling it around her shoulders, went up on deck.

Hammer was at the wheel. He nodded shyly then gazed resolutely forward as, embarrassed but determined, she passed him and opened the door in the side of the wheel shelter.

When she emerged, her chest hurting from holding her breath against the carbolic-laced stench, she saw Martin a few feet away. He had the heavy copper stern light on deck and was topping up the oil and trimming the wick.

She made her way forward to the companionway. Leaning against the side, she wrapped the shawl more closely and looked westward to the setting sun. As the huge orange ball sank towards the sea, the sky changed from deep rose to pale pink and gold. The small clouds that had speckled the sky during the afternoon had melted away.

'Looks like she's set fair again tomorrow,' Nathan said, appearing at the hatch. 'If the wind hold steady, we should make port in three days.' He nodded at her and went aft to take the wheel from Hammer.

Caseley watched the sun disappear, swallowed by the ocean. Jimbo and Martin moved about on deck. The port and starboard lights in the mainmast rigging glowed ruby and emerald. At the stern an arc of white light played over their wake. No longer warmed by the sun the breeze was chilly. She shivered and, bidding Nathan goodnight, went below.

Reaching the bottom of the stairs she heard Jago's voice. Pitched too low for her to distinguish the words, there was no doubting his anger. She hesitated, unsure what to do. Then she realised the voices were coming from Nathan's cabin, now occupied by Antonio Valdes.

Quickly entering the day room she closed the door. Warmth radiated from the crackling stove and the mellow lamplight made the cabin feel cosy. The chart was rolled up and pushed to the back of the table and the leaf had been folded down.

As she tossed her shawl onto her bunk there was a single rap on the door. She opened it and stood back as Martin staggered in, a loaded coalscuttle in one hand, a bucket half-full of steaming water in the other.

'Beg pardon, miss. I had to kick 'n 'cos I had both hands full.' He set the coalscuttle on one side of the stove, the bucket on the other, closest to the sleeping cabin.

'Thank you, Martin. How thoughtful –'

'Cap'n's orders, miss,' he blurted, blushing. ''E said you got the place to yourself til ten.'

'Oh. I see.' Recovering, she smiled at him. 'You must be busy enough without these extra duties. I'm very grateful.'

''Tisn't no trouble, miss.' As he reached the door he grinned over his shoulder. 'Handsome bit of cake that was.' He hurried out, pulling the door shut behind him.

Taking off her jacket, Caseley fetched her soap, towel, and nightgown. Starting to unbutton her bodice, she glanced up and realised that the skylight was an illuminated window revealing most of the day room to anyone who cared to look in.

Hot with embarrassment, she carried her things back into the tiny sleeping cabin and dropped them on the bunk. She could not pull the curtain over for that would cut out all the light. Instead she placed the bucket in the doorway and moved round behind it. There wasn't much room, but at least she could not be seen.

Twenty minutes later, after a strip-wash that left her feeling clean, fresh, and very tired, she pulled on her nightgown. After brushing and braiding her hair into a thick plait that fell over one shoulder, she put on her cape. Slipping her bare feet into her shoes she opened the door, starting as she came face to face with Jago.

'Where are you going?' He raked her with angry eyes.

'I – to empty this.' She hefted the bucket forward. 'Martin will need –'

'I'll see to it.' He was curt.

'Thank you.' She turned away.

'Caseley?'

She looked round. His voice held a note she had not heard before. In the lamplight his expression was forbidding and his eyes glittered.

'Yes?' Her heart thumped.

He stared at her, unspeaking. The tension emanating from him hinted at an inner battle. He shook his head. 'Nothing. Go to bed.' He turned and lifting the bucket in front of him, went swiftly up the stairs.

'Goodnight,' she murmured, and quietly closed the door.

Caseley woke with a start and for a moment could not remember where she was. Then it all flooded back. She lay, listening intently, waiting for a repeat of the sound that had woken her. But apart from the rattle of the steering gear, the creaking of the ship's timbers, and the hiss of water against the hull, there was nothing.

Pushing back the blankets she swung her feet to the floor and peeped round the half-drawn curtain into the day room. It was empty. The lamp was out and the grey light of dawn filtered through the skylight. She saw the bucket, once again half full of steaming water. It must have been the door closing that woke her.

She washed quickly and put on the same skirt and blouse she had worn the previous day. She had replaced the bucket by the stove and was in front of the mirror brushing her hair when the door opened.

She whirled round as Jago walked in, her hair flying like a red-gold banner. Their eyes met, held. She saw his hair was damp. His beard gleamed as if that too was wet. In one hand he carried a brass sextant, in the other a towel.

His shirt was open to the waistband of his trousers and she glimpsed black, curling hair on his chest. Realising suddenly that she had been staring, and hot beneath his amused gaze, she turned back to the mirror, wielding the brush with fierce strokes, sweeping through the tumbling mane until it crackled.

Jago dropped his towel on the bench seat and replaced the sextant in a lined wooden box lying on the table beside the open log. Aware of him close behind her, she lowered her arms and turned, ready to move out of his way. He reached up to stow the box in a locker.

'You slept well?' he asked without looking at her.

'Yes. I didn't expect to but – Yes I did. It must be all the fresh air.' She felt nervous, jumpy. 'And the movement. I'm hungry too.' She edged out from behind the table. 'Is breakfast ready?'

'Give the boy a chance.' His tone was mild but it brought a flush to her cheeks. 'Hold that a moment, will you?' He pushed the rolled-up chart into her arms and leaned down to raise the table leaf, slotting the supporting leg into place.

As he straightened she offered him the chart. Ignoring it, he lifted a lock of hair that had fallen forward over her shoulder, studying it as though mesmerised.

Common sense told her to step back, or knock his hand

away and bundle her hair into its confining net. But she couldn't move, couldn't breathe.

He lifted his gaze and their eyes met. She swallowed. Her heart skipped a beat. Holding the chart in one hand and her brush in the other, she felt trapped, helpless. She wanted to run, but there was nowhere to hide. Still his hand moved in her hair, running it through his fingers as if testing its weight, its texture.

'Listen to me.' He spoke softly. 'Stay away from Valdes.'

The words seemed come from far away. Then they registered, bringing her back to reality with a jarring thud.

'Why? You have refused my offer of help. You tell me I must not distract the crew. Señor Valdes provides pleasant company and conversation.'

Jago's lip curled. 'So I noticed. Nevertheless, I think it wiser that you do not spend time with him.' Gently he twisted her hair around his hand, preventing her from moving. 'Do I make myself clear?'

'What is your objection?' She pushed aside her doubts about the Spaniard, whose cheerful flirtatious countenance had twice cracked to reveal an entirely different personality.

'Did you not want us out of your way?' She moved, expecting him to release her hair. Instead he tightened his grip. Shock rather than pain caused her breath to catch and tears to form. She blinked them away.

'You are not stupid, so don't play the fool,' he grated. 'Valdes is a Basque. He has a silver tongue but few scruples. If he believes you have something he wants, he will stop at nothing – and I mean *nothing* – to get it. *Now* do you understand? You are playing with fire, Caseley.'

'No,' she began, intending to tell him she knew full well that Antonio Valdes was not serious, that his flattery and conversation were only a means of passing time. But she froze as she recognised an alternative interpretation of Jago's warning. If she had something? The documents? Was that why he had explained in such detail about the political situation in Spain?

No, it could not be. No one but she and her father knew about them. The package had come direct from Mexico, the seal unbroken. Even if by some terrible misfortune Antonio Valdes was aware of their existence, he could not know they were in her possession. Her father would never have betrayed that trust and she had said nothing. Nor would she. Even Jago had no idea of the real reason she was aboard. *Or did he?*

His warning echoed in her head. 'You have something he wants.'

Did Jago know? If so, how had he found out? Did it mean he was in league with Valdes? She could not believe that. Their patent dislike of each other was no pretence. But nor would it matter. Jago was half-Spanish. He would care about the country of his forefathers. He would have his own beliefs about what was right for Spain.

If he and Antonio Valdes were of the same mind, and were offered the opportunity to assist their chosen leader, where would Jago's loyalties lie? With the Cornishman whose schooner he commanded? Or with the Spaniard he loathed? Yet what if that apparent loathing was indeed a ruse?

All this raced through her mind at lightning speed. No matter what either of them suspected, they had no proof, and she would not break her oath of secrecy to her father.

Not knowing whom to trust, she could trust no one. She had to pretend the documents did not exist. Future conversations with Antonio Valdes would require extreme caution. But right now she needed to convince Jago that

Valdes's interest was purely personal.

'You –' Her voice cracked and she had to clear her throat. 'You are mistaken. Señor Valdes is a gentleman.' She desperately hoped he would interpret her trembling as indignation. 'He would not take advantage. Anyway,' she said recklessly as he shook his head in disgust, 'you are in no position to condemn my behaviour, or anyone else's.'

Immediately the words were spoken she wished them unsaid. His face darkened ominously and his eyes turned as cold as arctic seas. Releasing her hair, he gripped her shoulders, his fingers digging into her flesh.

The brush fell unnoticed to the deck. Her breath sobbed in her throat as he pulled her towards him and her hands flew up to fend him off. Her heart leapt in a dark tangle of fear and shocking excitement.

One hand snaked round her waist, the other grasped the nape of her neck, effectively immobilising her. One black brow rose.

'Jealous, Caseley?'

'Don't be ridiculous.' She meant it to sound scathing, a rebuff of his massive conceit. But the look in his eyes and the unyielding hardness of his body against hers were stopping her breath, sapping her will.

'Let me go,' she pleaded, her voice unsteady. She could feel her strength ebbing and a treacherous weakness stealing along her limbs. 'I – I'm sorry.'

He frowned. 'For what?'

'Anything. I should not have said ... Don't, please ... don't ...' Her voice faded to a strangled whisper as his head lowered to hers, blotting out the light.

'Hush,' he said against her mouth. For a moment neither moved. Then a tremor rippled through him. As Caseley's hands pushed against his chest, his lips covered hers.

Chapter Fourteen

She hadn't known what to expect: perhaps demand, even anger. But his mouth moved on hers with heart-stopping tenderness. Her eyes closed and she was falling, flying. His lips were warm, soft. Helpless against their gentle pressure hers parted.

Her heart cried out to him as her body lost its rigidity and became pliant. It fitted against his as if created for this moment, for him.

Her fingers spread, sliding through the silky black hair. Beneath the searing heat of his skin she could feel the rapid thunder of his heartbeat, and was awed.

With a groan he tore his mouth from hers, his breathing harsh, and she gave a soft inarticulate cry of loss. Gripping her upper arms he held her away, his face a taut mask. His eyes blazed with emotions she did not understand.

Releasing her without a word, he turned swiftly and strode out. She staggered against the table, hearing the clang of his quick footsteps on the stairs.

Bereft, she lifted a hand to touch her mouth. Reaction set in and she began to shake, hugging herself as she trembled. An aching void yawned in the pit of her stomach.

Shame and doubt bubbled up like marsh gas. He had a mistress. Why had he kissed her? A whim? Punishment for her defiance? Why had she let him? Not merely allowed, but responded, welcomed. She had been waiting without knowing what for. Now she knew. But that joyous moment of recognition had been shattered into jagged shards by his rejection and abrupt departure.

A wrenching sigh sobbed in her throat. Why had he come into her life? He had stirred hopes she had deliberately suppressed, disrupted an existence she had tried to fill with meaning by caring for her father, running the house, and shouldering the responsibility of protecting him and the business.

It would have been better if she had never met him. She would have dreamed, yearned, but she wouldn't have *known.* Knowing made loss agonising.

She pressed her fingertips to the throbbing ache in her forehead. The day had only just begun. There were meals to attend and the crew to face, as well as Antonio Valdes. She *had* to pull herself together.

She ran her tongue over her lips, tasting him. She could still feel the sensation of his mouth on hers, still smell his skin. She scooped up the now-cool water to bathe her face again and erase every trace. But it was too late. Jago Barata had left his mark on her as surely as if he had used a branding iron.

She could not begin to guess at his motive. He had seemed reluctant but driven. As his lips had touched hers, his hunger and barely controlled violence had shocked her. Yet she had not been frightened, nor had she fought.

His mouth had softened like a sigh, and he had stirred an aching sweetness so exquisite her heart had stumbled. Then he had gone, leaving a gaping wound.

With unsteady fingers she twisted her hair into a thick coil on her nape and anchored it with pins. She would not think about him. She could as easily stop breathing. His presence was all around. She was living in his cabin. She had slept in his bunk. His hand had penned the flowing writing in the log. And her body still quivered from his touch.

There was no escape.

Unwilling to face a truth she had no idea how to deal with, she avoided the mirror. Instead she tidied away her soap, flannel, and toothbrush, folded her nightgown, plumped the pillow, and straightened the blankets on her bunk. The tasks soothed her so that when Martin knocked she was able to open the door and greet him with a mask of calm firmly in place.

‘'Morning, miss. All right if I fetch the bread and milk? Breakfast'll be ready in a few minutes.'

'Thank you. I'll bring the bucket –'

'No, miss. Cap'n wouldn't like that. You leave 'n there and I'll fetch 'n d'rectly.'

Her stomach clenched into a small hard knot as she sat down opposite Hammer and Jimbo. Making an effort to smile she returned their greetings, dreading the moment when Jago would join them. Antonio came in, freshly shaved and trailing the scent of soap and cologne. Nathan followed, his expression betraying amusement and scorn. Caseley realised Jago must be at the wheel. That meant he would eat later.

Relief left her weak. For a moment she wondered if he might be avoiding her, but dismissed the notion. He had made it clear that her presence on board would not be permitted to affect the ship's routine.

So she had to hide a start of surprise when she heard Hammer ask Nathan why the skipper was on an eight to noon watch when he had already put in an extra two hours during the night.

The mate shrugged. 'He'll have his reasons. He want you to check the repair on the spare mainsail and re-stitch 'n if he's loose, all right?'

Hammer nodded, his mouth full.

'Going to strip and grease the dolly winch, he was,' Jimbo put in.

'That'll keep. Do 'n after.'

Antonio frowned at the boiled oatmeal Nathan ladled onto his plate, then turned to Caseley.

'Buenas dias, guapa señorita.'

'Good morning, Señor Valdes.'

He studied her. 'Something is wrong. What is it? You must tell me.'

Caseley looked at her plate, and carefully lifted a spoonful of oatmeal to which she had added treacle and a little milk. Surely it could not be that obvious? The others had greeted her quite normally. There had been no lingering glances or questioning frowns. He was guessing, she realised. More than that, he seemed hopeful. Pushing thoughts of Jago to the back of her mind, she closed a door on them.

'You are mistaken, Señor. Nothing is wrong. Why should you think there is?'

His gaze was speculative, assessing. 'Because –' he answered in Spanish, 'yesterday I was a brute. I told you sad tales of my country. These are not your problems. But to engage your interest, your sympathy, I did this cruel thing. I asked questions, wanting to learn about you and your family. My only excuse is that though Fate has brought us together, it is for so short a time. But you will be in my heart forever.' He brought his head close to hers. 'Do you believe in love at first sight, señorita? I did not,' he paused, 'until yesterday.'

Caseley looked away from his smouldering gaze, and toyed with her oatmeal, her cheeks on fire.

Nathan pushed the jug of milk towards her, his frowning gaze darting between her and the Spaniard.

She did not know what to say. For an instant she had

been tempted to laugh. But he was so abject, so sincere, she felt ashamed of the impulse.

Then, like a feather brushing over her skin, came realisation. His impassioned plea had been made entirely in Spanish. Despite telling him yesterday that she spoke little of the language, she had been too taken aback to interrupt or claim that she did not understand.

She glanced up, met his gaze, and saw only admiration. Maybe she had been wrong about him. Maybe her overwrought imagination had seen intrigue and threat where none existed. His forcefulness and inquisitorial manner had unsettled her. But, as Miss Amelia had often remarked, the Latin temperament was volatile, impatient, and passionate, and thus not easy for the cool, phlegmatic English to understand.

Caseley had wondered how Miss Amelia knew. Had she reached this conclusion through her studies of Spanish art and literature? Or had she in her younger days known a man like Antonio Valdes? Had she loved and lost?

'*Madre de Dios*,' he swore under his breath. 'I am a clumsy fool. My head counsels silence but my heart must speak. And the heart is always stronger, *no es verdad?* Your pardon, señorita, I beg you.'

Caseley was thoroughly unsettled. She had not invited his attention – had she? Could she, simply through not wanting to appear discourteous, have given him the impression that she welcomed his declarations? She didn't.

Perhaps someone more experienced might laugh them off and do so without causing offence. But she didn't have that experience. No one had ever spoken of love to her. Common sense told her he didn't mean it. He was exaggerating, though she had no idea why.

Nathan cleared his throat. 'Come on, miss. You got to

do better 'n that, else the skipper'll have my hide.' He indicated the plate she had hardly touched. 'Want a drop more milk do you?'

Unable to watch her himself, Jago had detailed the mate to do it and no matter what his own feelings were, Nathan would obey his captain.

'No, thank you, Mr Ferris, this is fine.' She made herself swallow a spoonful of the glutinous porridge. She knew she needed the nourishment. Nor did she want to put the mate in the position of having to report her. She sensed his discomfort, and none of this was his fault.

'What is this?' Antonio demanded in a low voice. 'The captain is surely exceeding his authority. It is unforgivable. I will speak with him.'

'No.' Caseley surprised herself with her firmness. 'That is not necessary. Captain Barata is responsible for my welfare while I am aboard. He is only saying what my father would say were he here.'

Antonio leaned towards her. 'What would your father say to you sharing the captain's cabin, señorita? Is that also necessary for your welfare?'

Caseley's face flamed. 'I – I – '

'Señorita,' he interrupted with smooth concern. 'You are a lady of sensitivity, as yet unmarried. Such an unorthodox arrangement must be deeply distressing for you. When I learned you were to travel with us I offered my cabin. I was told to mind my own business. It seems the captain is a law unto himself. But what are his reasons for forcing such embarrassment upon you? No man of honour would'

'Please excuse me, señor.' Caseley pushed her barely touched plate away and stood up.

'Can you trust him?' Antonio hissed. 'What does he want from you?'

'Miss –' Nathan began.

'It's all right, Nathan. I'm – I just need –' Shaking her head she fled.

She wanted to hide in the day room, not see or speak to anyone. She needed to think. She hadn't had time to wonder how the arrangements might appear to anyone else. The crew had made little of it. But they must be curious. Unless – Had this happened before? Were they used to seeing a woman on board?

No. Instinct told her that was not so. If they showed little reaction it was because they were well-disciplined and they trusted Jago. His reasons were not their business. But clearly Antonio saw something sinister in it, and he had reawakened all her doubts.

Jago had said it was for her protection. Against what or whom? *He* had kissed her. *He* was trying to stop her talking to Antonio. *Why*?

She hesitated at the bottom of the stairs. She did not want to see Jago. The memory of his kiss was still too vivid. Just thinking of it made her heart turn over. But she *had* to go to the wheel shelter.

Her heart quickened as she climbed the stairs. The breeze was fresh and tasted of salt. All the sails were full. She clung to the top of the gunwale as she made her way aft, the wind blowing into her face over the port quarter.

Jago stood behind the massive oak wheel, the wind billowing his shirt, his booted feet apart, balanced against the schooner's motion. His hands rested lightly on the varnished spokes and his gaze shifted from sea to sails then to the compass as he held their course, harnessing the power of wind and current to coax all possible speed from the graceful vessel.

The schooner's bow rose and she was suddenly conscious of the size of the seas around them. The deep water was inky blue and streaked with foam blown back from the wave crests. Carried forward on a rolling mass of water, *Cygnet* met a cross sea with her head down. As her prow carved a path through, a cloud of spray flew skyward and Caseley gasped as some of it caught her, stippling her blouse and trickling down one side of her face and neck.

'Get below,' Jago bellowed as she gripped the rail with one hand using the other to wipe cold salt water from her stinging eyes.

She shook her head and released the rain to lurch across to the wheel shelter.

'Are you sick?' He had to shout above the din created by the wind shrieking through the sheets and shrouds and the creaking blocks.

'No,' she yelled back, her face burning as she fumbled with the latch.

With a brief nod he looked down to check the compass once more. He might have been a stranger. Yet his strong arms had held her close and his mouth had caressed hers with a sweetness she would never have suspected in him.

She almost fell into the tiny shack. Fortunately the bucket was empty except for a puddle of carbolic whose powerful smell caught in her throat. She wondered which of the crew had the unenviable task of cleaning it and sympathised, realising how much she took for granted at home.

As she swayed back to the companionway she could feel Jago's eyes on her. The temptation to look round was almost irresistible. But pride gave her the strength she needed. He had walked away without a word. Even now, though they were alone on deck, not by a word or a smile had he so much as hinted that anything had occurred between them.

Maybe as far as he was concerned it hadn't. Maybe it

had slipped from his mind, an impulse acted on and dismissed. Not important enough even to be regretted. Simply forgotten.

She hurried back to the day cabin, her head down, nearly tripping in her haste to be alone as scalding tears spilled down her cheeks. Hurt, bewildered, hating herself and him, she curled up on the bunk. But the harder she tried to untangle her thoughts, the more confused she became. What to believe? Whom to trust?

At dinnertime, pride and reluctance to give Jago reason to criticise her forced her into the mess. She ate as much as she could, conscious of his rare glances, and remembered to thank Martin, who reddened and was at once teased by the rest of the crew.

Escaping back to the cabin, she brought a book from her bag and curled up in one corner at the stern end of the bench to read.

Jago came in a little later. The atmosphere changed in an instant, becoming charged with tension. Bending over the table to enter details of their course and the weather into the log he asked if she had everything she needed. She thanked him politely and said she did. Then he left. But the tension lingered on.

Towards late afternoon, Antonio Valdes knocked softly, claiming an urgent need to talk to her. She did not open the door, grateful for the barrier as she pleaded a headache. After sowing further seeds of doubt as to her safety under Jago's so-called protection, he left.

Tea followed a similar pattern. When, to settle an argument, Jimbo wanted her opinion about the best way to cook pigs' trotters, Jago answered, deftly steering the conversation away from her. Yet instead of feeling excluded or rebuffed, she was relieved and grateful. The men took their cue from him. While giving her an occasional nod or smile to acknowledge her presence at the table, they left her alone.

Only Antonio persisted in trying to draw her out. But after his third attempt to begin a private conversation with her in Spanish earned him a cutting rebuke from Jago, he subsided into simmering silence.

As soon as she had finished eating, Caseley excused herself, left the table, and went up on deck. Hammer was at the wheel and after a nod and smile, made a point of checking the compass and looking up at the sails as she went to the wheel shelter.

When she came out the sun had set, leaving a blood-red stain on the horizon. In the twilight, stars were beginning to appear. A cold pale moon hung low in the dusky sky. With nothing but sea all around her she felt very small and insignificant. She moved down the deck, staying on the seaward side, filling her lungs with cold fresh air as she gripped the rail and gazed out across foam-tipped waves.

Thinking about home she wondered how her father was. She did not hear Jago's footsteps. But she was suddenly aware of him behind her. She could feel his presence, the warmth of his body across the inches that separated them. Tension crawled along her nerves. She shivered, craving and dreading his hand on her shoulder or cupping her elbow. But he did not touch her.

'Come below.' His deep voice was gentle, but the words were an order. There was nothing to be gained by arguing. She obeyed without looking round.

When she reached the day room, Martin had lit the stove and the cabin was warm and welcoming. Her heart quickened and a mixture of fear and anticipation rippled through her as Jago followed her in and closed the door.

Chapter Fifteen

She walked to the table and stood with her back to him, waiting.

'I have a request,' he spoke quietly.

She stiffened, mentally sifting through all the requests he might make. Only one sprang to mind. She half-turned, not meeting his eyes. 'If this concerns Antonio Valdes –'

'Valdes is the least of my concerns at the moment. I want you to write some letters.'

She swung round in surprise, watching as he opened a locker and took out a metal box. Lifting the lid he removed several sheets of paper covered in his bold scrawl. Laying the sheets on the table, he took out fresh paper, a pen, and a bottle of ink. Clearing a space on the shelf, he set the box on it out of the way.

'As you see I have already made notes. The letters are to my father's agent in Madrid, the Bilbao port authority, the British consul there, and one to Señor Esteban Cervantes who is a ship broker in Bilbao with contacts in other Spanish ports.'

'Why me?

Jago sat down and pulled the log towards him. 'You have a neat hand and you write fluent Spanish.' He paused. 'Besides, I am very busy. You are not.'

It was no more than the truth. She slid onto the bench opposite. Picking up the scribbled notes she began to read through them, then looked across at Jago who met her startled glance with perfect calm.

She resumed reading, scanning the pages faster and faster. Then she went back and re-read to make sure she was not mistaken.

When she finished she looked up in disbelief. 'You are selling your schooner, *Cara*, and disposing of all your business interests in Spain?'

'Ah, my writing is not as poor as I feared.' He picked up his own pen and began to make entries in the log. 'I know I can leave the correct phrasing to you,' he said without looking up.

'Why?'

He reached up and tapped the barometer, making another entry on the page. 'You are practised at writing business letters for your father. The one concerning the steam pumping engine for the silver mine in Mexico was an excellent example. Write something along those lines.' His dark head was bent over the log.

'No, I meant why are you selling everything?'

He looked up then, turning the pen between his fingers. One corner of his mouth lifted. 'Caseley, I asked you to write some letters, not question my decisions.'

The flush started at her chest and rushed up to her scalp. His rebuke was far milder than she deserved. 'I beg your pardon. I did not – that was impertinent of me.'

She drew fresh paper towards her and lifting the first sheet of notes. But she could not focus on the words. This was his private business. Yet though he would not tell her *why* he was selling all his Spanish interests, and she certainly had no right to ask, clearly he did not object to her knowing.

In asking her to write the letters it was as if he *wanted* her to know. Why? Perhaps he was simply using her to get a tedious chore done quickly while keeping her occupied and away from Antonio Valdes.

Why had he said that Valdes was the least of his concerns? He had been concerned enough to forbid *her* any contact with the Spaniard.

Some sixth sense told her Jago was watching her. Feeling a warm tide creep up her face she peeped up from under her lashes and met his ironic gaze. Quickly picking up her pen she uncorked the ink, moved the notes to one side, dipped the nib, and began to write.

For a while the only sounds were the creak of the ship, the thump and hiss of water along the hull, and the scratch of pens. Then Jago broke the silence.

'Do you know the name of the ship carrying that engine to Mexico?'

Caseley looked up, shaking her head. 'I don't, but Uncle Richard should.'

'I called into the office the day before we sailed. Unfortunately he wasn't there.'

'Is it important?'

He shrugged. 'The cargo I'm collecting is also bound for Mexico. It would have saved time if I could have got it on the same ship.'

'Will there be room? The engine is not small and is additional to the load already booked in. What is your cargo?'

'Mercury,' Jago replied. 'Ten iron containers of quicksilver. My father needs it urgently at his mine.'

'Oh.' She nodded.

Jago watched her for a moment then started to laugh, a deep-throated sound, full of warmth. She glanced at him and her heart leapt, for the warmth was also in his eyes, along with a teasing light. 'Go on, then.'

'I don't know what you mean,' she retorted, feeling her colour rise and helpless to stop it.

'Yes, you do,' he shot back. 'You have a questioning

mind, Caseley. It's one of the things I –' He broke off abruptly. He was gripping the pen so hard she tensed, expecting it to snap. Then he continued. 'You want to know what the mercury is for.' He made it a statement.

'Yes,' she admitted. 'I did wonder.'

'It's used in the refining of silver.'

'I thought silver was found in nuggets, like gold.'

Jago nodded. 'It can be, has been, in some places. Nuggets weighing hundreds of pounds have been dug up in Mexico and Canada. But most silver is a by-product of other ores such as copper, lead or zinc. Before my father moved to Mexico and left them to me, he owned refineries in Oviedo and Ciudad Real in the south of New Castile. Mercury is used in the extraction process.'

Resting her elbows on the table, Caseley supported her chin on her fists. Heat from the crackling stove and soft lamplight made the turbulence of wind and ocean outside seem far away. The conversation's shift to less personal topics had helped her relax. Though the atmosphere in the tiny cabin still held the tension that seemed inevitable when they were together, over it lay a new and gentler intimacy.

'How does it work?' she asked.

Jago studied her, a faint frown creasing his forehead. As the silence lengthened and his scrutiny continued, she became self-conscious. Why did he stare so?

'You really want to know?' His tone held both surprise and irony.

'I would not have asked otherwise. Haven't you just commented on my curious mind? But if you're too busy –'

'No, I –' Setting the pen aside, he leaned back, stretching his arms out, his strong brown hands spread flat on the table. 'You constantly surprise me, though I should know better. First the ore is finely ground,' he said before she could respond. 'Then it is mixed with water and mercury and shaken. The mercury breaks up into globules and dissolves the silver in the ore. When this amalgam is heated the mercury evaporates, condenses, and is collected for further use while the silver is left behind. Inevitably some mercury is lost during processing, so my father has regular shipments sent out to him. But the fighting has caused disruption and shipments have been delayed.'

Glancing at the clock he rose to his feet, his black curls almost touching the deck-head at the edge of the skylight. He went to the door. 'I'll send Martin with some hot water. Don't worry about finishing the letters tonight. We won't arrive in Santander until late tomorrow.' He held her gaze for a moment.

His grey eyes seemed to pierce her soul and she looked down. She carried too many secrets and their weight was becoming an intolerable burden. The door closed quietly.

Alone again, she realised how easily he had captured her attention, re-directed it, allowing her to forget for a while her doubts and fears.

Self-disgust consumed her. She had only to listen to Jago to be drawn under his spell. Had it taken only a single kiss to demolish her defences, destroy her sense of balance? She had no idea where she stood in his estimation. Was *useful* all she would ever be to him?

Antonio had declared himself in love with her. Yet his fervent whispers inspired only laughter and unease, though good manners demanded she conceal both.

When Jago had kissed her, his heart had beat against her palm as hard and fast as her own, and Antonio's warnings had crumbled to dust.

She buried her face in her hands. Jago's kiss had shown her something she had never known. Then he had left without a word, leaving her tortured by dreams that had no future.

She was neither beautiful nor experienced in the arts of pleasing a man, and Jago Barata could have his pick of women who were both.

She pictured Tamsyn and Liza-Jane. Love had made them happy. They glowed with pride and contentment. For her, love was a double-edged sword of ecstasy and pain that would destroy her if she did not fight it.

Sitting up, she dropped her hands and looked at the notes. Her eyes burned and her head felt heavy. Smothering a yawn she gathered all the papers neatly into the tin. She still had another day in which to complete them.

She undressed, then brushed and braided her hair. Worn out by stress and the ship's plunging and rising, she climbed into the bunk, turned onto her side, and closed her eyes.

When she woke, grey light at the edge of the curtain told her dawn had broken. Sitting up and pushing the heavy plait back over her shoulder, she recalled troubling dreams and a vague memory of a quiet voice drawing her out of the nightmare that had smothered her. Her feverish body had calmed and she had slipped once more into sleep, this time deep and restful.

Hot water waited in the bucket beside the stove. After washing, she put on a clean shift and fresh bodice of cream cotton sprigged with tiny green and yellow flowers. She loosened her hair from its braid, brushed it thoroughly then twisted and coiled it into a net on her nape held in place by hand-painted slides.

She arrived in the mess as Jago was finishing his breakfast.

'Good morning.' His searching look as she sat down made her heart contract.

'Good morning,' she nodded round the table.

''Morning, miss,' Nathan, Hammer, and Martin responded then turned to Jago who was issuing the daily orders. Antonio did not smile and his narrowed gaze held bitter condemnation.

Guessing what was in his mind, Caseley was tempted to try and reassure him. The impulse swiftly passed. She owed him no explanations. She had done nothing wrong.

She ate a small dish of oatmeal and a ship's biscuit spread with treacle. After a cup of hot strong tea, she quietly excused herself and went up on deck, enjoying a sense of wellbeing she had never known before. Unwilling to examine it, she simply accepted, and was grateful.

Jimbo was at the wheel and bawled a cheery greeting. ''Morning, miss. 'Andsome day, isn't it?'

With her visits to the wheel shelter tactfully ignored by the crew, her embarrassment lessened each time.

When she emerged, Antonio was waiting near the companionway and begged her to come to his cabin. 'I have proof you are in grave danger,' he muttered urgently. 'Señorita, you are being led into a trap.'

Before she could ask him to explain, Jago appeared. Not sparing the Spaniard a glance, he took her arm in a gentle grip. 'Would you care to take a turn around the deck, Miss Bonython? Or are you ready to complete my letters?' While speaking he led her to the hatch and followed her down the stairs to the day room.

Unnerved by Antonio's hoarse warning and her inability to fight Jago's effect on her, she stopped at the door. 'Will you stop treating me like a – a prisoner?' she hissed as he leaned past to open it.

He raised one dark brow. 'I wasn't aware of doing so.'

'No, you call it protection,' she retorted, heat climbing her throat. 'I don't need it.'

'I think you do.' He was calm, implacable.

'I was only on deck a few minutes. I needed to – I wanted some fresh air.'

He nodded, guided her gently inside the cabin and closed the door. Only then did he release her arm. Without the warmth of her palm it felt cold and she rubbed it absently.

'What poison was Valdes dripping into your pretty ears this time?'

Caseley was shaken. How did he know? He could not have heard. *Pretty*? She struggled to concentrate. 'What do you mean? Why would he –?' His steady gaze stopped her. Why did she find it impossible to lie to this man?

'You have something he wants, Caseley. He will use any means he can to gain your confidence and destroy your trust in me.'

Pausing, he turned a page of the log over and back. 'The usual method for a man to get his way with an inexperienced, impressionable young woman is to tell her he had fallen helplessly in love with her. Even normally sensible and intelligent women are too easily taken in.'

'You speak from experience, no doubt,' she flung at him, mortified as she recalled Antonio's declaration.

'I have never found it necessary to resort to such tactics.'

No, he wouldn't have. She turned away and limped to the table, not wanting him to see her hurt, her shame. Was it so obvious that she had never been sought after, never desired, never been in love? She closed her eyes, gripping the edge of the table. Just for an instant she had believed Antonio's declaration. Jago knew, and pitied her. She cleared her throat.

'You don't like him.' Her voice sounded thin.

'No, I don't.' There was no emotion in Jago's reply. He

was simply stating a fact.

Caseley turned. 'Then why did you accept him as a passenger?'

'I owe his family a debt. They have business connections with my father. When I set up as a merchant-trader with my own schooner, they gave me cargoes.'

'But surely that was simply a business arrangement? Not a personal debt.'

Jago's chin lifted. 'To me it was a matter of honour. They had helped me. I was in a position to return the favour.'

'But how did he know you were going to Spain?'

'Valdes visited Bonython's office the day before we sailed and enquired for an urgent passage to Spain. Your Uncle Richard was out but had left word with Thomas Bonython regarding the cargo of pilchards he had arranged for me to carry to Santander. Thomas told Valdes I was due to sail the following morning. When he arrived at the yard I assumed he was the passenger Toby had warned me to expect.'

Caseley realised he had answered all her questions without hesitation, questions she wasn't sure she had the right to ask. But would he answer this one?

'Why don't you like him?'

Jago's features hardened. 'He has no concept of honour.'

Caseley's mouth twitched in an ironic smile.

'You find that amusing?' He was sombre and she thought she had never seen him look so haughty or so Spanish.

'No. As a matter of fact he said the same of you, because of …' Her brief gesture encompassed the day room and sleeping cabin and her face grew warm.

'I see.' Neither his tone nor his expression gave

anything away.

'You must have other reasons.' She wasn't sure how far she dared press, yet his explanation seemed too nebulous. Because she wasn't Spanish she might not fully appreciate their code of ethics. Even so, to her his dislike of Antonio Valdes felt personal.

'We have nothing in common,' he was brusque. 'Valdes lives on his wits and his family's generosity. It is years since I last saw him. But I have heard rumours of scandals and of his involvement with various political factions.'

Caseley's stomach tightened and it cost effort and willpower to remain perfectly still.

'Whether they are true I neither know nor care,' Jago went on. 'But right now he has you in his sights. Once Valdes steps ashore in Spain my debt is paid. Until then you are at risk, and I will do whatever I consider necessary to ensure your safety.' He did not smile.

Her gaze fell away and she shivered. Despite his flat tone she detected anger and impatience. Certain phrases he had used resurrected her uncertainty. It was as if he knew about the package and was giving her the opportunity to confide in him.

She clasped her arms across her body. Her heart was telling her what she wanted to hear, that she could trust him. It was a siren song, insistent and persuasive. But as she recalled the way he had treated her in Falmouth, how he had manipulated, blackmailed … then there was Louise Downing …

'You're trying to frighten me.'

The glacial façade cracked. His eyes blazed as his hand shot out and gripped the back of her neck.

'Being frightened would be wise, Caseley,' he growled as she gasped and her hands flew up to clutch his wrist.

'We are sailing to a country torn by civil war, where friendship counts for nothing against heritage and tradition. Santander is Basque territory. I learned to sail with Basques. I worked, ate, and slept with them. They were my second family. But I am Castilian, an outsider. Now, because of the unrest, I am suspect. Think about that, Caseley. I am your only protection. But I too could be in danger.' He released her and she stumbled backwards, trembling.

He thrust his hands into his pockets, as if fighting the urge to touch her again. 'For the love of God, see sense. Let me deliver the … contract.'

Had that tiny pause been deliberate? Was he telling her he knew whatever she was carrying was more valuable and more dangerous than any business agreement? No, he was only guessing. He couldn't be sure. Her instinct told her she could trust him. But trusting him would mean breaking her promise to her dying father.

As his gaze held hers, she wanted so much to tell him, to explain. She shook her head, the words torn from her. 'I can't.'

'So be it,' he muttered and strode out.

Chapter Sixteen

Caseley stared at the door. Doubts tore at her like talons; so did grief. Rousing herself she lifted down the tin. But as she worked on the letters her thoughts kept straying.

Tossing down her pen, she paced up and down the small cabin, rubbing her arms. Trapped, stifled, she wished she had never heard of Spain, Antonio Valdes, or Jago Barata.

She stopped, head bowed, staring at the wooden floor. She didn't mean it, not about Jago. In the short time she had known him he had caused her rage, frustration, jealousy – and unimagined happiness. He had transformed girlish dreams into a woman's desire, and kindled a spark of love that, no matter how starved of nourishment, or how low it burned, would never be extinguished.

Despite all the lacerating doubt and uncertainty, she could not regret that. Nor – even if it were possible – would she want to go back to being who she was before she met him.

Once they returned to Falmouth her father could tell him the truth about her journey. Would he understand? Or would he reject her for her lack of trust? It would be too late then to change anything. In any case, he would return to his house, and the possessive arms of Louise Downing.

She tensed against knifing pain. Quickly wiping her eyes, she returned to the table.

Addressing the envelope to Ramon Gaudara, she folded the letter and slipped it into the envelope for safekeeping.

Was the civil war the reason Jago was severing all his connections with Spain? That would still not explain his decision to sell his schooner.

As owner-master he could collect and deliver cargoes anywhere in the world. He was not confined to Spanish ports or waters. It did not make sense that he would sell the only vessel he owned outright.

Selling the silver refineries would bring him a large amount of money. What did he need it for? He had demanded and been given the post of senior captain with Bonython's. He would be sailing *Fair Maid* to the Azores in December at the start of the fruit season. His seamanship would ensure a fast passage and consequently a high price for his cargo. So *why?* And why *now?*

By dinnertime she had completed all the letters. After the meal, Jago returned with her to the cabin. She sat opposite him while he read each one. She had worked hard on them and, considering how brief his notes and instructions had been, she was pleased with the result. But they were going out in his name, so it was his opinion that mattered.

When he had finished, he gave a brief nod and bent over the table to scrawl his signature at the bottom of each sheet.

Caseley wrapped her arms across her waist. She knew better than to expect gushing compliments, but could he not have managed a simple thank you? Disappointment vied with anger and her effort to mask both made her tone sharp.

'Am I to take it they are satisfactory?'

He looked round. 'Do you doubt your own ability?'

'I – no – but –'

He cut across her confusion. 'Then you must know they are exactly what I wanted.'

'Would it have cost you so much to say so?' Rising, she turned away. As tears pricked she was furious at her weakness. What was she, a child? Praise asked for had no value. She knew she had done a good job. That should have been enough.

'I'm … sorry.' The word was uttered with difficulty as though unfamiliar to him.

Wearily she shook her head. 'It doesn't matter.' She waited for him to go. Instead he came up behind her. She could hear him breathing. *Don't touch me*, she prayed silently, her tongue paralysed by the knowledge that she wanted him to.

His hands, warm and heavy, clasped her shoulders. She caught her breath and her eyes closed. Slowly, deliberately, he turned her round.

She kept her eyes lowered.

'Caseley?'

She did not respond, terrified to meet his piercing gaze, all too aware that evasion was impossible, the truth would be there for him to read. Then what would she see in *his* eyes? Amusement? Irritation? *Pity*?

'Caseley, look at me?' he said softly.

She gave her head a tiny shake.

His hand came up and grasped her chin. Her skin burned beneath his fingers. She tried to pull away. His grip tightened.

'Look at me!' It was harsh, a command.

Her lashes lifted long enough for her to see his bearded face, his glittering eyes so frighteningly close, before tears splintered her vision.

He muttered an oath then his mouth came down on hers. He released her chin and his arms encircled her, drawing her against him.

Honed by the physical demands of handling a large

schooner in all weathers, his hard-muscled body was unyielding but warm. His lips trailed fire across her cheek and down her throat, then returned to her mouth with a tenderness that spoke of iron control.

Caseley felt a strange contraction deep inside and liquid sweetness surged through her limbs. She drew in a long sobbing breath as her hands slid over his shoulders and into the thick hair curling on his neck.

Crushed against his chest, she could feel his heart pounding, knew her own matched it. He released her mouth and as she rested her forehead on his shoulder, he laid his bearded jaw against her temple. His quick breathing feathered her ear. Her legs trembled uncontrollably. No matter what happens, she thought, I have had this moment.

'Caseley?' His voice was little more than a vibration.

'Yes?'

'Say my name.'

She opened her eyes.

He tilted her chin up with his forefinger. 'Say my name.'

'Jago.' She tested the syllables shyly, speaking them aloud for the first time. 'Jago.' She smiled.

He did not smile back. Stepping away, he slid his hands down her arms to grasp her fingers. 'Whatever happens in the next two days,' he raised her hands to his lips, kissed each one in turn, 'trust me.'

Caseley felt a dart of fear and a shudder rippled through her. Had he picked up her thoughts, or had she sensed his?

About to say more, instead he let her go. 'We should sight land in an hour. I want you to come topside. But you must stay beside me at the wheel. The wind is shifting and we'll have to change tack several times as we approach the harbour entrance.' He glanced at the barometer once more, frowning briefly. But when he looked at her, his expression softened. 'All right?'

Aware that his question had nothing to do with joining him on deck, she nodded. He left and she went into the sleeping cubicle to fetch the short jacket that matched her skirt. Events were in motion over which she had no control. Yet strangely she felt calm. There had been no confiding, no explanations. Yet without a word being spoken their relationship had changed.

Leaning against the gunwale a few feet from Jago as the deck canted, Caseley was relieved to be on the higher side. With all sails full, the schooner drove through the water at speed, her fine stem cutting a path and tossing aside a foaming bow wave that bubbled and sparkled in the sunlight.

Wind and sea had changed since she was on deck earlier that morning. Busy with the letters, she had heard the grating clank of the steering chains, the squeal of ropes through blocks, and the loud rippling snap of sails refilling as the course changed. She had not registered their significance.

Now with time to look, she noticed that instead of coming from one side of the stern, the wind was blowing over the port beam. No longer a steady breeze, it was fitful and gusty.

The sea had dulled to pewter grey, and dark rolling masses of water streaked with foam surged towards them from the southwest.

Caseley glanced at Jago. Meeting her gaze he gave a small shrug. Clearly he had no idea what was brewing either. To her surprise Caseley found his honesty a comfort. A smile that pretended everything was fine would have been patronising as well as shutting her out to worry alone. Recalling his frown as he checked the barometer, she looked from sea to sky.

Though the sun still shone, it was through a fine veil and a large ring encircled it. She knew that meant rain was on the way. The puffball clouds had become torn and ragged as they scudded across the filmy sky. A frisson of nervousness made her glad they would soon be safely in port.

The uneasiness gripping her now was different from that she had experienced earlier when Antonio Valdes came on deck. His eyes had darted from her to Jago and back. As bitter realisation thinned his lips to a tense white line, he had stumbled past her to the wheel-shelter.

She had adjusted to the increased pitching without even thinking about it. For Antonio Valdes, so sure of his invincibility, to have his advances spurned, his machinations foiled, and his *machismo* demolished by seasickness must be devastating.

Despite knowing that he would have used her for his own ends without a moment's hesitation, she still pitied him as he emerged from the lavatory, his colour a blotchy greenish-white as he wiped his mouth with a handkerchief clutched in trembling fingers.

It crossed her mind to offer help. But even before she intercepted Jago's warning glare, she abandoned the idea.

Not only had Antonio failed to sweep her off her feet, he recognised the bond between her and Jago. Though he had no idea of its significance, the fact that it existed rubbed salt into his wounded pride.

Having his seasickness exposed to their joint gaze made him a very dangerous man. Looking neither left nor right, his dignity in shreds, he staggered back to the companionway.

Jago beckoned to Caseley. 'You'll find Martin in the galley shack. Tell him to take an old bucket down to

Valdes. By the look of him he won't make the stairs next time.'

The afternoon wore on. Nathan took over the wheel while Jago fetched the sextant and took sightings.

'See that double flash?' Caseley followed his pointing finger. 'That's the Caso Mayor lighthouse.'

'What's the one on this side?'

'Santa Marina Island. Our course will take us between two islands, Santa Marina and Mouro. The river curves round past Magdalena Beach and Puerto Chico up to the wharves of the main harbour.'

At teatime there was none of the leisurely pace and chatter of previous evenings. Caseley ate with Nathan, Jimbo, and Martin while Jago and Hammer remained on deck. Antonio Valdes did not appear.

Afterwards Caseley went to the cabin. Dragging her bag out she lifted it onto the bunk and felt among her clothes for the package. From now on it would be safer to keep it on her person. As her fingers closed around it she heard the door open. Her heart leapt into her throat.

'Caseley?' Jago's voice reached her through the drumming of blood in her ears. Lifting the short flared skirt of her jacket, she pushed the bulky envelope into her waistband, smoothing the material flat again.

'Yes?' Leaving the bag where it was, she emerged from the cubicle, unrolling her gabardine cape.

'What do you want that for? Are you cold?'

She shook her head. 'Not at the moment. But it may be chilly later when we go ashore.'

'Go ashore?' A frown drew his dark brows together.

'You said we would be in port this evening.'

'So we will.'

'Then I must go ashore and deliver the c – contract.'

'*Tonight?*' His gaze was shrewd, penetrating.

She nodded, swallowing to try and lubricate her dry throat. 'My father said Señor Spinoza wanted me to go to his house the moment we arrived.'

'Surely he meant during office hours? We will not be moored up much before eight. How can you be sure anyone will be there?'

She shrugged helplessly. 'I – my father said as soon as we arrive. I must follow his instructions. That is why I'm here.' Would he try to stop her? What would she do if he did?

He gazed at her for what felt like a long time. Her fingers tightened on the cape. 'Please, Jago. I have no choice.' She saw a muscle jump in his jaw then he inclined his head in a brief nod.

'All right, come up on deck. I don't want you out of my sight.'

She glanced at him but there was nothing romantic in the grim set of his mouth and narrowed eyes.

'One moment.' He caught her arm as she reached him in the doorway. 'What is the address where you are to meet this…'

'Señor Spinoza. I have it here in my pocket.' As she felt for the folded scrap of paper her father had given her the evening before she left, her fingers brushed against the bulky shape of the package making is rustle. She felt heat flood her face and could not meet Jago's eyes as she passed him the address. *Please don't let him have heard.*

'What are you hiding, Caseley?' His quiet demand sent chills along her arms.

She had to tell him as much of the truth as she could without breaking her word to her father. 'I did not bring a purse or reticule with me, so I am carrying the contract in my waistband to leave my hands free for getting on and off the boat.'

His expression gave nothing away as he took the small piece of paper and Caseley folded the cape over her arm to occupy her trembling hands.

'I know this place,' he murmured. 'It's in the old town, not far from the harbour.'

She followed him up the stairs, taking up her position on the port quarter as he reclaimed the wheel. The setting sun was hidden behind a mass of grey and violet cloud and the sky had an eerie yellowish hue. Though it wasn't cold she felt gooseflesh erupt on her arms.

Ahead loomed the Spanish coast. In the fading light Caseley could just see purple mountains rising behind the smaller hills over which spread the town of Santander.

At Jago's command, Nathan and Hammer lowered the large foresail while Jimbo took in the flying jib. Next the square topsail was hauled up and the staysail dropped. *Cygnet* was now in the river. Shielded from the wind by rolling hills, the water was calmer.

Their progress had slowed and Martin was in the bow, checking the depth of the channel with a marked and weighted line, singing out the fathoms as the schooner made her way upriver.

'Why is he doing that?' Caseley asked.

'We're going in on an ebb tide,' Jago said, 'and the river has a lot of shifting sandbanks.'

'Wouldn't it have been safer to take on a pilot?'

'Anchor in the bay and wait until morning? Possibly. But I know this river well and I want to get home as quickly as you do.'

She stayed silent after that. Her fingers strayed to the package at her waist. She wanted to be rid of it as soon as possible. Naturally she wanted to see her father again, to watch his face as she told him she had done as he asked, and the documents had been safely delivered. But then what? What was there for her to look forward to?

Why was Jago so anxious to get back? He had his father's quicksilver to trans-ship – and there was also his house. He had only seen it once. He would want to see for himself how she had spent his money. And of course there was Louise.

Where do I stand in all that, Caseley wondered. She had refused to do any further work on the house. Jago had said Louise would not bother her any more. But he had not said he would give her up. If he did not, then the kisses that moved her so deeply, the attraction, antipathy, respect, dislike, admiration, and fury he stirred in her, had meant nothing to him. She was no more than a passing fancy.

Doubts crept in, quiet as cats, and tore at her with unsheathed claws. What did she have to offer a man as well travelled, as sophisticated and knowledgeable as Jago Barata?

It was almost dark when they reached the harbour. Huddled in the warm folds of her cape, Caseley watched as Jago guided the schooner in alongside one of the quays lit by brightly burning lamps. He ordered Jimbo to make fast the stern line only. The seaman leapt ashore, apparently unsurprised.

She caught Nathan's sleeve. But he only grinned as the bow drifted out and, caught by the current, swung the schooner round to face down river once more. Jimbo trotted down the quay, ready to catch the bowline Hammer threw to him.

'Why did J – the captain do that?' she asked quietly.

'To save time,' the mate explained. 'Skipper said we might want to get away quick.'

Once *Cygnet* was securely moored, Caseley looked expectantly at Jago and started towards the midsection of the schooner, ready to disembark. His hand shot out and caught her arm before she could take a second step.

'No one leaves this vessel until the cargo has been unloaded and the quicksilver brought aboard and stowed below.' He looked over Caseley's shoulder. 'That includes you, Valdes.'

'Enough of this foolishness,' Antonio snapped. 'You cannot keep me here against my will.'

'Nor do I wish to.' Jago was perfectly calm. 'But you have been ill. You are still weak and, I believe, feverish. A few hours' rest while we unload will help you recover. Believe me, señor, I have no wish to detain you. Jimbo, escort Señor Valdes to his cabin.' He walked away before the Spaniard could draw breath to argue.

'This way, sir.' Jimbo's gesture was polite, but his eyes were alert and his strong stocky body was twice the width of Antonio's slender frame.

To Caseley's surprise, instead of storming off in a rage, Antonio shrugged in apparent acceptance.

'I'm going to find the wharfinger,' Jago told Nathan. 'We'll get no help at this time of night. But the space is booked and paid for so he can't refuse to open the warehouse. Set up the winch and start unloading onto the quay.'

'Let me go with you,' Caseley pleaded softly. 'I can deliver the contract and be back on board before the men have finished unloading. Then I won't delay departure.'

Jago's glare froze her. 'Have you taken leave of your senses? You want me to let you go off into town, alone, at this time of night?' A harsh whisper, his voice vibrated with impatience. 'In the name of all that's holy, you live in a port. How could you be stupid enough to suggest such a thing?'

'Then send one of the men with me. I –'

'They are all needed here.' He bit the words off. 'When

the work is completed, *I* will take you to deliver this contract. Until then, you stay right where you are.' He sprang onto the gunwale then leapt onto the quay. Striding quickly towards a row of warehouses, he disappeared into a shadowed alley between two of them.

Chapter Seventeen

Caseley leaned over the schooner's side and looked down into the black oily water. In the lamplight she saw a rainbow broken by bits of cork and frayed rope floating on the surface as water slopped between the quay and *Cygnet*'s hull. She shivered.

Even with two sound feet she would be wary of jumping that gap. It wasn't very wide. But the schooner was riding two feet below the quay and the top of the gunwale was narrow, wet, and slippery. Hampered by her long skirts, it would be all too easy to slip and find herself trapped between the wooden hull and stone quay, unable to climb up and no one able to reach her as filthy black water filled her nose and mouth, dragging her down …

'Beg pardon, miss?' Nathan said, and she looked up gratefully. 'Mind brewing up a nice cuppa tea, would you? Only Mart got to help getting the hatches off, and all.'

'No, Mr Ferris, I don't mind at all. I'd be glad to.' Had it been the mate's idea or Jago's to keep her occupied? She rubbed her hands. 'It seems colder all of a sudden.'

'Weather's changing.' He lifted his head to sniff the wind. 'That there sunset was a warning. We'll have some blow in the next day or two.' He grinned at her. 'You get that tea, and I'll see about this here cargo.'

Caseley filled the kettle from the fresh water tank and set it on the stove in the galley shack after stirring up the fire. Then she went below to the day room to fetch more tea for the tin, and the condensed milk. Closing the day room door behind her she turned towards the stairs and gasped.

'Oh! You startled me.'

Standing in the doorway of his cabin, Antonio Valdes watched her. 'So,' he said softly, as he looked her up and down. 'I was too late.'

Unease battled anger and Caseley felt warmth flush her throat and cheeks. 'Please excuse me, Señor Valdes, I am busy.' She took a step towards the stairs but he blocked her path.

'Is he a good lover?' His mocking tone insinuated otherwise.

'I … he is not my lover,' she blurted in shock, then wished she had not spoken as he raised disbelieving eyebrows. Even discussing it with Valdes, she was playing into his hands.

He shrugged. 'My apologies, señorita. Perhaps you do not like men.'

'I do not like men who insult my intelligence, señor,' she retorted. 'Nor do I like men who pretend feelings they do not have.'

'You suggest I am guilty of this?'

'Can you deny it?'

He smiled with disarming candour. 'I underestimated you, señorita. I do not encounter many women whose brains match their beauty.'

'Then perhaps you should review your choice of company. Now if you would kindly step aside, Mr Ferris is expecting me on deck.'

He did not move. 'Señorita, I beg you, listen to me. Do not risk more danger. Give me the package. I will ensure it reaches those who have the best interests of my country at heart.'

So there it was. Out in the open at last. There could be

no more doubt about the true nature of his interest. Caseley frowned in puzzlement.

'Señor, I am sorry if the recent troubles have cost your family money. But I do not think one contract for the transport of iron ore will restore their fortunes. Please excuse me.'

His hand fastened around her upper arm. Fear flooded through her as rage and frustration contorted his face.

'Let go of me.' Somehow she held her voice steady though her stomach was knotting painfully. *Please somebody come.* If Valdes became violent there was little she could do to defend herself.

'You think you are so clever,' he hissed, lapsing into Spanish. 'Don't you see, you are playing right into his hands? Jago Barata is a half-breed. He does not live in Spain. His father fled to Mexico to avoid the troubles. What are the morals and loyalties of such a man? He has left the ship, no? Where is he now? You do not know. Who is he with? What are they planning?

'I have followed that package from Mexico. I care about the future of my country. The monarchy must be restored and Don Carlos must establish a new dynasty.' Saliva had gathered at the corners of his mouth, and his eyes had the feverish glitter of a fanatic. 'Spain needs his strength and his courage Give me the package, now!'

Booted feet clanged on the stairs and Jago appeared. There was icy anger in his narrowed gaze. 'Take your hand off her.' He turned. 'The men are waiting for their tea, Caseley. See to it, will you?' he said evenly.

She glanced from one to the other then ran up the stairs. As she reached the top she heard a fist connect with flesh, a sharp cry, then a muffled thud. Her pleasure at Antonio Valdes's punishment was unladylike and deplorable. She ought to feel guilty. But she didn't.

Hurrying to the galley shack she looked over her shoulder and saw Jago emerge from the companionway, sucking his knuckles. He did not even glance in her direction but went straight to the winch, sending Hammer onto the dockside to roll the barrels to the warehouse after Martin had unloaded them from the net.

Caseley carried out mugs of tea and the last of the cake. Nathan, who had been on the winch rope with Jago, called Jimbo up from the hold and beckoned Martin and Hammer back on board. While the men talked softly, sipping and chewing, Jago took Caseley to one side.

'We won't be finished for several hours. Drink your tea, then go below and get some sleep.' He didn't give her a chance to protest. 'There's nothing you can do to help. I'll call you the instant the hatches are battened down. You have my word.' Still she hesitated, but his next words convinced her.

'I have no wish to frighten you, but it's likely we'll run into bad weather on our return trip. You'll get little rest then. Make the most of this chance.' It made sense.

'And, Caseley?' She looked up. 'Lock the door.'

A brisk tapping woke her from a fitful sleep. She had not removed any of her clothes, so it took her only moments to refasten her skirt and button her jacket. Pausing only to slip her feet into her shoes, she hurried to unlock the door.

Jago stood on the threshold. 'Ready?'

'I just need a moment.' She turned to re-enter the sleeping cubicle, limping badly, wishing there was time to wash her face and clean her teeth. Tendrils of her hair had escaped the confining net and curled on her forehead and in front of her ears.

'Put on your cape. We must go at once.'

Slinging the cape over her arm she returned to the day

room, tucking her wayward hair back into the net. 'What's happened? What's wrong?' Her ankle turned again and she winced.

'Are you all right?'

She nodded quickly. 'It's just my foot. It's always stiff when I first get up. It will be fine in a moment.'

'Are you sure?'

She sensed there was more behind the question than concern for her comfort.

'Yes, truly. It's better already.' She put her weight on it, rocking back and forward as she checked that the package was secure in her waistband. 'Now, please tell me what's wrong?'

'Valdes has gone. I didn't expect – But when I sent Hammer down to check, he'd disappeared. Did you hear anything?'

Caseley shook her head. 'Does it matter?' He must have accepted that she wasn't going to betray any information concerning the documents. 'Perhaps he has returned to his family.'

'Not yet. He hasn't given up, Caseley. We don't know where he is or how many friends he may have locally. So, yes, it matters.'

She bent her head, pretending to fasten her cape, knowing her fiery blush must give her away.

'Come on.' He put his hand under her elbow. 'Let us finish this charade.' His tone was unexpectedly bitter and she dared not look at him.

She felt sick with a fear that had nothing to do with the dangers attached to delivering the package. If Jago knew what it contained – if he hated her for not trusting him – she wrenched her thoughts away. She had a job to do for her father, the most important job of her life. Focus on that. Forget everything else.

As they crossed the deck, Caseley saw that *Cygnet*'s gunwale was just above the level of the quay. She noticed Martin filling an iron cooking pot with water and marvelled at the boy's stamina. He had worked alongside the men all night and was now preparing breakfast.

But where were the others? She was about to ask when Jago called her name sharply from the quay. She scrambled onto the barrel he had placed as a step. He held out his hands and she grasped them as she put her feet on the gunwale and jumped down onto the quay, automatically taking her most of her weight on her sound foot.

He kept hold of her hand and she ran to keep up with him as they quickly crossed the deserted wharves, weaving between silent sheds and warehouses.

They left the harbour area and as they turned onto a cobbled street that climbed towards a small, whitewashed church with a square tower, dawn was breaking.

Tall, flat-walled houses with oblong windows and small iron balconies bright with geraniums lined both sides of the street. But the height of the buildings filled the narrow thoroughfare with shadows. Dark doorways and alleys between the houses resembled gaping mouths.

Caseley slipped on the damp stones. Jago's grip stopped her falling. In the momentary silence as she regained her balance and flexed her foot, she heard a soft slithering on the cobbles behind her. She looked round quickly but could see nothing in the gloom. Her throat was tight and dry.

'Someone is following us,' she whispered.

He did not appear surprised, merely nodding briefly. 'It's not far now. Once we reach the church –'

Whatever words of comfort he had intended to offer remained unspoken as he glanced over his shoulder.

The sound of soft laughter from higher up the hill made them look forward again and Jago clasped her hand tighter.

'Sitting ducks.' Antonio Valdes regarded them with malicious pleasure as he and another man came slowly down the hill towards them.

A chuckle from behind them made Caseley whirl round and she clutched Jago's hand as fear bloomed inside her. Two more men were coming up the hill.

All three wore heavy dark trousers that ended just below the knee, coarse stockings criss-crossed with leather thongs, and crude shoes. They had dark waistcoats over their shirts, loosely knotted scarves or kerchiefs at their throats, and on their heads the bright red woollen *boina* of the Carlist cause.

Jago drew Caseley towards him. 'They will try to separate us,' he warned.

Fear had robbed her of speech. She had never imagined Valdes would go to such lengths. How naïve, how foolish she had been. She could feel Jago's heartbeat against her back, slow and steady. His body was tense and one arm encircled her waist.

'Get the girl,' Valdes growled.

The men were closing in, moving forward slowly and relentlessly. Now she could see they were carrying short staves. Their eyes gleamed with savage excitement. Swarthy and unshaven, they grinned as they slapped the wooden clubs against dirty hands. She could smell their stale sweat.

'Once you've got it,' one whispered hoarsely to Valdes in heavily accented Spanish, 'what about her?'

He shrugged. 'Do as you like.'

'No,' she whispered, pressing back against Jago, raw fear turning her blood to ice water and her legs to jelly.

She felt Jago fumble at his belt and saw the flash of a blade as he held his hand low and slightly away from his body. He turned his head quickly, gauging which of the two pairs were nearer, then gave a piercing whistle. Thrusting Caseley behind him, he lunged with lightning speed at the two men on the lower side.

Neither was prepared for the sudden attack. One slipped on the damp cobbles and fell backwards. As Jago caught the other a sweeping blow, the man yelled in pain, dropped his club, and clutched his arm. His shirtsleeve turned red and wet, and blood oozed between his fingers and dripped onto the cobbles.

The man who had fallen scrambled to his feet and lunged forward as Antonio darted towards Caseley.

'Take Barata,' he panted to the man beside him and seized Caseley's arm, trying to dodge the punches she was aiming at his head and shoulders. She kicked at his shins but was hampered by her skirt and petticoats. Terrified, she fought with all her strength as he tried to wrench her away from Jago.

Then she heard the sound of running feet and the sickening thud of fist on flesh. Valdes released his hold.

'Don't you fret, my 'andsome. We'll see the buggers off,' Nathan grinned and pitched into the battle.

Leaning against the wall, Caseley dragged in sobbing breaths and tried to control the trembling that racked her. The three Basques were wielding their clubs with horrific ferocity. They weren't defending themselves. They wanted to kill.

But Hammer, Jimbo, and Nathan were no easy prey. Using only fists and razor-sharp reflexes that allowed them to duck the blows, they quickly disarmed the attackers. Then they separated them.

Jago had re-sheathed his knife and as Hammer reeled

back after taking a fist to his temple, Jago felled the Basque with a right cross, followed by a left hook. The man's head snapped back and he was unconscious before he hit the cobbles.

Aside from the quiet order from Antonio and the Basque's query about what to do with her, the incident had taken place in silence. Though the fighting was vicious, apart from gasped breaths, grunts as a fist landed, and the scuffle of feet on the cobbles, there was little noise.

A hand closed around her ankle and Caseley choked back a scream. Looking down, she saw Antonio Valdes sprawled at her feet. He twisted his head to peer up at her, his narrow face contorted in a smile that radiated malice.

'You stupid bitch. You think you've won? How do you intend to get back to England?' His weak laugh became a cough.

Caseley stared at him for a moment. *Cygnet.* Martin was alone on the schooner. Rage filled her. Stamping on his wrist, she wrenched her ankle, free then bent and slapped his smiling face with all her strength. The force of her blow split his lip and smashed his head against the cobbles. She ran to Jago.

'The boat,' she gasped, dragging him free. 'Valdes has done something to *Cygnet.*'

Jago didn't ask questions. 'Nathan, get back to the wharf as fast as you can. Martin's in trouble.'

Seizing Caseley's arm he hurried her up the street, past the church and into an alley. Halfway along there was a heavy wooden door studded with iron nails. To one side a rope led through a small hole in the stone archway surrounding the door. Jago tugged it hard.

The wait seemed interminable but was probably no more than half a minute. The door opened to reveal a short plump man with receding hair dressed in dark clothes.

'Señor Spinoza, please,' she said quickly. 'I am Caseley Bonython. My father is Teuder Bonython, the consul for Mexico. But he is unwell and could not come himself. This is Jago Barata, my father's senior captain.'

Stepping back, the man gestured for them to enter and closed the massive door. They followed him across a small courtyard then through a maze of cool passages, finally emerging into a wide hall. Opening a door on the far side, the man ushered them into a spacious, book-lined study containing a huge carved desk, a brass-topped hexagonal table and several leather armchairs.

'Señor Spinoza will be with you shortly.' He inclined his head politely and would have left had Caseley not clutched his arm.

'Please ask him to hurry. We must get back to the harbour. We were attacked on our way here and –'

Gently detaching her hand, he glanced from her to Jago then walked out.

Chapter Eighteen

As Caseley withdrew the crushed, wrinkled package from her waistband, the door opened. The man who entered was about sixty, tall and gaunt, and wore a full-length belted robe of crimson quilted silk with a white silk scarf knotted like a cravat at his throat.

Seeing the silver hair, small goatee beard, and the fine-boned aristocratic features of a grandee, Caseley was shaken. He was exactly as she had imagined Señor Rodriguez. The other man remained near the door, silent and watchful.

'Señor Spinoza?' Caseley asked the tall man.

He nodded. 'You have something for me?' His tone was polite, but Caseley noticed he had not bothered with greetings.

At her hesitation Jago muttered, 'For God's sake, Caseley, give it to him so we can get out of here.'

She glanced at him, holding the package tightly, feeling its altered thickness. Remembering her father's instructions, that she was only to hand over the documents if she was told the name of the place where the young king was, she moistened her lips.

'I believe you have visited England, sir,' she said.

He smiled slightly. 'I did, many years ago. I have a young acquaintance at Sandhurst Military Academy. He is staying with one of the instructors whose address is One, The Terrace. Apparently it is known as Tea Caddy Row, though I have yet to discover why.'

Caseley offered the crumpled envelope and the thin man took it. But when he saw it was already open his face changed and as he raised his eyes to hers she glimpsed steel beneath the velvet courtesy.

'I beg your pardon, sir. I had to be certain.' Turning away, she withdrew the second envelope with its distinctive and unbroken seal from within her blouse. Her shaking fingers fumbled as she refastened the buttons.

'You are your father's daughter,' the thin man said.

Jago placed an impatient hand on the small of her back. 'Forgive us, sir, but we must hurry.' He propelled her towards the door.

'Please accept our sincere thanks, Miss Bonython. You also, Captain Barata. *Vaya con Dios.*'

As they raced back to the harbour, she was so relieved to have honoured her promise and delivered the package, she assumed Jago's silence was due to concern for Martin and the others.

Though she ran as fast as she could, her uneven gait and the slippery cobbles would have caused her to fall more than once but for his firm grip on her hand.

Her breath burned in her throat, her heart pounded, and she could not suck enough air into her lungs. Beneath the heavy cape and fitted jacket her cotton blouse and shift clung to her skin as perspiration beaded her back and trickled between her breasts. Again she stumbled, and once more he pulled her upright and forced her to keep running.

People were beginning to appear and paused to stare with mingled curiosity and suspicion. But none got in their way. A swift glance at his set features convinced Caseley he would simply have knocked aside anyone who tried to stop them.

The sun had risen. But instead of the pastel shades of a

mellow autumn morning, low grey clouds with flame-tipped ragged edges filled the eastern sky.

They passed the warehouses and reached the wharf. As they rounded the corner Caseley saw black smoke belching from *Cygnet*'s wheel shelter. She was too breathless to speak. But Jago cursed with bitter fluency as they covered the last few yards and saw Martin, his face smeared with soot and tears, helping Hammer hurl buckets of water onto the flames.

The staysail was set. Jimbo and Nathan, their faces contorted in effort, were hauling on the mainsail halyards, but the weight of the gaff and enormous canvas sail was too much for them.

Catching sight of Jago and Caseley, Nathan yelled to Jimbo to cast off. Hopping nimbly onto the quay, Jimbo loosed the bow line. Jago swept Caseley up into his arms and threw her over the gunwale. Then, waving Jimbo back on board, he cast off the stern line himself and jumped the widening gap between quay and ship.

Lifting Caseley to her feet, he took her hands and wrapped them around the polished spokes of the wheel.

'Head her into the channel,' he pointed. 'Aim for that buoy.' Then leaving her he hurried forward bellowing, 'All hands to the mainsail! Martin, put that bloody fire out!'

Caseley clung to the wheel. Still breathless and shaking from their headlong dash, she didn't have time to worry about the enormity of the task Jago had set her.

She glanced shoreward. Men were gathering on the quay. Was Antonio there? She couldn't see him. Nor did she recognise the men who had attacked them. Under the staysail, the schooner was drawing away from the quay. The menace in the crowd's silent watching made her throat close and she swallowed. Then smoke drifted across, obscuring the scene and she quickly looked ahead.

With Jago and Nathan on one rope, Jimbo and Hammer on the other, the four men hoisted the peak and throat halyards controlling the inner and outer edges of the sail, hauling on them evenly to send up the gaff to which the edge of the sail was laced, parallel to the boom.

The rhythmic squeal of blocks and rattle of mast hoops finally stopped. Jago passed the throat halyard under a cleat to hold it fast, while Nathan threw his full weight on the taut rope to pull the edge of the sail nearest the mast up tight. Nathan's effort enabled Jago to take in a few more inches of rope. When the throat halyard was finally secured, Hammer and Jimbo swiftly hoisted the peak, made it fast then coiled the loose ends of rope over the belaying pins. Not a word had been spoken.

Jimbo ran forward to trim the staysail and hoist the jib as Hammer and Nathan scrambled aft once more to help Martin who was working feverishly while sobbing with shock and exhaustion.

Jago eased out the mainsheet. The boom swung to starboard and the sail filled. Caseley felt new weight on the helm. Clenching her teeth so hard that they ached, she eased the wheel over. *Cygnet* responded. Bowsprit pointing towards the river mouth, the schooner surged forward.

Caseley could hear a low crackling, and felt the heat through the back of the wheel shelter. Thick smoke and choking fumes billowed from the open door as the man drew bucket after bucketful of water from over the side and hurled it into the paint store.

Gulls screamed overhead and further down the river brightly painted fishing boats scurried back to the protection of Puerto Chico, the little harbour.

Caseley's knuckles were white as her grip on the

spokes tightened. Everyone else was making for shelter. They were heading for the open sea and the approaching storm.

They had no choice. She knew that. Had they stayed in port – it did not bear thinking about.

'I reckon we've beat the bugger,' Jimbo yelled in triumph, his sweating blackened face appearing round the wheel shelter.

The smoke was thinner, paler now it was mixed with steam, and the voracious crackling had stopped. But the fumes still caught in the throat, and were joined by the acrid stench of charred wood and burnt paint.

Jago came to the wheel. 'I'll take it now.' His tone was curt and he didn't look at her as she stepped aside.

'Hammer, see what can be salvaged,' he shouted over his shoulder. 'Chuck the rest overboard. Nathan, you and Jimbo set the lower topsail, then the foresail and secure all hatches. Martin,' he beckoned the boy forward. 'What happened?'

Caseley leaned against the shoulder board, massaging the stiffness from her fingers as she listened.

Martin's eyes were red-rimmed and bloodshot, his face and clothes smeared with oily soot. Wiping his nose on the back of his hand, he shifted from foot to foot.

'I was in the galley when they came,' his voice was hoarse, rasping from the smoke. 'Three of 'em there was. One had blood all down his arm. They had torches. I went for your gun, Cap'n. I – I thought it would scare 'em off.' He rubbed one bare grimy foot against the other.

'How else could you have defended the ship?' Jago said calmly. 'You were here alone.'

A smile lit the boy's weary face. 'Gave 'em some shock, I did. They didn't expect that.' His expression clouded. 'One was trying to burn through the bow mooring line. Another had just throwed his torch down the fo'c'sle. That's when I fired. I got'n in the leg.' He faltered.

'Good.' Jago nodded. 'What was the third man doing?'

'Trying to smash the day room skylight. But when he seen me coming, he kicked the door of the paint store and chucked his torch in. Then he jumped back on the wharf with the others. Laughing they was – not the one I shot. He was on the ground. I didn't know what to do first what with smoke coming out of the paint store *and* the fo'c'sle. I thought of all our clothes and gear down there –' he stopped.

'Good lad. Fire is far more dangerous below deck than above.'

'But by the time I'd put 'n out the paint store was well alight. Soon as they bast – Basques,' he corrected quickly, his gaze darting to Caseley, 'seen Jimbo and Hammer come back they took off, dragging their mate with 'em. Jimbo told me to keep going with the buckets while they made ready to leave soon as you got here.'

'Where was Nathan?'

'He come just a couple of minutes later with bags of fresh bread rolls and oranges. He said we wouldn't have time for revittling, so he'd took care of it.'

Jago grasped the boy's thin shoulder. 'I'm proud of you, Martin. You showed great courage and presence of mind.' The boy shrugged and shuffled his feet, but the dirt on his face could not hide his blush of pride. 'Where did you put my gun?'

'He's over there, Cap'n, on the hatch cover.'

'Put it away, then clean yourself up and turn in for a couple of hours.'

'I'm all right, Cap'n.'

'Do as you're told, boy. I'll need you later.'

'Aye, sir.' Martin shambled forward to collect the gun, rubbing his eyes, his mouth opening in a wide yawn.

'Jago?' Caseley said. 'Shall I make tea?'

He nodded briefly, checked the sails and compass then glanced over his shoulder to see how Hammer was doing. Looking anywhere, Caseley realised, but at her. 'While you're in the galley,' he added, 'see if the oatmeal can be salvaged.'

She hesitated, wanting to ask him what was wrong.

'Go on, then,' he snapped. 'What are you waiting for?'

Stung by his tone, she turned to the companionway, fumbling with the fastening on her cape. He was tired. They all were, but responsibility for the ship and crew rested squarely on his shoulders. Her presence had been an added burden.

But they had both achieved what they had set out to do – he had his cargo, she had delivered the package – so why was he so angry? Was he blaming *her* for the attack?

As she thought about it she realised he had every right. Had she not been aboard it would not have happened. *Yes, it would.* Whoever had carried those documents would have been a target. Had her father been fit enough to make the journey himself Antonio Valdes would have employed different tactics. But the objective would have been the same.

Roughly folding her cape, she wedged it behind the chocks on which the dinghy rested. She was too hot and sticky to wear it and it would be awkward in the galley. But there wasn't time to take it below and she didn't want it blown away.

The wind whined and moaned in the rigging. As another gust caught her, Caseley felt its force like a giant hand on her back and was glad to reach the shelter of the shack.

She lifted the lidded iron pot from the stove top and put it on the zinc sheet on the floor. Then she riddled out some of the ashes, fed a few sticks and some more coal into the stove, and opened the damper to coax a flame from the glowing embers.

Taking the kettle she went out, holding tightly to anything within reach as the deck heaved under her feet. The fresh water tank was just over half full. Thank heaven Martin had reacted so quickly. Had the water been contaminated or the tank punctured, they would have had to put into one of the French ports. It might have been days before they could leave. And Jago was anxious to get home.

At the back of her mind, warning bells were ringing. Something wasn't right. But the harder she tried to fathom what it was, the more it eluded her.

Back in the galley she set the kettle within the fiddle rails to boil, then crouched and lifted the lid off the iron cooking pot. Inside a thick, black tarry substance coated the sides and bottom. That must have been the source of the smoke.

She gritted her teeth and scraped loose as much as she could then lurched across to the rail with the pot.

'What are you doing?' Jago demanded.

'It's burnt,' she shouted back and tipped the mess into the dark rolling water, momentarily dizzy as it came up towards her then fell steeply away. Turning, she crossed to the fresh-water tank, but before she could draw the dipper out, Jago shouted again.

'Have you no sense? You use seawater for a job like that.' He sounded furious.

Caseley flushed. 'I'm sorry. I didn't –'

'Think? That seems to be a habit of yours. Don't just stand there, get some food ready.'

She flinched. There was no teasing note to take the sting out of his criticism, only barbed impatience. He *meant* to hurt.

Caseley turned away, catching Nathan's eye. He winked in sympathy. But his expression turned harder and puzzled as he glanced towards the man at the wheel. He grabbed a bucket with a rope tied to the handle and swung it over the lee side, drawing it up full.

'Here you are, miss.' He set it on the deck be the galley doorway. 'You'll find a tin of sand just inside there. Use a handful or two on a cloth. Scour it out 'andsome, that will.'

'Thank you. Nathan …' she hesitated. 'Can I ask you something?'

The mate regarded her steadily. 'Depends.'

She recognised the warning. She could ask, but he might not answer. 'I've never been at sea in a storm. I know it's going to get worse, and I'm sure J – the captain knows exactly what he's doing, but …' she glanced nervously at the straining sails.

Nathan followed her gaze, and his stern expression softened. 'Think we're carrying too much canvas, do you?'

Caseley looked at the iron pot and shrugged. 'Like I said, I don't –'

'Nathan!' Jago bellowed.

The mate ignored him. 'The minute the skipper sees the wind driving her head under, we only got to release the ropes from they pins and the sails will drop. There's far more danger in being close to shore in a storm. So he's making searoom before the wind get too strong and we have to reef down.'

'Nathan, get over here!'

The mate lifted his head, his ruddy features tightening.

'Aye, *sir.*' She wasn't alone in finding Jago's hostile behaviour unusual.

The kettle boiled. Despite the sand, it was going to take time to get the pot clean, so Caseley put it aside and made the tea. Leaving it to brew, she collected her cape and went towards the companionway, clutching at the hatch cover and skylight for support.

'Given up already?' Jago snorted.

She winced and a lump formed in her throat, making it ache. Why was he doing this? She opened the hatch door and latched it back. 'I'm going to fetch the milk and some jam for the rolls.' She looked at him over her shoulder. 'Do you want yours in the mess, or would you prefer it where you are?'

His gaze held hers for a moment and in his smoky eyes she saw self-loathing and a plea. Startled, she felt her heart contract. Immediately he looked away.

'Everyone stays on deck.'

Cold and distant, his tone was totally at odds with the powerful emotions she had just glimpsed.

Retrieving the rolls, Caseley split and spread them with jam, then poured the tea. Unable to fill the mugs more than halfway without the tea slopping over the rim, she realised with growing dread that the sea was much rougher. Setting the mugs and the plate of rolls on a battered tray, she made her way carefully aft.

Working in the snug warmth of the shack, she had managed to shut everything out, clinging for comfort to the normality of domestic chores. But out on deck ink-dark seas loomed over the gunwale. Spindrift fogged the air. The wind tore at her hair and clothes as the first drops of rain splashed into her face.

She glanced up, gasping as a wall of foam-streaked water bore down on them. The stern lifted and Caseley staggered, crying out as the tray tilted and the mugs began to slide. But Nathan reached her just in time and grabbed the tray as the sea passed beneath them.

'All right, miss. I got 'n.' He grinned. She tried to smile back but her mouth wouldn't respond. Though she told herself there was no need to be frightened, that the crew were experienced sailors who regularly faced storms like this, her body wasn't listening. Her throat was dry, her skin dewed with the sweat of fear. She shivered as her heart galloped.

Nathan shouted to Hammer and Jimbo. Dressed in oilskins and sou'westers, they skittered along the canting deck, brightening at the sight of food.

'Take a mug down to the boy, shall I, skipper?' Jimbo said through a mouthful of bread and jam.

Jago nodded and, swallowing his tea in two gulps, replaced his mug on the tray Nathan held and took a roll. 'Hammer, fetch my oilskins, and Nathan's while you're down there. Where are you going?' he demanded as Caseley followed Hammer towards the companionway and Nathan took the tray back to the galley.

'For my cape,' she pointed, glancing at the darkening sky.

He shook his head. 'Go below.'

'But what about dinner?'

'Martin will see to it. That's his job.'

Something snapped. Not stopping to consider the consequences of matching his anger with her own, Caseley whirled round as large raindrops fell onto her unprotected head and soaked into her jacket.

'If you tell him to, Martin will cook dinner, tend the fires, help on deck, and work until he drops. He would die sooner than let you down. But he's totally exhausted. If you put him to work now he's quite likely to have an accident. That may not bother you, but I'm not prepared to have it on *my* conscience.'

She paused only to take a breath, her chin high. 'No passengers, you said. *I* can cook. *I'll* make dinner.' Turning her back on him she limped furiously towards the galley, slinging to the rigging as the schooner pitched and rolled.

'Miss Bonython!'

The icy rage in his voice froze her and apprehension shuddered down her spine. Yet though every nerve was stretched tight, she turned and met his gaze.

'*You* dare lecture *me* about conscience?'

'I want to help, that's all.' Head down, she dived into the galley. Sinking down onto the little stool she closed her eyes. Never in her life had she spoken to anyone like that. Nor had she ever seen such anger directed at her. She loved him and hated him, and it was tearing her apart.

She pressed her fingers hard against her forehead and sucked in a deep sobbing breath. Then she reached for the cooking pot and another handful of sand.

Chapter Nineteen

Cygnet drove on through steepening seas. Focused on each task, Caseley took no notice of the rain lashing the roof of the little shack or the water washing over the schooner's deck. She heard orders shouted, the thud of running feet, the rattle of blocks and mast hoops, and the clacking of the patent reefing gear as the fore and mainsails were reefed down.

Having got the pot clean, she needed fresh water to rinse it out and prepare the vegetables. But her cape was still jammed behind the dinghy, and without some form of protection she would be soaked to the skin in seconds.

Looking round the cramped galley she found a piece of old sail canvas. It was stiff and smelly but would have to do.

Holding it over her head and shoulders with one hand, she screwed up her eyes against the driving rain and stumbled out to the tank.

The wind shrieked, whipping the tops off the waves so the air was full of salt spray. The rain was so heavy and the cloud so low, it was impossible to tell where sea ended and sky began.

She struggled back to the galley, water streaming down her face and the canvas to soak into her long skirt. She set the bucket down and immediately half of it slopped onto her shoes and ran over the floor. Rinsing the pot twice she threw the water down-wind out of the door, then lurched outside again to the salt beef barrel.

The smell of the meat made her feel sick. As she fought nausea, swallowing hard, she considered abandoning her attempt to cook a meal. The men would understand. They knew she had no experience of conditions like this. No one would think any the worse of her. They were probably amazed she had stuck at it so long.

Clinging to the barrel as the deck heaved and dropped beneath her feet, she recalled Jago's bitter taunt. 'Given up already?' That had been an hour ago. It had got much worse since then.

'Damn you,' she whispered as the rain hammered onto her back. Slamming the lid back onto the barrel, she fastened it down with fumbling fingers then, clutching the chunk of gritty fat-marbled beef, slithered back to the shack.

She made up the fire once more, deeply grateful for its crackling warmth. Hunched on the tiny stool, a chopping board on her knees, she cut up the meat, potatoes, onion, and turnip and scraped it all into the deep pot, covered it with fresh water, and jammed on the lid.

She rinsed and wiped her hands on a scrap of towel, fitted extra guard rails round the stove top to prevent the pot sliding off, then peered out of the doorway, clinging to the frame.

The seas were white and breaking. The topsails had been taken in, so had the aft gaff. The schooner was running with the reefed foresail and the staysail.

As the bow reared, two figures, oilskins slick with rain and spray, struggled to loosen the foresail halyards. The wet ropes had contracted and were wire-taut. The schooner climbed, the reefed sail filled with a deafening clap, and the staysail split.

Feet pounded forward along the deck. In the flying spray Caseley could just make out two figures releasing ropes and hauling in the tattered sail while a third unlatched the scuttle to dive below to the locker for the spare.

Salt stung her eyes and burned her face. Petrified, she could only cling to the doorframe. How long could *Cygnet* take such punishment?

A mountainous sea toppled aboard just in front of the mainmast and washed down the foredeck, swirling round the windlass in a welter of foam, reaching the knees of the men working frantically to free the torn sail.

One of the men slipped and fell, hitting his head on the windlass as he went down. Caseley's hand flew to her mouth and she choked back a scream of panic.

Working with desperate urgency to free the split sail so a replacement could be bent on, the man in front hadn't noticed. His mate lay face down in the water that streamed across the deck and out of the scuppers.

Another huge wave broke over the side, sweeping the unconscious figure against the gunwale.

Heedless of the danger, Caseley dashed forward. Icy water filled her shoes and soaked the bottom of her skirt and petticoats.

'Caseley! No!'

She heard the roar of anguish, fury and warning but kept going. Rain beat down and within seconds her hair was a wet, straggling mass. Her jacket offered little resistance to the spray-laden gale and before she reached the foredeck she was soaked to the skin. But all her thoughts were focused on the man sprawled against the gunwale.

Gasping against the force of the wind, she staggered along the deck, grabbing whatever offered a handhold, until she reached him. Crouching, she turned his head. It was Jimbo. A cut above his ear oozed blood. The swelling had spread to his temple and was already beginning to turn purple. His eyes were closed, his face pinched and white.

The tough, chirpy little man who amused them with his tales and had pitched into the vicious fight with no weapons but his callused hands, looked shrunken, vulnerable, and suddenly much older.

Nathan turned, his arms full of torn canvas. His eyes widened in horror. 'Get back! Get away! It isn't safe here,' he yelled against the howling wind.

'I can't leave him,' Caseley cried. 'He'll drown.'

Another wave crashed over the gunwale driving the breath from her body as the achingly cold water cascaded past, soaking her to the waist.

She clung desperately to the windlass with one arm and Jimbo with the other, holding his head above the foam. As it drained away through the scuppers, she clasped her hands under his shoulders and began to drag him backwards towards the companionway.

Hammer emerged from the fo'c'sle with the spare sail, slamming and latching the hatch behind him. His jaw dropping as he saw Caseley, he lunged forward, ready to help.

'No,' she panted. 'I can manage.'

'Come on, Hammer,' Nathan bawled. 'We're losing way. If she broaches to, skipper'll be mad as hell.'

Caseley choked on a hysterical giggle. If they turned side-on to these seas, Jago Barata wouldn't have time to be furious. He'd be drowning with the rest of them. *She wasn't ready to die. She had only just started to live.*

The schooner nose-dived once more and she had to strain to prevent Jimbo's dead weight dragging her back towards the bows. Her fingers kept slipping on the wet oilskin. Her back felt as if it was breaking and her arms were being torn from their sockets.

Cold to her bones she sobbed for breath. Black spots danced in front of her eyes and she bit her lip to stop herself screaming as she felt her fingers slip. She adjusted her grip once more. Then as *Cygnet's* head came up she managed to drag Jimbo a few feet further.

Hammer and Nathan staggered along the deck.

'Where shall us put 'n?' Hammer was asking. 'Mart's just coming up, bleddy fo'c'sle's awash.'

'My cabin,' Nathan said, rain and spray dripping off his chin. 'All right, my bird, we got 'n.' He had to prise Caseley's fingers loose.

Dimly she heard Jago shouting to Hammer to take the wheel. Painfully she straightened up, clinging to the smooth heavy frame of the skylight. Every muscle ached and she was shaking violently.

There was movement around her, scuffling and grunts as Jimbo was manoeuvred through the hatch and down the stairs. Then a hand closed around her upper arm.

Blinded by rain and spray she raised her head, blinking to clear her vision and felt her heart wrenched as she focused. There were dark shadows beneath Jago's eyes and lines of strain she had not seen before. His lips were bloodless, his expression chilling.

Silently he guided her ahead of him down the stairs, his firm grip holding her up when she would have fallen. As they passed the mate's cabin she heard the rustle of oilskins, Jimbo moaning, and Nathan berating him for having two left feet.

They reached the day room just as Martin clattered down the stairs wearing oilskins two sizes too big for him.

'Make a pot of tea, now,' Jago ordered before the boy could speak.

'Aye, Cap'n.' The boy whirled round and raced back up again, slamming the hatch door.

'Get those wet clothes off.' Shutting the door Jago pushed her towards the sleeping cubicle. Stripping off his waterproof and sodden coat, he crouched in front of the stove, his wet shirt clinging to his broad back and muscular shoulders, and began to set a fire.

Cygnet pitched and Caseley collided with the door frame, sliding slowly down the wall. She wasn't even cold any more. She just wanted to sleep.

Jerked to her feet, she was shaken roughly.

'Open your eyes. Damn you, Caseley Bonython, look at me. You are going to get undressed and into dry clothes.' He shook her again. 'Do you hear me?' His fingers dug into the tender flesh below her shoulders.

She felt her face crumple and hot tears seeped through her lashes and slid down her face. 'I'm tired.'

Cursing under his breath, Jago held her up with an arm around her waist and unfastened the buttons on her jacket. Water dripped from her skirts onto the floor in a steadily widening pool. Pulling the jacket off he tossed it aside and reached for the waistband of her skirt.

Vaguely aware of what was happening, Caseley struggled weakly.

'Keep still,' Jago snapped, pushing the heavy skirt and petticoats down over her hips.

'Leave me alone.' She tried to fend him off, fighting the lethargy of cold and exhaustion that had sapped her strength.

'And let you die of lung fever? Not on my boat.'

'It's not your boat,' she mumbled.

'While I'm master she is. Now get the rest of your clothes off.' Releasing her, he reached into the cubicle, took one of the blankets from the bed, and shook it out. 'Do you hear me?'

'Yes, I hear you,' she flung back. 'But I'm – I can't –'

She could feel her face burning. 'Please look the other way.'

'For God's sake,' he said through gritted teeth. 'I've seen naked women before.'

'No doubt you have. But I'm not Louise Downing.' The moment the words left her lips she wished them unsaid. He held the blanket out to her and, as she took it, turned away.

'No, you aren't. There is no comparison.'

Stiff and cold, her fingers dug into the rough wool as she tore her gaze from the wet cotton clinging to his broad back and fumbled with the buttons of her blouse.

She had walked onto the knife and he had twisted it. He had only been using her: first his house, then the letters she had written for him here on board. Had she been a challenge?

He had blackmailed her into obedience and she had completed her own destruction by falling in love with him. He had never lied. She wasn't important enough for that. He knew she knew about Louise and had made no secret of his desire to get back to Falmouth as quickly as possible.

'Are you done?'

Blinking back scalding tears, she clenched her teeth determined not to allow a quivering chin to betray her, and hastily tore off her remaining garments. Gathering them into a bundle she tossed them onto her skirt.

'Yes,' she whispered, wrapping the blanket around her.

'Then come over here by the stove.' His voice was rough as he picked up her shoes from where she had kicked them and set them to dry. He went into the cubicle again, this time bringing her towel.

'Turn around.'

'I –'

'Your hair is dripping. It will soak the pillow.' He turned her firmly around and removed the slides and net.

As the heavy coil fell loose down her back, Caseley heard his soft intake of breath, felt his fingers brush her neck and shoulders as he lifted the wet mass to wrap the towel around her head and squeeze the water out.

The crackling stove radiated heat and now she was free of her saturated clothes, the aching cold was gradually ebbing. Though scratchy against her bare skin, the rough blanket offered comfort.

He began to massage her scalp through the towel, his strong fingers soothing. The tautness at the base of her skull started to ease. Her eyes closed, then flew open again as she realised what was happening. Not only was she falling under his spell once more, his quickened breathing told her he knew it.

She whirled round, careless of the pain as she wrenched free. Her bronze-gold tresses tumbled over her shoulders and the towel fell to the floor between them. She glimpsed hunger in his eyes before shutters came down and his features hardened.

'Leave me alone.' What she had intended as an angry demand emerged a weary plea. Backing away she caught her heel in the blanket, bumped against the table, and fell onto the bench seat. Could she possibly look any more awkward and ungainly? *No comparison.* It was a blessed relief to sit down.

About to speak he clamped his mouth shut and turned away, raking a hand through the wet curls plastered to his scalp. He spun round, making her jump.

'Had I left you alone, do you really believe Antonio Valdes would have been so polite? Do you imagine he would have stopped at seduction, or even rape?' His tone was brutal.

'He would have thrown you to his thugs, watched while they had their sport, then left you to die in the gutter. You have a lot to answer for, Caseley. Your lies might have cost me the *Cygnet* and my crew.'

'I never –' she flinched and fell silent as he raised a warning finger.

'There was no contract.' His scorn was withering. 'Ricardo Spinoza has as much interest in iron ore as I have in dressmaking.'

She gaped at him. 'You *knew*?'

'From the moment you stepped on board.' His words fell like stones into a pool, the ripples spreading ever wider.

Caseley swallowed. 'How?'

Jago slid onto the seat opposite, rested his forearms on the table. As he placed one hand over the other she saw grazes and bruising on his knuckles. *He had hit Antonio and fought the Basques to protect her.*

'Your Uncle Thomas is a frightened man. My guess is he's in deep financial trouble. Not only is he scared, he's bitter. All it took was a couple of drinks, a little sympathy, and he was telling me how much he resented your father checking his every move. Especially when he found out a contract had been drawn up for a company your father admitted did not exist. A contract that was a cover for a special assignment that would make all your father's years as a consul worthwhile.'

Caseley closed her eyes. He had sworn her to secrecy, trapped her in a web of deceit. *No one* must know, he had said. But aware he had little time left, he had been unable to resist the temptation to tell Thomas, as proof he was still a man of consequence.

She opened her eyes, saw him watching her, and looked away.

'Sam mentioned the package from Mexico,' Jago went on. 'He was fascinated by the stamps and seals. My father's last letter spoke of aid from ex-patriots supporting the restoration of Alfonso to the Spanish throne. Toby warned me to expect a passenger who had urgent business in Spain.'

'Señor Valdes?'

'Having followed the package from Mexico, he called on Thomas. Smoothing your uncle's ruffled feathers with liberal doses of charm and money –' he raised one eyebrow and her protest remained unspoken. 'He extracted the information he needed. Guessing you would be carrying the package as your father was unlikely to trust anyone else, Valdes allowed me to think he was the person I had been told to expect.'

Caseley clutched the blanket tighter. All she could do was listen.

'Then you turned up with that ridiculous story. Had the contract been genuine, *I* would have dealt with it on your father's behalf. So the pieces began to fall into place.'

Bitter anger swelled inside her. What a blind fool she had been. 'You knew. All the time, you *knew*.' Suddenly she recalled incidents whose significance had escaped her at the time.

He had never asked her why Valdes would go to such lengths to capture a contract. He had not asked because he already knew. He had warned her off the Spaniard, but never said why. And she, unused to dissembling, had dared not call his bluff and ask, for fear of letting something slip.

He had *expected* the ambush. He had been carrying a knife, and had sent Nathan, Jimbo, and Hammer on ahead because he anticipated trouble.

He had known which was Señor Spinoza's house.

Shocked and anxious after the attack, she had not noticed when he led her to a concealed side entrance instead of the front door.

Though neither of them had given any sign of knowing one another, the silver-haired Spaniard had accepted Jago's presence without question, even during her handover of the documents. Not once had Jago asked about the *second* envelope.

'You –' her entire body burned with rage and mortification. 'Why didn't you say something?'

'Why didn't you?' he countered immediately.

'My father swore me to secrecy.'

'Some secret.' His contempt had the sting of a whiplash. 'I daresay half Falmouth knew.'

Caseley's chin lifted even as her lips quivered. 'Not from me.'

'No. You kept your word to a sick old man, and nearly got yourself and the rest of us killed.' He passed a hand across his face. 'Why wouldn't you trust me?'

'Trust you?' Her voice cracked on a laugh that was half sob. Hadn't she yearned to do just that? Hadn't she ached to confide in him, draw on his strength, and share the awesome responsibility? But she had given her word. *Oh Father, how could you?*

Yet she could not find it in her heart to blame him. He was old and ill. He had seen so many of his hopes destroyed. Even this, his last and most important task as consul, he'd been forced to delegate. Jago Barata had known all this, and had said nothing.

'What reason have you ever given me to trust you? You barged your way into my life, bullied and blackmailed me to get me to do what you wanted.' Her breath hitched. 'You made me think … made me hope … What sort of a man are you?' She hurled the words like missiles, desperate to hurt him as he had hurt her. 'You have a mistress in Falmouth you can't wait to get back to, yet that didn't stop you forcing your attentions on me.'

Had she not been so devastated by his revelation, so hurt by his duplicity, she might have recognised the tightening of his features and swift turn of his head as the guilt and self-contempt they were. But in her misery she saw only impatience, the arrogance of a pirate who accepted no terms but his own, who had always taken what he wanted, heeding neither refusal nor rebuff.

He started to reach across the table.

'Keep away,' she warned. 'Don't touch me.'

He let his hand rest on the table. 'Or what? You'll scream? Who would hear you?'

Fear crawled along her nerves. He was right. While *Cygnet* was fighting for survival in the teeth of a storm, the crew, *his* men, had their hands full.

He lifted a handful of her damp dishevelled hair, closing his fist on it. 'I haven't known a moment's peace since I first laid eyes on you. And for that you will pay.' Opening his fingers he let her hair spill over the grey blanket like liquid bronze. 'But not here, not now.'

Gathering the remnants of her dignity, she tilted her chin. 'Spare me your threats.' Her knuckles gleamed white as she drew the blanket close. 'I owe you *nothing*. There was a time when I thought we might be friends.'

Her throat tightened and she swallowed to clear it. 'I was wrong. Once we reach Falmouth your problem is solved, for I never want to see you again. Until then, I will keep out of your way and you will oblige us both by ignoring me. I am not your *responsibility*.'

She slid out of the seat and crossed to the cubicle.

'Do you really hate me so much?' he asked quietly.

She paused in the curtained doorway, digging her

thumbnail hard into the pad of her index finger. It was a trick she had used before. Inflicting a small pain to hold off the larger one about to engulf her. She glanced over her shoulder, willing her voice steady.

'I do not hate you, Captain Barata. To hate someone they have to matter.' She walked into the cubicle and pulled the curtain across. Curled into a ball on the bunk she closed her eyes in silent, desperate agony.

Chapter Twenty

The storm passed, leaving in its wake a heavy swell and an exhausted crew.

Kept busy repairing damaged sails or splicing and whipping frayed and broken ropes, the men did not linger over meals. Instead they took every opportunity to catch up on sleep. They had all appreciated the stew. But Caseley had been unable to swallow more than a couple of mouthfuls.

On Jago's orders, Jimbo had rested for twelve hours. But he had refused to stay in bed any longer.

Caseley approached Nathan at the wheel. 'I realise this is an imposition, but would you mind if I used your cabin for the remainder of the voyage?'

After a moment's hesitation ripe with surprise and speculation the mate nodded. ''Tis all right with me, miss. But you better check with the skipper.'

Caseley went down to the day room, knocked then opened the door, and went in. Jago was seated at the table writing in the log.

'May I speak to you?'

'Yes.' He continued writing in his bold scrawl.

She cleared her throat. 'Now Jimbo has moved back to the fo'c'sle, I would like your permission to move into Nathan's cabin until we reach Falmouth. He has no objection but said I must ask you first.'

He raised his head then leaned back against the panelling, studying her with piercing intensity.

It cost her dearly to hold his gaze as she forced herself to add. 'I think you will welcome my absence and the return of your privacy.'

The silence stretched. Then he nodded. 'As you wish. When do you –'

'Now. I'll just collect my things.' Braced for a biting comment, his agreement came as a relief. Yet she was acutely aware of him watching as she removed her bag.

Wearing her spare green skirt and a pin-tucked cream shirt-blouse, she had pushed her other clothes, stiff with salt after drying in front of the stove, into her bag. Even looking at them brought back painful memories.

Nathan's cabin was not much bigger than Jago's sleeping cubicle. After stowing her bag, Caseley sat on the bunk for a few minutes. But with the only light coming in from gaps at the top and bottom of the door, she was suffocating. Putting on her salt-stained jacket she quickly buttoned it then hurried up the brass stairs to fresh air and the wide expanse of sea and sky.

The crew gave her friendly nods when their paths crossed but focused on their work, eager to get home.

Jago spoke little. When he did his tone was cool.

It was for the best, she told herself. He had shown he was not to be trusted. Wretchedly miserable, she grieved for the intimacy they had shared.

As they crossed the Bay of Biscay heading towards Falmouth she realised how hard he was driving himself. From dawn until nightfall he was either at the wheel, supervising and helping with repairs, or bent over the charts and log.

No matter what hour of the night she slipped from the mate's tiny cabin, unable to sleep, desperate for escape from her tormented thoughts, she saw light from the oil-lamp under the day-room door.

Did he never rest? With a sudden fierce yearning for revenge she hoped not. Why should he be granted the blessed relief of oblivion when it eluded her?

Before meeting him she had been trying hard to come to terms with the limitations of her life. Yes, she had been lonely. Especially when there was no task demanding her attention, when the household slept and the new day had yet to dawn.

In those dark hours she pined for a man who might love her in spite of her limp, her boyish figure, and her coppery hair. A man she could love and respect, a man to share her thoughts with, to have children with, grown old with. Yes she had yearned, but it had been manageable.

Until *he* came, shocking her into quivering awareness, kindling wild hopes and soaring dreams, only to trample them. He had broken her heart, leaving her nothing but aching misery and the pitiful rags of her pride.

At least he had never known the depth of her feelings for him. But that was small consolation.

Midmorning on the fourth day after leaving Santander, *Cygnet* sailed into Falmouth. The sun shone in a cornflower sky, the sea sparkled like sapphires. Only a short time ago they had been fighting for their lives.

Quay punts and rowing boats criss-crossed the water ferrying goods and passengers to and from bigger ships moored to huge buoys.

Jago was at the wheel. Acutely conscious of him, she had chosen a spot well out of everyone's way. She could not have borne to stay below.

'Right, boys.' Those two laconic words were all Jago said. Yet within minutes the foresail and jib had been dropped, the square topsail hauled up, the mainsail reefed a couple of points, and the peak lowered.

She drank in the sights and smells. Nothing had

changed yet everything was different. She had not wanted to make the voyage. But the events and emotions she had lived through had changed her forever. Right now her heart felt like a raw wound. But even the deepest wounds healed. Eventually.

Just before they reached the yard slipway and quays, Nathan, Hammer, and Jimbo lowered the mainsail. At Jago's nod, Martin released the staysail halyard. The canvas dropped into a pile on the foredeck and the schooner glided gently in alongside the wharf.

After securing the fore and aft lines, Hammer and Jimbo moved about the deck furling and lashing the sails. Martin began to unfasten the hatch cover and Nathan set up the winch.

She gazed across the yard over the sheds to the little tower on her father's house, its windows glistening in the sunlight. Home. No longer enough. But it was all she had.

She started to turn away. A shout made her glance back. Toby was hurrying towards the ship. His trousers hung in baggy folds from the belt beneath his belly, and his rolling gait made him rock from side to side. Worry furrowed his face as he beckoned urgently.

'Quick, my 'andsome. They want you uplong.'

She knew at once. 'He's not …?' She could not bring herself to say it.'

Toby shook his head. 'No. Doctor's with 'n now. Ben come over and told me and said for you to get on home the minute you come in.'

'I'll just fetch my things.' She whirled round and bumped into Jago who caught her arms to steady her.

'I've already sent Martin down.' As he spoke the boy appeared, his young face puckered in concern as he held out her bag and cape.

Shaking off Jago's hands, she seized her belongings

from Martin. 'Thank you,' she managed and the boy touched a knuckle to his forehead in salute. Her world was crumbling. It was too soon. Months, the doctor had said. Why now? Why so *soon*?

'I'll come with you.' Jago was close behind her as she limped to the schooner's side where Toby waited.

'No!' she rounded on him, her voice low and intense. 'He's the sick old man who nearly cost you the *Cygnet* and the lives of your crew. Remember?'

He shook his head, abrupt and impatient. 'I spoke in the heat of the moment –'

'Stay away.' Her voice broke on a sob.

Brilliant sunshine glinted on Jago's black curls as he stood like a rock, allowing the tide of her hurt and fear to smash against him. 'If there is anything you need, anything I can do –'

'*I* can give my father everything he needs,' she broke in, not allowing him to finish. She hated the sympathy in his eyes, hated her need, the longing for his support and strength surging through her, hated *him.*

'I managed alone before. I'll manage now. Go to your *friend*, Captain Barata,' she hissed, heedless of the round-eyed stares of the crew who, sensing something was wrong, had moved towards them. 'Go and find the peace you have missed so much. You need never see me again.'

She tossed her bag and the gabardine cape onto the wharf, then stepping onto the barrel and up onto the gunwale, jumped down into Toby's arms, wincing as the hard landing jarred her foot.

'All right, are you?' Anxiety creased his lined, weathered face, and she knew he was not referring solely to her concern over her father.

Not trusting herself to speak, she nodded quickly. As she snatched up her things, she heard Jago snap at the men to get back to work. There was a cargo to unload and transfer.

She hurried away from the schooner, the pain in her chest excruciating. *Jago*. She kept her gaze resolutely forward. Aware of Toby's worried glances, she hoped he would interpret the scalding tears that streaked her cheeks as fear for her father.

'See you across the road, shall I?' he offered as they reached the yard gates.

She shook her head. 'No. I'm all right, Toby. You get back. I know you have lots to do.'

'We're all thinking of 'n. And you too, my 'andsome.'

Impulsively, seeking comfort as much as giving it, Caseley leaned over and kissed the bristly cheek. 'Thank you.' Her voice wobbled.

Rosina met her at the door. 'Doctor's upstairs, my bird. He said you was to wait down here and he'd be with you d'rectly. I'm going to make you a nice cuppa tea.' As she spoke she took Caseley's bag, dropped it in the hall, and steered her firmly past the stairs and into the dining room. 'Kettle's boiled and I got a tray all set. Now you stay there.'

She pulled out one of the carver chairs and gently pressed Caseley down into it. 'Don't you move, mind,' she warned, and Caseley knew the housekeeper's sharp eyes hadn't missed a thing.

Resting her elbows on the polished table, she buried her face in her hands as her thoughts flew like sparks from a burning log.

A few moments later she heard footsteps in the passage, a muffled exchange of words and the tinkle of china. Sitting up she took a deep breath and braced herself for what was to come. Dr Vigurs walked in, closely followed by Rosina.

'Good morning, Caseley. No, don't get up.' He studied her with a deepening frown and she realised he was seeing her pallor and the dark circles beneath her eyes.

'Father –'

'Is resting quietly. You will see him very soon, I promise. First I need to talk to you. And you appear to be in need of a good meal and a few minutes to compose yourself.'

'I'll go and get –' Rosina began.

'No, nothing to eat. I'm not hungry right now. Thank you, Rosina.'

Shaking her head, the housekeeper left the room.

Dr Vigurs pulled out another chair and sat down, half-facing Caseley. 'Pour the tea, my dear,' he ordered gently.

Starting, she straightened up. 'Of course. Forgive me. It's –' Her hand shook as she lifted the white china pot patterned with roses.

Removing his pince-nez, the doctor polished them carefully with a spotless white handkerchief. But she was aware of him watching her. Replacing his spectacles he helped himself to sugar, and motioned to her cup, indicating she should drink.

She took a sip then replaced the delicate china onto the saucer with a clatter, raising anguished eyes. 'Please, you must tell me – how – how long?'

'A matter of hours. He had the attack two days ago. To be honest, I did not expect him to last the night. But against all odds he hung on. He has asked for you several times.'

The lump in Caseley's throat was so painful she could hardly speak. 'He's not in pain, is he?'

The doctor shook his head. 'Not any more. He's tired, Caseley. He's ready to go. I believe he is only waiting to see you. No,' he pressed her hand as she started to get up.

'Finish your tea. You have had a shock. You need time to gather your strength.'

She nodded, lowering her head, gripping the fragile china cup with stiff fingers as she blinked back scalding tears. After a moment she looked up. 'What happened? What caused the attack? I know you said – But he was delighted to be back at work, especially going to the yard. Something must have –' She broke off as the doctor glanced away, visibly uncomfortable.

'What? What is it? I have to know. Please?'

Robert Vigurs's features were sombre. 'My dear, I am so sorry to add to your troubles, but financial irregularities have been uncovered within your father's company.'

Caseley started so violently her cup fell over, spilling dregs of tea onto the lace tray-cloth. 'I don't believe it. Not *Father*. He wouldn't –'

'No, no, my dear. Forgive me. I did not make myself clear. Your father is in no way – The person responsible is Thomas Bonython. I understand the situation came to light when a money-lender demanded, with certain unpleasant threats, the return of his loan plus accrued interest.'

Caseley stopped breathing. *Jago was right.* She wanted to ask the doctor if he knew any more details, but held back. This was a family matter. She would speak to Uncle Richard later. She stood up. 'Thank you for telling me. I'll see my father now.'

Leaving Rosina to see him out, Caseley walked up the wide carpeted stairs. Her mind flashed back to a spiral of chased brass treads.

She lowered herself carefully onto the edge of the large bed. Her father's head and shoulders were propped up on snowy feather-filled pillows. His eyes were closed, his breathing shallow, and beneath the network of purple thread veins on his cheeks and nose, his complexion was ash-grey. He looked thinner. But the deep furrows of pain, the grooves of anger and disillusionment, had smoothed out. His face looked waxen.

It was then she realised that, despite the doctor's warning, she had not really expected her father to die. She had heard the words without accepting the reality.

She looked down at the man who had always been a giant, strong, forceful, and full of life, with hands like hams and a voice that could reach from one end of the yard to the other. During her absence he had withered into frailty.

Her vision blurred. Biting hard on her lower lip, she lifted his cold hand in hers.

Creased like fine tissue paper, his eyelids flickered and parted, opening slowly. As his dull gaze focused, Caseley smiled down at him.

'I can't leave you for a minute, can I?' she scolded softly.

One corner of his mouth lifted. 'Took your time, didn't you, girl?' His voice was weary and slurred, but the glow of pleasure in his eyes was nearly her undoing. She longed to lay her head on his chest, cling to him, and beg him not to leave her, not yet, not so *alone*.

She swallowed the agonising stiffness in her throat and kept her voice low to disguise the thickness of tears. 'Can I get you anything? Some water?' Her own mouth was dust dry.

His hand moved in hers and he turned his head a fraction on the pillow. 'Did it go all right?' The words rustled from his lips like autumn leaves.

She nodded. 'Señor Spinoza sends you his kindest regards. He said the new King of Spain has reason to be very grateful to you. So too will the Spanish people when Don Alfonso puts an end to the rebellion and restores peace.'

Teuder's rheumy eyes shone. 'He did? He said that?'

Caseley nodded.

Her father sucked air into his failing lungs. 'You didn't have any trouble?'

'None at all,' the lies were easy on her tongue. 'Everything was just as you said it would be.'

'And Jago, did he –?'

His name sent a tremor through her. She could not speak of him, even to her father. Fighting for composure, she gently pressed the frail hand.

'All the crew were very kind to me. Jimbo told some amazing yarns. The bad weather you warned of hit us on the way back. But *Cygnet* rode it out. She's a beautiful ship, Father.'

He nodded; too tired to press now he knew the mission had been successful. The groove between his shaggy brows deepened. 'Is it out yet? Do they know in the yard?'

'Know what?'

'About Thomas.'

'No. No one knows,' she said firmly, not knowing or caring if it was the truth.

'It mustn't get out.' Anxiety quickened his breath, making it rasp in his throat.

'It won't.' Caseley placed her hand over his, trying to soothe.

'I paid off Colenzo. But if word gets round ...' He coughed weakly and she heard bubbling in his chest.

'It won't, Father. I'll take care of it.' Lifting his hand she pressed it to her cheek.

His eyelids drooped and tension drained out of him like water through a sieve. 'It's yours, girl,' he muttered. 'The yard, the business, all of it. Changed my will. Don't let it fail, Caseley.' His eyes lost focus. 'Ralph would have drunk it all away.' His voice trailed off. Then he rallied, his eyes opened and fixed on her face, urgent, pleading. 'Listen, girl, you must –' His face contorted in pain.

Smothering a cry, her heart beating wildly, she clutched his hand in both of hers. 'It's all right. Don't try to talk.' Tears splashed onto her hand. 'Rest now.'

The spasm passed. His breathing grew fainter. Then, his lips barely moving, he whispered, 'Philip?'

Caseley sat and held his hand, felt it grow cold. Eventually she laid it gently on the coverlet and rose stiffly to her feet. Her eyes burned and her throat ached. She went downstairs to the kitchen.

Rosina and Liza-Jane were preparing lunch. Ben came in from the garden as she was breaking the news. He put an arm around Liza-Jane's thin, shaking shoulders. Rosina sobbed quietly into her apron.

Caseley didn't think she would ever cry again. She was numb.

'Some sorry I am, miss.' Ben's open face was full of sympathy. 'I remember what 'twas like when my father went.'

'Thank you.' Many people would say those words in the next few days. Most would be thinking of their own losses, not hers. Few would care the way Ben, Rosina, and Liza-Jane did.

'Ben, will you go across to the yard and tell Toby? I think it's best if he tells the men. I'll let him know the date of the funeral as soon as it's arranged.'

He nodded then bent his head. 'Come on now, maid,' he murmured in Liza-Jane's ear. 'Best get moving. We want to give mister a proper send-off.'

Their closeness was too much for Caseley and she looked quickly away.

Rosina wiped red-rimmed eyes with the corner of her

apron. 'We all loved 'n, though he wasn't always easy.' Her mouth quivered. 'Place won't be the same.' She sniffed then pulled herself together. 'Put the kettle on, Liza-Jane. Miss Caseley, if it's all right with you, I'd like to lay 'n out. You want it done proper, with respect.'

'Thank you, Rosina. I have to go out for a while.'

'But, Miss Caseley,' the housekeeper began, clearly startled.

'I'm going to see Dr Vigurs, then I'll call on Mr Nancholas.'

'Ben can fetch the undertaker. There's no call for you to –'

'There's something else I must do,' Caseley interrupted and went upstairs to put on a clean jacket. As she left the house the housekeeper was still protesting, visibly concerned.

The doctor was busy with a patient so Caseley left a message with the sour-faced housekeeper. 'Please ask the doctor to call when it's convenient. Tell him there's no urgency,' she added in the new calm voice that seemed to belong to someone else.

Mr Nancholas expressed his deepest sympathy in hushed tones while making washing motions with his hands. He urged her to inspect his range of coffins and suggested they decide upon the number and types of cab she would require for the cortège. Caseley shut off the flow by inviting him to call at the house later that afternoon. He was still washing and mouthing condolences as she closed the door behind her.

She went into the office and told Richard.

'Oh, my dear.' Taking both her hands in his he squeezed them. 'I am so very sorry.'

The genuine sympathy and kindness in her uncle's words and gesture caused a wrenching pang. But leaving a few minutes later she was still dry-eyed.

She reached the house in Florence Terrace, unaware of the route she had taken or the people she had passed.

'Are my aunt and uncle in?' she asked when the stocky maid opened the door.

The girl nodded and stepped back. 'In the drawing room they are. Want me to show you in? Only I got–'

'No, thank you. I know the way.'

Rose nodded, closed the front door and stomped back to the kitchen.

A door off the hall opened. 'Rose? Who –?' Margaret Bonython froze, paling so the rouge daubed on the flesh covering her cheekbones stood out in two bright patches. Shock and guilt chased across her face. 'Caseley! What – what a surprise.' Her forced smile was more a grimace.

Without waiting for an invitation, Caseley walked past her into the stuffy over-furnished room.

Thomas was huddled in a tall wing-backed chair beside the brightly burning fire. His face was the colour of clay, his eyes puffy and bloodshot. He flinched when he saw her. Her gaze went to the glass in his trembling hand and she smelled the pungent aroma of whisky.

'I suppose *he* sent you,' Thomas said. 'I can't work today. I'm not well.' His gaze slid away from hers. He did indeed look ill.

Caseley sat down, her back very straight. She folded her hands in her lap and looked from one to the other.

'I know.' She saw Thomas flinch.

'What did he want to tell you for? He had no business …' He gulped the whisky, the glass clattering against his teeth.

Margaret wrung her hands. 'It was simply an unfortunate misunderstanding. Anyway, it's all settled now.' Her mouth stretched in a travesty of a smile.

Caseley remained silent. 'Thomas only *borrowed* the money,' she blustered. 'He was going to pay it back. If that stupid Luke Dower hadn't got himself arrested by the customs men –'

'Margaret –' Thomas croaked.

'Oh, be quiet,' his wife snapped.

'Luke Dower?' Caseley held her aunt's gaze.

'It was all his fault,' Margaret babbled. She leaned forward in an armchair upholstered in emerald green velvet, determined to convince. 'Thomas didn't know anything about the gold coins. It was supposed to be honest business. He was to be an agent, handling goods for clients abroad. Only Luke never paid Thomas when he should have. Then your dear father decided to check the books.' Her mouth pursed. 'So Thomas had to borrow off Colenzo to repay what he'd borrowed from the business.'

'Are you saying that if Father had not returned to work when he did, Uncle Thomas would not have had to borrow from Colenzo?' Caseley's calm seemed to reassure her aunt.

'That's right. I knew you would understand.'

'He would simply have continued stealing from the family business?' Caseley went on as if her aunt had not spoken. 'He would have entered into further arrangements with known criminals in order to make more money for himself?'

Margaret's eyes bulged and her mouth sagged open then snapped shut like a trap. Indignation swelled her bosom.

'It was all your father's fault. How are we supposed to maintain any kind of standard on the pittance he pays? Keeping up appearances costs money. Not that *you* would understand. You don't know the first thing about style. Prices are going up all the time. We have a position to uphold –'

'So you would *steal* to maintain it?'

Margaret didn't even hear her. 'I told your father it wasn't our fault. I told him he would have to pay Colenzo off for the sake of the family name. Like I said, no one need ever know. Luke Dower won't talk. Even if he does, Thomas will swear he had no idea there was anything dishonest –'

'Margaret,' Thomas pleaded.

'Shut *up*,' she spat, her expression venomous. She turned back to Caseley. 'Everything will just go on as normal. That's in everyone's best interests, isn't it? It won't do your father any good to make a fuss, him being a consul and everything. That's what I told him anyway. Now it's all tidied up we'll say no more about it.'

Caseley stood up. 'When did you discuss this with my father?'

'When? The day before yesterday. Of course it all fell on my shoulders. *He*,' she glared at the slumped figure of her husband, 'wasn't fit for anything.' She turned a suspicious gaze on Caseley, her mouth pursing again. 'Not that it's any of your business. There's no call for you to be hanging around the office, not now your father is back. Far better that you leave business matters to those who understand them.'

'Like your husband?' Caseley suggested.

Margaret flushed an ugly brick colour. 'You mind your tongue, miss. We all know why you spend so much time in the office and down at the boatyard. Got your eyes on that Spaniard, haven't you? It's disgusting. Your father should know better.'

Caseley walked to the door. Her heart drummed against her ribs as she turned to look from her uncle's drunken misery to her aunt's malice.

'My father died this morning,' she said through stiff lips. 'The pair of you killed him.'

In the silence that followed her footsteps were loud on the hall's tiled floor. She pulled the front door closed on Thomas's groan and Margaret's shriek, and drew a deep, shuddering breath. Never had she felt so tired.

Chapter Twenty-one

It was nearly four when she got home. Messages of sympathy were beginning to arrive. Liza-Jane, her eyes pink-rimmed and swollen, had time for little but answering the door.

Rosina brought a bowl of chicken soup to Caseley in the dining room, refusing to leave until she ate it all. ''Tis nice and easy to swallow, bird.

'I can't, Rosina. My stomach hurts.'

'It probably think your throat have been cut. You're hungry, bird. That's what's wrong. Come on now. You want to do your best for your father, you need to keep your strength up.'

Caseley lifted the spoon and sipped. For a moment she feared her stomach would rebel. But as she swallowed the hot aromatic soup, she felt the knots loosen. After several more mouthfuls, warmth slid along her veins and the dull ache at the back of her skull receded.

Rosina talked of the past, reminding Caseley of incidents long forgotten, laughing and crying over Teuder's irascibility and his kindness, so often hidden beneath noise and bluster.

'You could get 'n to do anything so long as you convinced 'n it was his idea all along. Men!' She stood up, shaking her head with a fond sad smile. 'Break your heart they do, but 'twould be a dull old world without them.'

Caseley was spared having to respond by the sound of the front door slamming. She had seen questions in

Rosina's eyes. They were too close for the housekeeper not to have recognised that aside from her father's death, she was deeply unhappy.

'You stay there, miss.' She patted Caseley's shoulder. 'I'll see what's going on.' She hurried out. Hearing her voice, sharp and scolding, Caseley tensed.

The door swung open and her brother lurched in. His clothes were creased and stained, his hair dishevelled, and he needed a shave. Under his arm he carried a large, flat, oblong object wrapped in brown paper. He had the slow blink she had come to dread and seemed to be having trouble focusing.

Caseley turned away, propping her elbows on the table as she covered her face with her hands.

'Wass' matter? Why's Rosina been crying? And skinny Liza? For God's sake, I was only away a couple of nights.'

Caseley looked at him. She felt distanced from everything and oddly calm. 'It isn't about you, Ralph. Father died this morning.'

'Oh.' He dropped the parcel onto the table then slumped into a chair, resting his head against the high wooden back. 'Sudden, wasn't it?'

Evidence of his dissipation was clear in his slack mouth, sallow complexion, and the pouches of skin beneath his muddy eyes.

'Is that all you have to say?'

'What do you expect?' he retorted angrily. 'Grief? Why should I pretend something I don't feel? We never got on, you know that.' He rubbed a hand across his eyes. 'I've been staying with Jason.'

'Why, Ralph?'

'Why what?'

His vacant expression ignited a spark of anger that flared hot and bright. 'Why stay with Jason? Why not come home? Why be drunk at this time of day?'

He didn't answer and her anger died as quickly as it had flamed. How nice it would be to go to sleep and not wake up.

With unsteady hands Ralph ripped the paper off the parcel to reveal a freshly painted canvas. He pushed it towards her.

Lifting it she turned it towards the light, looking carefully at the portrait. Posed against a background of crimson drapes a pretty girl with corn-coloured hair wore a low-cut bodice that framed her white shoulders in a froth of lace. She caught her breath as she saw it: the sulky wilfulness behind the sweet smile, a restless boredom in the china blue eyes. She glanced away then looked again. But it wasn't her imagination. It was there, real and clear. She looked at her brother in awe.

'Ralph, it's brilliant. But –' She stopped, reluctant to add to his misery.

'But,' he agreed, his careless shrug not deceiving her for an instant.

'They didn't like it.' Caseley stated. How could they?

'The Tidburys said it was nothing at all like their daughter. How, when she was the prettiest girl in the entire town, had I managed to make her look so plain? The Lashbrookes, including her husband Edwin, simply looked uncomfortable. They know that painting is a true likeness, but prefer to pretend it isn't.'

'And Frances?' Caseley was curious. 'What did she say?'

'She burst into tears and wanted to know why I hate her so much. I don't hate her. I hardly know her.' He shrugged. 'I painted what I saw.' His hands, long-fingered, talented and grimy, hung over the arms of the chair. 'Anyway, they refused the portrait.'

'So you went and got drunk for two days.'

Tense and furious he half-rose then fell back onto the chair, his features softening into the familiar expression of petulance and self-pity. 'How could I expect you to understand?'

Caseley laid the canvas down. 'I understand this. You have to choose. If you can see Frances Lashbrook's character reflected in *her* face, you can see the same, good and bad, in other people. Ralph, you can commit yourself to your painting, honour your vision and talent, and accept the rejections that are bound to come. Or you can give up, live in a bottle, and be a failure who lacked the courage even to try. If you choose to paint I'll help you all I can. But I won't give you the money to drink yourself to death.'

'What money?' he sneered. 'You haven't got any. Now Father's gone, the house and the business will be mine.'

'No, they won't.' She spoke quietly.

It took a moment to register then Ralph's head jerked. 'What do you mean, they won't?' Shock had sobered him.

Caseley stood up. 'I was with Father when he died. Just before … the end he told me he had changed his will.' She watched all colour drain from her brother's face.

'He didn't – You can't mean – You?'

'I didn't know, Ralph.' She guessed what was coming. 'Truly, I didn't. He was worried about your drinking. I think he saw everything he had worked so hard to build being frittered away.'

His face distorted, ugly with rage. 'You sneaky, manipulating bitch! It's mine. I'm the eldest. I was his only son, for God's sake. It's mine by right.'

'I'm sorry,' she whispered.

'What the hell will *you* do with the business? What do you know about running a boatyard? Or are *you* going to sell it? It's probably worth a bit. You could buy yourself a husband.'

Clasping her upper arms, holding the hurt inside, Caseley went to the window. She felt as brittle as fine glass, but tried to make allowances for Ralph's disappointment. Their father's decision was a bitter blow to him.

The sun was going down: another day almost over and her last link with childhood broken.

'I shan't sell,' she said, talking to herself as much as him, exploring possibilities. 'I learned a lot helping father during his illness. With Richard and Toby to advise –'

The door slammed and she fell silent.

The funeral took place three days later. The parish church was packed. The doors were left open so those left standing on the steps or in the road could hear.

Caseley had closed both office and yard for the day. Dressed in their Sunday best, their faces shaved and scrubbed shiny, hair slicked flat, every man and boy who worked at Bonython's followed a red-eyed Toby into the church.

At the graveside, with Richard and Helen on one side, Margaret, Thomas, and their daughter, Charlotte on the other, Caseley said her silent farewell. Ralph had not appeared.

As the finality of the moment hit her, she swayed. A hand gripped her arm, drawing her gently back. Her eyes burning behind the black veil, she glanced round, hoping, needing so desperately … and looked into Richard's kind face, furrowed in concern.

Of course he had not come. Why would he? She had told him she never wanted to see him again. He had sent a note of condolence, his bold scrawl instantly recognisable.

Her heart had thumped, her fingers unsteady as she opened the envelope. The wording had been formal as befitted the occasion. Yet he had signed it, 'As ever, Jago.'

What did he mean, *as ever*? What was there between them but lies, blackmail, and mistrust? Was that what he wanted her to remember? She needed no reminding.

Crushing the paper into a ball she had been about to hurl it into the fire. But she couldn't, and tossed it onto her deck instead. That night, unable to sleep, she had crept out of bed and lit the lamp. Sitting at her desk she smoothed the crumpled paper flat, and gazed at those three words for a long time.

The following day she was up early. Life had to go on and responsibility for all her father's employees now rested on her shoulders. Passing the yard on her way to the office, she caught sight of *Cygnet*, easing away from the quay.

Stopping, she looked for the tall, bearded figure. Nathan was at the wheel. Hammer, Jimbo, and Martin moved swiftly about the deck, setting the smaller sails. She did not see Jago.

Recovering, she hurried on along the road. He was probably below in the day room, bent over the chart table, plotting their course. The image was so vividly, painfully real that she stumbled and almost fell.

With a hand against the high wall, she fought for mental balance. It should be getting easier, not more difficult. She should be missing him less, not more.

He was out of her life. It was a mutual decision. The problems between them were insurmountable. He had passed through her life like a shooting star. Brief, brilliant, tantalising her with a wish, a hope.

She was glad he had sailed again so soon. There would be no embarrassing encounters at the office. She would not have to face those mocking grey eyes. She would be able to work without hoping for, yet dreading, his footstep on the stairs, his cynical smile at her temerity to imagine she could succeed in a man's world. Far better he had gone.

Nodding to Sam she entered her father's office. A neat pile of letters had been stacked in the centre of the desk. She took off her bonnet and hung up her cape, now washed free of salt and neatly pressed. She looked at her mother's bureau. Then walked round behind her father's desk.

She had just sat down in his chair when the door opened and Richard entered. His round shoulders and puckered features made him appear more mole-like than ever.

'What's to be done about Thomas? He sent Charlotte down with a message that he is still unwell and Margaret is prostrate with grief.' He clicked his tongue.

Caseley sighed, turning the ivory letter-opener over in her fingers. 'I don't know. What are your thoughts?'

Clasping his lapels, Richard paced to and fro. 'We cannot ignore what he did. But as a partner he has a financial interest in the company. It would cost more than we can afford to buy him out, especially now. Not only have we lost the money he embezzled, we've also lost the amount Teuder had to draw to pay off Colenzo.' He stopped, shamefaced. 'Forgive me, my dear. I don't mean to reopen old wounds.'

She waved his apology away. 'It must be faced. Though it was a shock to learn how much was involved, and that Father had emptied his personal account to repay the debt.'

'Your father was an honourable man, Caseley.' Richard paused in his pacing to look at her. 'He knew the business could not have withstood such a drain on its working capital. Has it caused problems at home?'

She made a small, helpless gesture. 'I haven't told Ralph about Uncle Thomas. But he's threatening to contest the will anyway.'

'What about the bequests to Rosina, Liza-Jane, and Ben? Short of selling the house, there's nothing left to pay them.'

Caseley looked away, her eyes filling even as she smiled. 'They all insist they don't mind. Rosina said it was a lovely thought. But what they never had they can't miss. And none of them will be a party to anything that involves selling the house or the yard to give them a few pounds. All three are prepared to work for nothing if we can keep a roof over our heads.' Clenching her fists on the desktop, she raised her head to meet her uncle's concerned gaze. 'We *must* go on.'

For the rest of the day she immersed herself in work, making notes of matters to be discussed with Toby.

After one of her consultations with Richard over fees and cargoes, she paused in the doorway of his office, hugging a leather-bound ledger against her chest.

'On my way here this morning I saw *Cygnet* leave.' She strove to sound casual.

'Mmmmmn,' her uncle nodded, still studying a page of figures. 'She's gone up to Penryn to load granite for London.'

'Do –' she cleared her throat. 'Do you know if Captain Barata found a ship to take that quicksilver to Mexico?'

Richard glanced up. 'What? Oh, yes. Fox's had a barque due to leave the day you got back. They delayed it until the next tide to allow enough time to transfer the cargo.'

'That was good of them.'

'It was. Do you have a note of the date of Lloyd's final inspection of *Fair Maid*?'

'Yes. It will be in the diary.'

'I'll send Sam for it.'

'Give me ten minutes.'

When Sam brought in the afternoon mail, Caseley was puzzled to find a letter addressed to her from solicitors, Knuckey & Son. She knew of them. They had an excellent reputation. But as far as she was aware they had never handled any of her father's business.

The envelope was heavy in her hand and she could feel an object at the bottom. As she slit open the envelope, tension tightened the back of her neck as possibilities raced through her mind. Was Ralph really going to contest the will? Had Thomas and Margaret taken legal advice, and now planned to cause more trouble?

Removing the thick folded paper, she tipped the envelope and a key slid out onto her palm. As she recognised it her heart leapt into her throat. Her fingers closing on the key, she read the letter. Then she read it again.

Though couched in polite terms the words amounted to an order. The following day she was required to go to the house of Captain Jago Barata on Greenbank Terrace to ascertain whether all the work ordered by her had in fact been completed. A key was enclosed.

She could not go back there. It held too many memories, too many poignant reminders of her foolishness. The wounds had only just beginning to heal. And yet …

She had loved the house. Its indefinable atmosphere had captured her imagination. Choosing colour schemes, selecting wallpapers and fabrics, searching shops for furniture to complement each room had given her such pleasure.

Could it really do any harm to take one last look now all the tradesmen had finished? To see at least some of her ideas translated into reality? But what if Louise Downing had had her way? No, she wouldn't have. Jago had said as much. *Jago.*

At least she would be alone. Alone to remember, to think of what might have been, to bleed. Why should she put herself through that?

When she reached home that evening she had still not decided whether to go. As she took off her bonnet and cape in the hall, she could hear Rosina and Liza-Jane gossiping beyond the open kitchen door.

'She ditched 'n for Redvers Edyvean.'

'She never!' Liza-Jane gasped. 'He must be sixty if he's a day.'

'He also got two grocery stores in Falmouth and one in Penryn.'

Despite her tiredness and all the weight on her mind, Caseley could not help smiling at Rosina's dry retort as she rubbed stiffness from the back of her neck.

'Well, that wasn't the story *I* heard,' Liza-Jane said amid a clatter of dishes. 'My cousin Doreen do work for Mrs Bowden who live next door to that place of his up on Greenbank.'

Caseley froze, unable to breathe.

'Doreen couldn't help but hear the row. Going at it something terrible they was. He was mad as fire that she had turned up at his house uninvited, and about her going down the yard asking questions about who he'd took to Spain. He wouldn't let her in past the hallway. He said she had no business there, and she wasn't never to come back. She was screaming and yelling.

'Well, I wouldn't put my tongue to some of the things

Doreen told me. But the gist of it was that she's gived him a bleddy good time and he didn't have no right to cast her off like a bleddy old shoe. He told her she wasn't in no position to complain. She'd started it, and she knew the rules. It was finished, he said, and if she had any sense she'd take the fifty pounds and keep her jealousy to herself 'cos she had most to lose and his patience was running out. Doreen said it all went quiet then. Next minute she seen Louise leaving. That was last week.'

'She certainly didn't waste much time,' Rosina commented. 'I reckon she's putting it out about she and old Edyvean. *She* always done the dumping before. Fifty pounds, eh? I'd say she done all right.'

Caseley's heart was beating hard and loud as she went upstairs to her room. Closing the door she leaned back against it. *Jago had ended his relationship with Louise.* Momentary joy evaporated as she realised it made not the slightest difference. He had left her first. He appeared to be severing all connections.

That had to be why the solicitor wanted all the loose ends neatly tied up. Was he selling the house? Would he still sail Bonython schooners? Or when *Cygnet* returned from London would he cut that last link with Falmouth and disappear to a new life in some other part of the world? Selling his interests in Spain would make him a very rich man. He could go wherever he chose.

After another virtually sleepless night and a morning during which she found it increasingly difficult to focus on the piles of papers covering her father's desk, she made her decision. She would go to the house. She must, to exorcise the past.

Because she would be out of the office for the afternoon she told Richard about the letter. She expected him to comment or ask questions, but he simply nodded.

'Don't worry about coming back. It's been a difficult time for you. Take an hour or two for yourself.'

'Are you all right, Uncle Richard?'

He glanced up, but only for a moment. 'Perfectly. Why do you ask?'

'You look a little flushed. I hope you haven't picked up Aunt Helen's cold.'

'No, I'm perfectly well. If I don't catch you before you go, I'll see you in the morning.'

Lunchtime came. Too tense to go home and risk Rosina's sharp eyes, Caseley went to Clara Powell's teashop on the corner of Church Street. Unable to face eating anything she ordered a cup of hot chocolate. Its soothing warmth loosened some of the knots in her stomach.

She paid off the driver. The cab turned in the middle of the road and headed back towards the town centre.

Caseley walked up the granite steps onto the pavement that ran high above the rutted road and walked along to the house. She hesitated at the open gate at the bottom of the path. A single rose bloomed in the weed-choked bed. The moss on the flagstones had been scraped off by the constant passage of feet.

The outside of the house was transformed. Within freshly painted frames, sparkling windows reflected the sunshine. The gossamer ropes and dead spiders had been swept from the porch and the steps scrubbed. So glossy was the black front door with its new porcelain knob and polished brass knocker, Caseley could see herself reflected in it. No longer shabby and neglected, the house looked proud, imposing. *Like its owner.*

She stood in the porch, fingering the key. Were it not for the letter she wouldn't be here. But now that she was, she might as well take a look.

She unlocked the front door. It opened without a sound on newly oiled hinges. Shutting it behind her she stood for a moment in front of the closed inner door. It was not too late. She need go no further. She drew a slow breath.

Chapter Twenty-two

Opening the inner door she stepped into the hall. It smelled fresh and new. She saw gleaming paintwork and new frosted glass globes with fluted tops on the gas mantles. Cream embossed paper added light and dimension to the space. The terracotta tiles glowed.

Her chest was painfully tight. As she pressed one hand to her breastbone she realised she had been holding her breath.

It was less than a month since she had followed Jago Barata into this house. Virtual strangers, captor and hostage, they had talked that day of childhood and loneliness, of destiny and courage and being true to oneself. That day she had begun to love him. What a blind, stupid *fool* she had been.

Tears gathered on her lashes and spilled down her cheeks. She clenched her fists. Why persist in this self-torture? How could she escape it? In spite of everything she loved him still. She should not have come. She could not have stayed away. Nor could she leave, not yet.

She walked slowly through rooms freshly painted and newly papered. Curtains complemented carpets on floors that had been sanded and varnished. Comfortably furnished, the rooms were not cluttered and so appeared lighter and more spacious than they really were. It was exactly as she had imagined.

Though she had walked in reluctantly, her heart had said *home*. She had seen through the neglect, and felt the house waiting. Unoccupied for too long, it needed people to bring it back to life.

Her breath hitched and she swallowed a sob. In such a short time her life had changed irrevocably. Her father was dead and she had not had time to mourn. Too many people needed her: Toby, Uncle Richard, Rosina. She hadn't seen Ralph since the day of their father's death.

She walked into the master bedroom and looked at the pretty paper echoing the green and white flower-sprigged tiles surrounding the fireplace. Trailing her fingers along the gleaming foot rail of the brass bedstead, she stared at the bed's bare springs and saw white sheets, piled pillows, and her father's face contorted, then waxen as death smoothed away his pain.

She gripped the rail, her knuckles white and aching as she recalled Jago talking of his children yet unborn, mocking her blushes, angry for reasons she did not understand. She shook the rail, making the metal springs shiver and squeak as anguish tore her throat.

How was she to cope? Ralph, Aunt Margaret, Uncle Thomas, no money in the bank, the house to run, the business to manage … How could she go on? How could she not? Sinking onto the bedstead, she rested her forehead on her hands and abandoned herself to grief.

The sound of footsteps on the landing outside jolted her upright, dashing away tears with one hand while she fumbled for her handkerchief with the other.

If one of the workmen had returned for something he'd forgotten, she didn't want to be discovered weeping. They would know about her father. But they also knew about Louise Downing.

The door flew open.

'No.' She barely heard her voice through the roaring in her ears. Black spots danced across her vision and the room swayed.

Then Jago's arms were around her and her tear-wet face lay against his broad shoulder. Hearing the thunder of his heartbeat she wondered why it was so fast.

'Don't, Caseley.' His voice was hoarse. 'Please don't cry. I can't bear it.'

She felt him kiss the top of her head. Then he rested his cheek against her hair, holding her so tightly she could hardly breathe. It was a dream. She would wake up in a minute and he would be gone. But the warmth of his body, his unique scent, and the pressure of his arms were no mirage.

Easing his hold he tilted her chin. Looking into his face she saw exhaustion in the shadows under his eyes and strain in the lines that bracketed his mouth.

'Forgive me,' he whispered. Then his mouth covered hers in a kiss of such aching tenderness that fresh tears slid down her temples and into her hair. Holding her fast with one arm, he cupped her face gently with his free hand and kissed her again and again.

He was here. He did care. Everything else could wait. She put her arms around him, felt his warm breath on her cheek and heard a soft groan. At last he raised his mouth from hers.

'What are you doing here?' Caseley's voice was husky from weeping. 'I saw *Cygnet* leave.'

'Under Nathan's command.' He rested his face against hers. 'I arranged for him to pick up another crewman at Penryn.'

'Why?'

'I had business here. With you.'

Caseley loosened her hold enough to lean back and look into his eyes. 'What business? And how did you know I would –?'

'Be here? I instructed Mr Knuckey to write and send the key. I hoped you would want to see the house finished. Come, sit down.'

Allowing him to guide her to the window seat with its padded cushion that matched the curtains, Caseley sat with his arm around her shoulders. She recalled her uncle's reaction.

'Uncle Richard knew.'

Jago nodded. 'I have spent a lot of time with him this past week. Once I explained my plans he could not have been more helpful.'

She stiffened at the implied betrayal. It was happening again. Jago Barata was prying into her family's affairs behind her back. And her trusted Uncle Richard was helping him. She tried to draw away but his arm tightened.

'No, Caseley, you must listen.' She opened her mouth to protest but he silenced her with his own. She could not fight. Instead she welcomed his gentle exploration, deeply moved by delicacy in his touch, stirred by the powerful emotions she sensed he was holding back. When at last he raised his head, they were both breathless.

'I *had* to talk to Richard. I needed an honest assessment of the shipping agency and the yard's present position, financial status, and future potential.'

'Why?'

'Because I want to buy it.' He placed his fingers gently on her lips to silence the refusal her eyes signalled. His next words took her breath away.

'If I asked you to marry me *before* I bought the business, you might – you probably would – assume my proposal was simply a means to get my hands on the yard. But if I already own it, that objection is void. If you refuse to sell, I will accept your decision. Instead I shall put into the business the equivalent of its market value. We will be equal partners.' A wry smile warmed his eyes. 'You would never settle for less.

'Richard will run the agency as he has always done. We will appoint a new accountant. The yard remains as it is, including the name. But Thomas goes. I will buy his share separately and give him a fair price.' Anger hardened Jago's features. 'But neither he nor that poisonous wife of his will ever set foot on Bonython property again.'

Caseley stared at him. 'Is there nothing you don't know?' Then like the sun appearing from behind a cloud she realised. 'Is this why you sold all your interests in Spain?'

He shrugged. 'What better reason could I have?'

Gently freeing herself she stood up. He rose as well, but did not follow as she walked to the window, rubbing her arms. It was too much to take in all at once.

'Caseley, please. Say you'll marry me.' He was not used to asking for anything and it showed. 'I've been out of my mind since you left *Cygnet.* I've spent most days with Toby, learning about the yard. I've nearly driven him mad.' He drove a hand through his black curls. 'Every evening I've been with Richard, going over the books. You mustn't be angry with them. I threatened them with dire consequences should they let a word slip.'

She felt a pang of sympathy for her uncle. It was not easy to stand against Jago Barata. In truth, it was impossible.

'I paid the tradesmen large bonuses to ensure everything was completed quickly while maintaining the standards you had set.' He joined her at the window. 'This house needs you. You belong here. I saw it that first day. Everything you've done here,' he gestured, 'the colours, the furnishings, I didn't know the house could look and feel so – so like a home. You couldn't have done it if you hadn't cared.' He raised his hands in silent supplication.

Still, she did not answer.

'Is it Louise?' He started forward, stopping abruptly as she moved back. 'It's over. I ended it the day we got back. It never meant anything. I'm thirty-four years old and I've never been married. Of course there have been – liaisons.' He took two quick steps forward and grasped her shoulders. 'But I have never loved, until now. Until you.'

And there it was. She stood calm in his grip, unafraid despite his strength and the seething emotions he was wrestling. He loves me, she thought in wonder.

'You once said there was no comparison between Mrs Downing and me.'

He shook his head impatiently. 'There isn't.' He studied her, frowning, and she saw the moment he realised. 'Oh God. Caseley, I'm so sorry.'

'It hurt,' she admitted.

'There's no comparison because she can't hold a candle to you. No woman could. Don't you understand? I love you. I've fought it every inch of the way. I didn't believe – There had to be a catch. I've always done as I pleased. But every time we were together I realised how different you are from the women I've known.'

'Defiant, argumentative, disobedient,' she smiled up at him through her tears. But this time they sprang from relief, and happiness too great to contain. He loved her. Jago loved her.

'Brave, beautiful, spirited, and loyal. I've treated you badly –'

'No –'

'Yes. But I'll spend the rest of my life making it up to you. Caseley, please be my wife. I need you. Come and live with me here.'

She laid her hand along his cheek, felt the warmth of

his skin through the close beard. 'What about Rosina and Liza-Jane?'

'What about them?' He was impatient. 'They'll come too, of course. We'll need them, especially when the babies come. And Ben. That back garden is a wilderness. There's a ruined cottage under the brambles by the back wall.'

'About Ralph –' She watched his face set.

'He is not your responsibility.'

'I know,' she said softly. 'But he's my brother.'

'Then I suggest you give him half of whatever the sale of your father's house fetches. It's more than he deserves. Then he is on his own. It's the only way, Caseley. He has to grow up sometime.'

She had to ask. 'You would not allow him to live here?'

'No,' he said flatly.

She turned to the window and gazed out across the harbour, past the yard and the docks, towards the lighthouse and the open sea.

He came up behind her, slipping one arm around her waist, the other across the front of her shoulders, holding her close.

She leaned back against his solid strength, safe within his protecting arms. This was what she had dreamed of, yearned for. This was home. *He* was home.

'My dearest Caseley,' he said against her ear, 'we have agreed arrangements for the business, your relatives, and the household staff –'

'There's just one more thing.' She turned her head against his shoulder to look up at him.

'God give me patience,' he muttered. 'What?'

'Will you still be taking *Fair Maid* to the Azores in December?'

He frowned. 'Yes, but –'

She smiled up at him. 'You'll be away for months. Can I go with you?'

His gaze reached into her soul as his arms tightened around her. 'There's nothing I'd like better. I'll speak to Toby in the morning.'

'What about?'

'It's a long way to the Azores, sweetheart,' he murmured, trailing his lips along her temple. 'A lot of nights at sea. If you think we'll be spending them in separate bunks, you are very much mistaken.'

Delicious heat flooded Caseley's body.

Roughly, Jago turned her around. 'Say it, Caseley,' he demanded. 'Say you'll marry me.'

'I love you,' she looked into slate-grey eyes she had seen as hard as granite, and cold as a winter sea. Now they held a warmth and gentleness that was for her alone. 'I'll be your partner, your friend, your …' she felt a blush climb her throat, 'your lover.'

'And wife.'

'And wife.'

'At last,' he murmured, and rested his forehead against hers. 'I know you're in mourning –'

She leaned back to meet his gaze. 'Jago, I really don't want a lot of fuss. Could we not be married by special licence?'

He reached inside his coat. 'I'd hoped you might consider it.' He held up a folded paper. 'There'll be gossip.'

She shrugged. 'I'm used to that. Then I was alone. Now I'll have you beside me.'

Dropping the licence onto the window seat he cupped her face and rested his forehead against hers. 'For always, Caseley.'

Romantic Fiction from

Accent Press

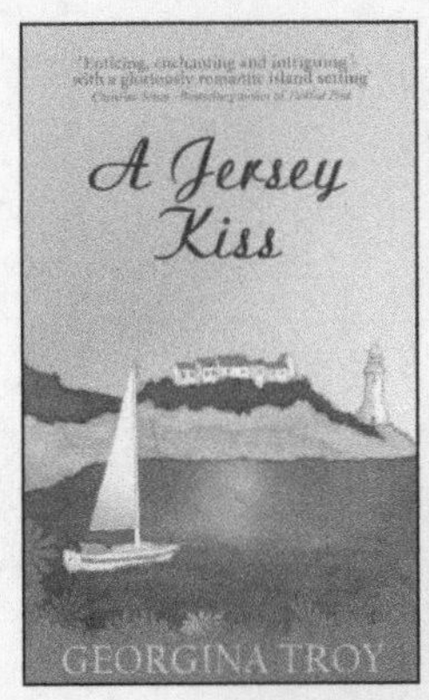

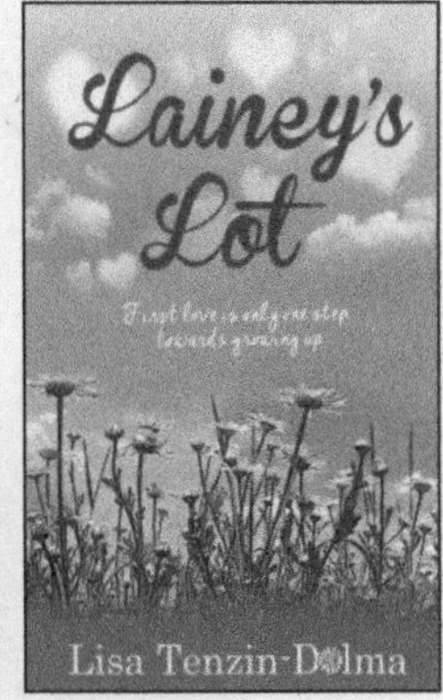

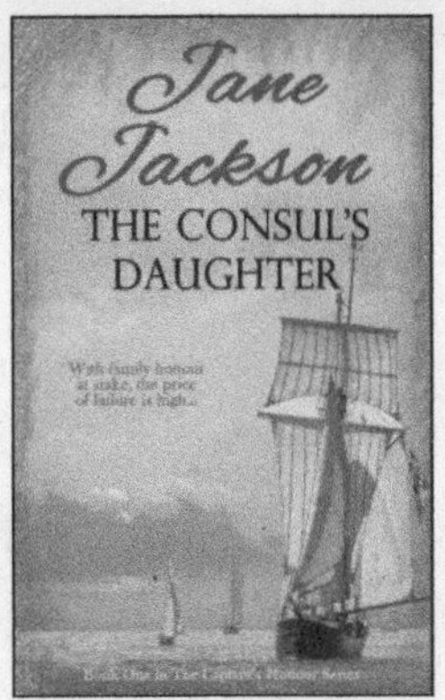

Nominated for the 2016 RNA Awards

Jane Jackson

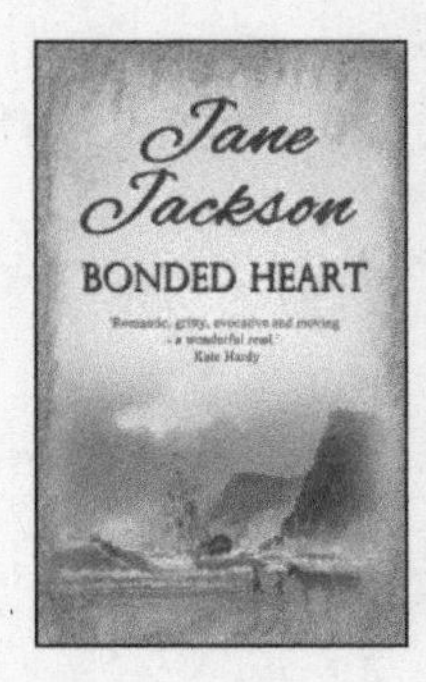